Tales of
MAGIC REALISM
By Women

Dreams in a Minor Key

EDITED BY SUSANNA J. STURGIS

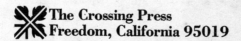
The Crossing Press
Freedom, California 95019

For the crew at the *Martha's Vineyard Times*,
the cutting edge of the far side
of the left hand of darkness —
my kind of place.

The first two sections of "Bapka in Brooklyn" by Batya Weinbaum appeared in slightly different form in *Word of Mouth*, Irene Zahava, ed., The Crossing Press, 1990; "Bottles," by Alcina Lubitch Domecq, has appeared in the original Spanish in the author's collection *Intoxicated* (Mexico City: Joaquín Martiz, 1988), and in Ilan Stavans' English translation in *The Albany Review* (Winter 1989/90); "Penguin Flight," by Rosalind Warren, was previously published in *Fiction Network* 5; "The Man Hanged Upside Down," by Lucy Sussex, first appeared in *My Lady Tongue & Other Tales* by Lucy Sussex (Melbourne: Heinemann, 1990).

Library of Congress Cataloging-in-Publication Data

Tales of magic realism by women: dreams in a minor key/edited
    by Susanna J. Sturgis.
      p. cm.
    ISBN 0-89594-500-2
    ISBN 0-89594-474-X (pbk.)
    1. Fantastic fiction--Women authors. 2. Science fiction--
Women authors. 3. Literature, Modern--20th century. 4. Magic
realism (Literature)
    I. Sturgis, Susanna J.
    PN6069.W65T35   1991
    813' .08762089287--dc20   90-28899
                                        CIP

CONTENTS

1 INTRODUCTION/Susanna J. Sturgis

6 THE GIFTS OF DIAZ/Valerie Nieman Colander

13 HEADING WEST/Kristine Kathryn Rusch

21 PENGUIN FLIGHT/Rosalind Warren

29 MEMO TO THE UNIVERSE/Gwynne Garfinkle

37 DEGREE DAYS AT HOME/Ellen Gruber Garvey

46 FLORA'S COMPLAINT/Kathleen J. Alcalá

54 EDGAR ALLAN POE IN THE BRONX/Lorraine Schein

63 THE MIRACLE OF SANTA MAIA/Kathleen de Azevedo

76 THE MONUMENT/Lianne Elizabeth Mercer

102 BOTTLES/Alcina Lubitch Domecq
(translated by Ilan Stavans)

105 IN UNISON, SOFTLY/Mary Rosenblum

122 OLD NIGHT/Stephanie T. Hoppe

136 HEARTS OF SAND/Conda V. Douglas

145 THE MAN HANGED UPSIDE DOWN/Lucy Sussex

173 BAPKA IN BROOKLYN/Batya Weinbaum

MAGIC REALISM:
What's in a Name?

by Susanna J. Sturgis

On the peripheries of fantasy, in the heart of reality, exists a dimension where the two mingle with barely a raised eyebrow. The settings are recognizable, if sometimes unfamiliar: an apartment building, a high-tech office, a grand hotel, art galleries, a highway through Montana. The women too: their relationships fail, they work for a living, they postpone their most cherished desires, they search for their roots.

And then . . .

Reality turns a somersault, twists and backflips and lands in an unexpected place. The artist scrapes away a bit of paint on her canvas; something covered over is revealed.

We live, many of us North Americans, in a paved over, painted over, homogenized world. Some of us suspect what we've lost, maybe glimpse it in the treetops, the stars, the back of the mind. Perhaps we go looking for it. Perhaps it comes looking for us.

Crossing worlds, sensations intensify, perceptions are heightened; often the old words fail to describe the feelings. Familiar places become strange, multi-dimensional. How does the world look from a new angle, once you have seen

1

what you were not raised to see?

It's not a new question for feminists, for writers and artists of any persuasion.

So what is this stuff? How about a catchy two- or three-word phrase to describe it to prospective readers, reviewers, and literature teachers?

Well.

The stories that have coalesced into *Dreams in a Minor Key* came to me as an editor of fantasy and science fiction (f/sf). That's what the writers called them, or would let them be called. Yet, as I read for what eventually became *The Women Who Walk Through Fire* (The Crossing Press, 1990), these stories drew together and pulled off a bit to one side. Not that these women weren't walking through fire too, but they seemed to have something in common that most of the others did not.

I *knew* them, the art critic, the midwestern Jew in search of her heritage, the photographer in search of the wild, the landscaper with a terror she can't share. I might get to where they were, with ingenuity and at some expense, perhaps, but without supernatural or uninvented technology.

"Magic realism" I started to call these tales, a term I picked up from English-speaking reviewers of Latin American literature in translation, or maybe from occasional references in f/sf journals. When I proposed a "magic realism" anthology to the writers whose work is gathered here, Lianne ("Monuments") Mercer wrote back, "I haven't heard that term before; I like it." Kathleen ("Flora's Complaint") Alcalá speculated, "The term must have been invented for American readers and writers, because no such distinction is made in Latin America. I simply write stories in the storytelling tradition of my family."

For the record, *Benét's Reader's Encyclopedia* traces the Spanish original — *lo real maravilloso* — to Cuban novelist Alejo Carpentier, who "was searching for a concept broad enough to accommodate both the events of everyday life and the fabulous nature of Latin American geography

2

and history."

Writers write what they write. It's publishers, booksellers, and critics who need a name for it. As a critic and former bookseller, I know those names are convenient, probably necessary. As an editor of women's f/sf, I get downright cranky, watching potential readers drift away because something is called "science fiction," or "feminist."

Science fiction (along with fantasy, horror, and other tendrils of speculative fiction) is called a "genre." Publishers devote separate lines to it; bookstores display it on appropriately marked shelves. When mainstream publications consider f/sf titles at all, it's usually in group reviews wherein each book, no matter how excellent or portentous, receives at most a paragraph or two.

Novels about middle-aged white male college professors, by contrast, are rarely referred to as genre fiction. Those are reviewed in *The New York Review of Books*, but novels by C. J. Cherryh or Octavia Butler generally are not. (For them you consult "specialty" publications like *The New York Review of Science Fiction*.) Fantastical elements are more often celebrated in fiction translated from another language, ignored or disdained if published in English as fantasy or science fiction.

Brooklyn geography and history is as fabulous as the Latin American, and if that claim seems excessive, Batya Weinbaum will reassure you in "Bapka in Brooklyn."

Magic realism exists within the realm of f/sf, or speculative fiction; at the very least, it shares a long frontier and a common language. All the same, gates open for magic realism that would be slammed in science fiction's face. Some gates. At least part way.

But magic realism is no model of decorum. It's paradoxical, shifty, rebellious, quirky, and loud. Sort of like . . . science fiction?

Invited to a literary soirée or — better yet — a science fiction convention, devotees of magic realism and fans of science fiction might retreat to opposite corners and eye

3

each other with suspicion. ("My God, what has she got on?" "Have you ever heard *anyone* talk like that?") After half an hour or so, would they be on their way together, laughs of recognition punctuating their search for the art show or the bar or the panel on world-building?

I like to think so. Both magic realism and f/sf delight in stretching, transcending, toying with, and otherwise playing havoc with boundaries, political, literary, and otherwise. Dancing, as Ursula K. Le Guin put it so well, "at the edge of the world," between night and day, past and future, real and unreal until the demarcation line dissolves in a swirl of color. Truth is, the imagination slips those lines with impunity, and not all times and cultures are as fettered by the rational mind as the U.S. in the late twentieth century.

Alice Walker's *The Temple of My Familiar* grew from a magic-soaked soil. So did Toni Morrison's *Beloved*. And the stories (surprise!) of Nathaniel Hawthorne and Edgar Allan Poe (who is remembered here in Lorraine Schein's "memoir," "Edgar Allan Poe in the Bronx"). Perhaps linear, rational, "mainstream" prose is a temporary glitch in literary history?

These writers manage to switch off the internal editor that restrains the imagination with hydraulic brakes: "No one would believe that! Are you crazy?" If they're walking down a city street and a paint-peeling fire hydrant grins up at them, they stop for conversation.

They tap into the world beyond our skins, older and deeper than the Age of Reason. Conda ("Hearts of Sand") Douglas draws on Navajo wisdom, Lucy ("The Man Hanged Upside Down") Sussex on the Aboriginal people of Australia, Kathleen ("The Miracle of Santa Maia") de Acevedo on Brazil. Stephanie T. ("Old Night") Hoppe's narrator is caught up in the magics or horrors of old Europe.

How do worlds held apart by custom come together? As women of different classes, cultures, ages, places, the question is posed for us, as we encounter each other, our own pasts, the histories of our people, the life of the land we live on. What we glimpse of the answers may disorient, terrify, horrify us — and exhilarate and empower us at the very same time. It doesn't yield to idealistic prescriptions or rational explanations. To what, then?

Courage, I think, to venture wherever the question leads.

THE GIFTS OF DIAZ

by Valerie Nieman Colander

Bellina clapped her hands and the finches flew up, scattering into the branches of ancient trees that shaded the porch.

"Fly away, friends," she called. "The sun is setting. Diaz will be coming home soon."

She counted the hours of his absence by the color of the sunlight, pink at morning, white as a bleached stone at noon, yellow in afternoon and orange at evening. Now the sunlight on her bare legs was orange, and Diaz would be on his way from town.

She went out of the black shade of the trees and stood in the dust of the yard, looking north. The road to town twisted across the valley, into the blue folds of the hills. It was as narrow as the ribbons he brought for her hair. It disappeared and reappeared like visions of Heaven in his magical nesting boxes.

Bellina shaded her eyes with her hand. Far away on the road a wavering dot climbed from a valley of disappearance.

She felt suddenly how dusty she was, how gray with the sweat of garden-work. She ran into the house, poured cool water from a pitcher into the broad bowl decorated with roses, washed from her skin the long solitary day. On her neck and wrists and ankles she rubbed a lotion that smelled of wildflowers and crushed leaves. She put on a cotton dress

6

the color of the distant hills and a bracelet set with pink-veined turquoise and a shawl knitted of gossamer silver. All these things were the gifts of Diaz.

At last she heard the sound of the horses' hooves, and the squeak of the wagon wheels, which sounded thin as the voices of the finches.

"Diaz!"

"My own Bellina." He swung down from the seat of the wagon. He was covered with the dust of the road, so that his eyes were startlingly dark and lustrous in his face. "Have you missed me?"

"Oh, I have had friends to see me," she said coyly.

He frowned (the lines cutting like water-channels in the brown land of his face) and said, "Who would come here?"

"The birds. And the shadows of the clouds when they passed over."

"Bellina. You would tease the man who has watched the rumps of horses from morning until night, only to bring you gifts?"

She clapped her hands and laughed. "What have you brought me?"

He went to the back of the wagon and lifted up a sack of flour and another of sugar. He had coffee, and a new metal pot. She lit the lamps as he brought in a bolt of blue canvas cloth. And finally he reached under the seat of the wagon and found a burlap sack, tied at the top and lumpy with small things jumbled together.

He opened it and took out five boxes and set them on the table.

One was wrapped in red paper, another in pink, a third one in green. There was a very small one wrapped in blue. The final box was wrapped in gold foil which reflected the lantern-light and made it brighter than the sun, and it was tied with a filigree bow of silver.

"Now, my Bellina, choose one. But—"

She looked up.

"You must save the gold box for the last."

7

Her heart fell. Never before had Diaz reserved any of his gifts.

She touched the pink box, but in her grasp it appeared small and mean. She lifted her hand and took the red one. She gave it back to him.

This was the way of Diaz' gifts. Always there were several, to be selected at the times he named. Always he would open the chosen box and present the gift to her.

Diaz bent his head over the package. Bellina thought that he was a handsome man. He had glossy black hair which she cut with her stork-billed scissors, and a black mustache, and a nose that curved proudly like the arch of a horse's neck.

The paper unfolded in his fingers. The box itself was white, with a lid held on by red wax seals. Diaz broke these with his thumbnail.

He set aside the lid and reached in, gently, with his forefinger and thumb, and took out a rose.

"Oh!" she said.

Bellina held out her hand and he laid the white rose across her cupped fingers.

It was no heavier than a blossom, freshly cut, but the rose was cool and firm. Its petals were made of porcelain; when she held it to the light, the light came through the petals as moonlight through a window. The stem was green glass, and the thorns were sharp and tipped red as though with blood. As it lay there, warming in her hand, she smelled the fragrance of damask rose, fresh and strong on the evening.

"It will never wilt?"

"No drought will ever brown these petals, my Bellina."

She held the rose by its stem, amazed by its beauty. But as she turned it, the petals caught the reflected light of the gold box.

"What is town like?"

Diaz, who was mending a harness strap as he sat on the steps in the sun, did not even look up at her.

8

"It is noisy and dusty."

Bellina twirled around once, lightly, on her toes, the flowered skirt of her dress following her movement in a wide sweeping curve.

"I know that there are many people there."

"Yes."

"I think to myself it must sound like the finches, when they are quarreling. Then I clap my hands and make them fly! And maybe only one will stay. Like me."

Diaz grunted as he pushed the awl through the stiff leather.

"Is it something like that?"

"Do you remember when I came here?"

Bellina remembered. She had been a little child when the man Diaz had ridden down the valley, following the path of a road which was then only a faint trace.

"I came from a town, like that one."

Diaz had stayed. When her father was dying, he put her hand into Diaz' large one and made them married.

"You do not wish to know about towns. They are full of violence and deception. A man does not live so long in town."

Bellina bent down a branch and touched the dark, waxy leaves of the old tree, the leaves that never fell.

"Are there women in town?"

"Yes. But they are not happy."

She looked north, as far as her eyes could see, along the twisting line of the road that Diaz' wagon-wheels had made.

She thought often about the gold package, the more so because it sat upon the kitchen table, bright as a new coin on the worn oilcloth.

After two weeks had gone by — or was it three? the days went by like birds—Diaz had opened the pink box and presented her with a comb for her black hair. The comb, too, was black, and beneath its shiny surface were pinpoints of white, the dust of stars. As Bellina held it in her hand it seemed that the motes wheeled slowly within the black.

9

It was nearly summer, and the sun moved each day southward along the ragged edge of the land. It might have been that, on that day, the sun shone more brightly through a notch in the encircling hills. Or that the warmth of summer was a brighter pink in that early morning. In any case, the summer sunlight on that particular morning burst through the trembling window-glass and made the gold box and the silver filigree blaze like the throne of God himself.

Bellina sat down at the table and rested her elbows on the edge. The brightness was such that she squinted against it; she almost could not look at the package.

"There is work to be done," she whispered to herself. "Diaz works; I hear his singing. Am I to sit here like a lizard, enchanted by the sun?"

But in her own thoughts were words that did not come like those, scoldingly to her lips. "A sign, this glory of the sun. Am I yet my father's little child, always to wait for the giving? And there sits a package to be undone."

There was a pounding in her chest. She put her hand to her breastbone and pressed back against the pressure.

"And if I were to die, now?"

Bellina reached for the gold box. The wrapping was warm under her fingers.

She untied the silver bow and smoothed it upon the oilcloth. Faded red showed through the filigree; the roughness of the surface was agreeable to her fingers.

The paper opened itself, a leaf unfolding.

Inside, the box was peacock blue and sealed with green wax. She pressed her thumbnail to the wax, watched it whiten as it split apart. A piece of wax fell away.

Bellina lifted the cover.

It was dark inside the box. It was a shadow on the northern hills at evening, purple and thick. Bellina tilted her head and bent closer.

The shadow swirled — Oh! — and lifted like a veil. On the peacock-colored cardboard of the box rested a butterfly.

At first she thought it was porcelain and glass, fashioned by the same artist as the rose, only thinner, yes, thin

10

as a butterfly's wing. The scales were iridescent peacock, green and blue and shading into violet. But as she watched the wings lifted slightly.

She set her forefinger close to the butterfly's head. It touched her skin with its uncoiled proboscis, then walked up her finger, carrying its wings gracefully.

Bellina raised her hand into the morning sunlight. The butterfly opened its wings (silk, but with the depth of color of velvet) and then closed them, upright.

Its delicate feet loosened their grasp on her forefinger and it fell as heavily as such as creature of the air could fall.

Bellina felt her heart beat convulsively.

She knelt.

The butterfly crawled feebly along the planks. With each step, its luster faded. Its wings lay flat and the tips were snagged by the splinters on the rough wood.

The box.

Bellina sprang up, gathered the box and paper and ribbon from the table. She held the open box in the butterfly's path, urgent with fear and the hope that within that waiting shadow the butterfly would be new and perfect once more.

The butterfly dragged its body across the edge. Its wings were transparent, every scale blown away as if by some great wind. The veins showed, black.

There the butterfly died. Its body crumbled into dust.

Her tears came and they shone in the sun that refused to shift or be dulled by the rasp of the day. Her hair fell, suddenly loose, and it was gray with the burnt-out stars of the shattered comb.

There were small sounds, like the rustle of birds' wings, all through the house. She knew that the gifts of Diaz were falling into dust. Bellina held her hands in front of her eyes, expected that they, too, would crumble, but like the sun they were strong, beating with a life of their own.

A thin shadow thrust itself across the floor, covering box, and ribbon, and all.

"No, my own Bellina."

She thought her chest would pull itself so tight that she would not be able to breathe.

"No, please. You cannot have done this."

Bellina scraped the fine dust which had been Diaz' last gift into a little pile, and blew it into the box. Then she threw back her unbound hair and stood.

Bellina wore a dress that she had long ago made for herself, from the plain hard denim cloth with which she also made Diaz' pants. It was faded and the hem had come loose, but it was solid on her back and hips.

Diaz stood on the porch. Bellina thought, he looks like my father.

"I only wanted the most beautiful things for you, Bellina," he said.

"I know."

"Tell me that you will stay." His voice rattled, an old man's voice. "Tell me that if I ride now for town, and if I find the gift which will undo all this, that when I return you will be here."

She looked down at her bare feet. The dust was thick between her toes.

"What is the name of the town?"

"What?"

"What is the name of the town, where you go?"

"And if I should tell you that it is called Gehenna?"

"Then that is where I go, Diaz."

Bellina held the peacock-colored box in the crook of her elbow. She went out through the black shade of the ancient trees. A leaf fell and, surprised, she did not try to catch it nor to step aside. Its sharp stem raked her shoulder.

She did not look back. She was certain that, if she did, she would see Diaz fade, stand for a moment like a ghost, an empty glass, and then collapse into a mound of fine dust.

HEADING WEST

by Kristine Kathryn Rusch

She drives in the cool Montana dusk, her car rattling around her. The sun is setting, filling her eyes with light almost too intense, pasting her contact lenses to her eyeballs. Behind her, the moon rises, a fiery circle in her rearview mirror. She thinks she sees smoke in the skies of Bozeman, smoke from the Yellowstone fires that have burned all summer, but the grayness could simply be incoming clouds. Her hands keep sliding on the wheel and she is afraid that she is nodding off.

She doesn't completely understand her compulsion to head west. During most of her life, when things got bad, she would look in the direction of the setting sun. When she learned to drive, she would drive to the west side of town, stopping on the outskirts, thinking that if she could only go to the ocean, she would be safe.

Two mornings ago, after she and Peter had fought for the final time, she cashed her paycheck, grabbed extra checks for her own account, and got in the car. She had only meant to go to her sister's, three hundred miles due west in Sioux Falls. But she didn't stop in Sioux Falls. She drove until she reached some small roadside motel stop in the middle of the Dakotas, slept late and continued west the following morning.

13

She laughs. At the age of thirty, she is finally running away from home.

The old-timers in Tom's Green Grill in Bozeman swear they have seen her before. The old-timers claim that, on nights that the full moon rises in the Montana skies, women like her appear on the horizon like an early dawn.

On this night, the six old-timers sit in their booth, the second one in from the door, behind the refurbished Wurlitzer jukebox. Tom's is a fifties-style diner, with real movie posters on the wall, 45s hanging near the jukebox, a large silver cash register box hiding the computer, and plush green decor. A drunk and two bums sit at the counter, nursing their coffee in an attempt to stay warm. The old-timers talk about everything and nothing, the same conversations they have held from those first days, back in the fifties when the old-timers were younger, when Tom's was a real diner, not an updated eighties imitation.

The woman comes through the door at seven-forty-five. Her hair falls softly about her shoulders, making her seem younger than she probably is. She stands confidently, slinging her purse over her shoulder and clutching a romantic-suspense novel in her right hand. The old-timers stare at the cover. The bosomy blonde is enjoying the embrace of a tall, handsome, weathered man. All of the old-timers are weathered. But they were never handsome. In all the years of driving truck, they have only kissed a few women between them. Perhaps none at all, after subtracting wives and hookers.

Tom comes out from behind the grill and grabs a menu. "Smoking or non-smoking?" he asks, and the old-timers think, not for the first time, that such a question would never have been asked in a real fifties diner.

"Non," she says.

Tom smiles. "Don't like smoking, huh?"

The old-timers all glance at the full ashtrays, the cigarettes in their hands. Perhaps the cigarettes are the reason for the loneliness, the reason that the old-timers have kissed so few women. Perhaps, if the smoking stopped, women would flock to the booth, baring their breasts like the blonde on the book cover.

"It's not that," the woman says. "I'm allergic."

She seems grateful to make conversation. The old-timers recognize that feeling from their long years alone on the road. As she passes the table, they notice that her eyes have that glazed look from staring at endless stretches of pavement too long. There is a story among truckers that some roads capture a driver: land, concrete, and sky going on forever. One of the old-timers whispers that she looks as if she has escaped that road and the others nod. They have all been thinking the same thing.

They watch her order, they watch her read, and they watch her eat, knowing what she will encounter under the cool Montana sky.

She thinks, as she walks from the restaurant, that she is too tired to drive any farther. The food, the smoky scent in the air, the darkness, are all conspiring to stop her western movement, at least for the night. She gets into her little car and drives off in search of a motel.

The chains are all full, except Super 8 which does not take a check. She glances at the cash in her wallet. Two hundred dollars is not enough to travel with. She doesn't know what she was thinking when she left. She contemplates paying cash, but something stops her. Her money must last until she gets wherever it is that she is going. She decides to try the Best Western again. They may have had a late cancellation.

As she drives, she passes a roadside motel across from Tom's Green Grill. The motel's blue neon sign baldly glaring "The Rainbow Inn" has stood in the same spot since 1954; she is sure of it. She finds herself swinging into the parking lot, stopping before the window with the ancient fading sign that reads "Office."

The man behind the fake wood counter seems startled to see her. Perhaps the place doesn't get many single women guests.

"We don't have any vacancies," he says.

She looks at the blue neon sign. There, beneath the motel's name, the little red vacancy sign glows. "Better turn on the 'no,' then," she says.

The man shrugs. "Sorry. I'm sure the chains'll take you."

She makes sure her smile is friendly, so that he knows there are no hard feelings. "They're all full. Know any place that I might try?"

He bites his lower lip, gazes up at the sky, at the smoke half-clouding the moon. "You're from out of town, aren't you?"

She nods, thinking his question odd. Of course she is from out of town. If she is from town, she would not need a room.

He turns, grabs a key from the rack behind the desk. The key clangs as it hits the fake wood. "Here," he says.

The tiredness hits her again. A place to stay, finally. "How much?" she asks.

"Twenty-two-fifty."

Even the price is good. The chains were going to charge her at least double that. "I don't suppose you would take a check."

"We don't normally." He glances around, seems to see no one. "But tonight, what the hell. Sometimes you have to take a chance, you know."

She knows. She pulls out her checkbook and begins to write.

The desk clerk takes her check and places it in the money drawer. He hates it when strange women arrive on moon-filled nights. Some of the women scream and carry on as if something awful is happening to them. Others stay in town long after they should have left, watching doors with a wistful expression. The women are safe at the chains, nothing happens there, only at the locally owned hotels and motels. He has heard the story from all the other clerks, has

16

seen it a few times with his own eyes.

If she stays here, he assures himself, he can make sure she will be all right.

The old-timers watch through the window of Tom's Green Grill. They see her get into her car and drive it around to the other side of the motel. She opens the car door and pulls out a small duffel bag, and her book. After closing the door with her hip, she lugs everything up the twisting metal stairway. She stops in front of B-17, sets her duffel down, opens the door and lets herself in.

The old-timers know the room is B-17 because they know the old hotel. They have watched people go in and out for thirty, almost forty years. Tom refills the coffee pot on the table. They say little, these old friends. They know that it will be a long night.

The room is larger than any hotel room she has ever seen, except perhaps her honeymoon suite. And she didn't enjoy that room, not with Peter's hands pawing her, pulling the pins from her hair, forcing her to join him into the heart-shaped bathtub when she wanted to remain beautiful for at least another hour. She had worked so hard on her looks, only to have him spoil them within fifteen minutes.

Funny old memory. Strange she thinks of it now.

She closes the door, turns the deadbolt and puts on the chain. The room seems almost homey. An old leather hideabed sits against the wall, two armchairs grouped around it in a living-room arrangement. The king-sized bed seems dwarfed by the room. The red bedspread doesn't seem garish, more the touch of a maiden aunt indulging her one and only pleasure. The television is new. She turns it on, and the familiar voices from an old sitcom soothe her.

She sets her bags on the dresser and explores the bathroom. It is clean, with new fixtures. Everything is much better than she expected it would be.

She comes back out and sits on the bed, suddenly bored. She is alone in Bozeman, Montana, where she knows no one. It is nine o'clock at night, too early for bed, too late to walk or test the pool. Her book has lost its appeal. The man on the cover looks too much like Peter and, she decides, a woman traveling alone should never read about women in jeopardy.

She flicks the channels, finds nothing, sighs, and returns to the old sitcom. The television will stay on, as company only. She gets up and goes into the bathroom. A long, hot bath will do her good. It will wipe off the road grime, clear the smoke from her lungs, and help her concentrate on the little voice in the back of her head, urging her to go west.

The old-timers glance at the clock on the wall behind the counter. Nine-thirty is almost too early, but she seems to be exhausted. They think of her soft brown hair, her tired eyes, the bosomy blonde on the cover of her book. They glance at each other and nod, happy that she appeared on the night of a full moon.

With a single movement, they all turn and watch out the window. In the parking lot across the street, the moonbeams coalesce and rearrange themselves into the shape of a man. He stands for a moment, glowing slightly, and then clothes appear on his naked frame: jeans, boots and a workshirt, just like the old-timers wear. He walks across the parking lot, his glow diminishing a little as a cloud races across the moon.

The desk clerk is checking in another guest. This man is tall, demanding with a nasal voice. The desk clerk is glad that he will not work in the morning. This guest will complain as he checks out, about the carpet, the television, the free continental breakfast.

The desk clerk hands the man his key, and files the guest registration form. The screen door bangs as the guest leaves. The desk clerk looks up. The quality of moonlight is different tonight, glowing a bit. And then he remembers when he has seen such light before.

He scans the iron stairway. Up along the hallway, a man with a moonlight sheen stands in front of B-17. The desk clerk runs for the door just as the moonlit man slips away into nothingness.

The man materializes in front of the door as she comes out of the bathroom, a towel wrapped around her damp skin. She doesn't scream because she can see the door chain through him, and realizes that she hasn't heard the door open. He smiles at her. She stands completely still, the warmth she received in the bath slipping out in the room's chill. "What do you want?" she asks.

But she knows the answer. She has seen it in a dozen eyes over the years, felt it in the brush of twenty outstretched hands. He takes a step toward her and she begins to tremble. Either he is real or he is a hallucination. She must deal with him. She must not let him know she is scared.

With a single, swift movement, she grabs her clothes from the bed. "I am going to get dressed," she says.

"No, please." He holds out his hand, and it is weathered and rough, like his face. His features are as rugged as the man on her book cover, but his eyes are filled with hesitation.

He takes a step forward. His lips are kissable, his hair baby fine, and he has a glow about him that she has never seen before. She can get lost in a man like him.

"Let me stay," he whispers.

She considers for a moment, thinking how nice it would feel to have someone caress her again, touch her as if she were loved. She takes a step toward him before remembering Peter, remembering the free, heady feeling of going west.

"No," she says.

The desk clerk pounds on the door, his fear a lump in his throat. The thin wood rattles beneath his fist and he knows that, if he has to, he can break into that room.

"Miss? You okay? Miss?"

He thinks he hears voices, faint inside. Perhaps he is

not saving her. Perhaps, in his own way, he is making matters worse.

The door opens. The woman stands there, wearing a sweatshirt and jeans. Her feet are bare and the edges of her hair are slightly damp.

"Everything okay?" he asks. "I thought —"

"I'm fine." Her smile is knowing. She understands why he is here. She pulls the door back and he glances inside. The room is empty, except for her things scattered about the furniture.

"Sorry," he says, a little sheepishly. "I just had this feeling . . ."

"It's okay," she says, closing the door ever so slowly. "Sometimes I get strange feelings too."

The glowing man has stepped out of the wall beside the desk clerk, just outside of the clerk's range of vision. For a brief second, the glowing man looks at the old-timers. They stare back, feeling his wistfulness echo their own. Then the moonbeams disperse, float away, leaving nothing on the balcony except one confused desk clerk staring at a gently closed door.

The old-timers lean back in their booth. It is just as well, one says, and they all agree. After this kind of night, they usually argue. Does she count among the women kissed? Or is she simply a shared fantasy, untouchable and uncountable?

A cloud covers the moon. The old-timers sigh and turn away from the window, resuming conversations started thirty, maybe forty years ago.

She rolls over in the king-sized bed, and reaches up to shut out the light. Her gaze falls on the book she has placed on her end-table. The man's body is perfect, the lamplight leaving a slight sheen on his reproduced skin. Dream lovers. She smiles. She will have time for them later. Right now, she is heading west.

PENGUIN FLIGHT

by Rosalind Warren

Even though I made the phone call, it was really Steven who put me on that plane. I wanted to fly out at dawn. "Let's wait till after breakfast," he said. "Change to a later flight."

By that time everything was sold out except a few seats on Doomed Flight 211, although, of course, they didn't start calling it that until it crashed. The booking lady didn't say, "The only seats we have left are on Doomed Flight 211." So I booked a window seat.

Doomed Flight 211 was an evening flight. The drive to the airport reminded me of too many other drives. Steven and I had had a lot of good times driving around San Francisco. I knew that by the time he got back from the airport, Mary would probably have moved herself into the apartment.

I can't say that I took the whole thing like a good sport or that there were no hard feelings.

I didn't say good-bye. I just got into the metal-detection line. He stood there and watched me. I knew he was feeling lousy. I had nothing to do but watch him waiting for me to finish waiting in line. A tall, skinny, smart-but-jumpy-looking guy wearing blue jeans, a black T-shirt, and a cowboy hat. Twenty-four years old and still wearing a cowboy hat. And I was still in love with this jerk.

21

"Go away," I called over to him. "Beat it. Get lost."

A couple of people looked around. He just stood there, looking miserable. I could tell he wanted to cry. I wanted to go over and give him a hug and say, Hey, it's not the end of the world. Forget that, I thought to myself. Didn't want to lose my place in the metal-detection line. Standing there with all the rest of the bozos emptying their change and car keys into little plastic containers and asking the attendants about their camera film getting clouded.

"Won't nothing happen to your camera film," the attendant is saying. Then this bozo walks on through and right away the alarm goes off.

"You got any metal on you? Put all your metal in this plastic container."

"Oh—metal?" the guy asks. "Where? In this container?" He is wearing a suit and carrying a briefcase. He must have been on an airplane sometime in the past couple of years.

"Oh no," says the attendant. "Not *metal*. We're collecting drugs today. Coke, ludes, reefer . . . Anything you got." He sees me smile and winks at me. "Just put the stuff right in here and keep walking." The other attendants are snickering.

I got on the plane in a daze. I didn't once look back at Steven, which took some effort. I found my seat. After we took off they began showing recycled nature shows from television and I began to drink. First there was one about otters. The next one was about hippopotamuses. Soon I was on my fourth drink and they were telling me about penguins. I noticed that there was a whole pile of empty airplane salted nut bags on the seat-back table in front of me. How had I managed to get my hands on so many? It seemed important to count them. There were twelve. They were very bright around the edges, illuminated, like a medieval manuscript. This was because of the drinks, which the insurance broker sitting next to me had bought me.

We had just learned that penguins have no natural predators when there was a loud "WHUMP!" and the plane began to drop.

22

I can tell you what went through my head the instant the plane began to drop because it was just one word and that word was "whoops." Here I was on a plane that looked like it was going to crash and nothing went through my head but "whoops." A lot worse has gone through my head when I've blown out a tire on the freeway.

I must have been in shock, although it's hard to say when the shock started. I'd been all shook up ever since Steven told me he was dumping me so he could get married to Mary. By the time my plane went down, I figure I was going on two solid weeks of shock. I barely knew Mary existed and suddenly the idiot wants to marry her. Knowing that the two of them were probably going to end up miserable together didn't make me feel any better. All I could think of was all those years of me and Steven down the drain. We weren't just high school sweethearts—we were nursery school sweethearts. One day I climbed up to the top of the jungle gym at Miss Nancy's Nursery School and there he was. I was only four at the time. It just wasn't fair.

After he told me about Mary, I cried for days. I didn't understand it. He didn't understand it either. He started smoking again. We both lost weight. Finally, he drove me to the airport and put me on the plane to Philly. We couldn't even stand to be in the same city. So then of course my damn plane crashes.

I assumed the emergency crash position, but after a few moments I unassumed it because I couldn't see anything from there but my knees. The penguin movie had gone off. The little pile of empty salted nut bags was long gone. The overhead luggage racks were popping open, suitcases were flying around, and everyone was screaming. I didn't scream. I'm just not a screamer. I never scream on the roller coaster either. The insurance broker next to me was struggling to dislodge one of those little airsickness bags from the seat-back pouch in front of him so he could throw up into it. Neatness counts.

I didn't feel sorry for myself. I felt sorry for the real people: the mothers who had babies with them, the young

23

couples on their honeymoons, and the teenagers who were going to die without ever having sex. I was mostly sad about Steven, and angry at him for booking me on some damn messed-up flight that was crashing because he was so lazy he couldn't drive me out to the airport early in the morning the way I'd wanted it.

The plane stopped falling and went into a glide. Everyone made a sighing noise like "ooohhhhh." The penguin movie came right back on. That penguin movie was eager to get itself across to us. A big group of penguins waddled across a stretch of ice and plopped into the water. Each one paused for a second on the edge of the ice and looked down at the water before jumping in. They looked very thoughtful, as if they had some other option besides jumping in and they wanted to think the whole thing through before going forward. I was watching the movie intently. It was as if as long as I could keep that movie on, the plane wouldn't crash. A stewardess was lurching up the aisle. Then the scene shifted to a penguin couple. They were standing together kind of poking each other with their beaks.

"Only the strong get to mate," proclaimed the narrator. The plane started falling again and I passed out.

When I came to I was sitting in the middle of a two-lane blacktop—still in my airplane seat. Nobody else was around. There weren't even any cars on the road, just me in my airplane seat. My seat belt was still fastened. It was very dark and quiet and all the stars were out.

I unfastened my seat belt and stood up. I felt sore, but not in any particular place. I hauled the seat off the road because it was a hazard for oncoming cars. My cousin Allen had been hospitalized once after hitting a twin bed on the New Jersey Turnpike. It fell off the roof of the van in front of him and Allen crashed into it. Flipped his car right over. The guy in the van just kept on driving.

I didn't think this was heaven. It looked too much like Ohio.

It was hard to know what to think.

"I have just experienced a miracle." I tried that out. Too melodramatic. I thought of kneeling down and kissing the blacktop, but I didn't feel like it.

What had happened to everyone else? Where was the plane? It had been such a big bastard. Where the hell was it?

I started walking. I didn't know which way was the right one, so I walked in the direction my seat had been facing. After a while ambulances and police cars started going by headed in the other direction. I didn't turn around and go back toward where the airplane was. There were things there I didn't want to see.

It was a beautiful night. Warm and clear. The sky seemed very high up. I hadn't seen so many stars in years, since before me and Steven dropped out of school and moved out West.

A beat-up Volkswagen was coming down the road. At the last possible moment I stuck out my thumb. With my luck it was probably a serial killer cruising for fresh victims. But when I got in, the guy driving looked fine, although he was much too tall to be driving a bug. He was all hunched over in there. He was dressed the way my friends tend to dress, in jeans and a T-shirt.

"Where am I?" I asked, after I got in.

"You're on the Gerald R. Ford Freeway," he said. "Just outside of Holland."

"What state is this?" I asked.

"Michigan," he said. He turned to look at me. "Are you okay? Is that where you want to be?"

I thought about this for a moment. The answer was no. Where I wanted to be was back on the playground at Miss Nancy's.

"Did you see a plane just crash?" I asked him.

"No," he said. "Are you sure you're okay?"

"I was in a plane that just crashed," I said. "But I walked away."

Walked away. I liked the sound of that.

An ambulance went screaming by.

"I have to make a phone call," I said.

We stopped at a Texaco station. He filled her up and cleaned the windshield while I called my older sister Louise in Philly, collect. I told her that I was in Michigan, and that I thought my plane had crashed but that I couldn't locate it. She thought I was stoned. I could hear my niece Molly, who is not yet one, making baby noises in the background.

"Put Molly on," I said.

"Only for a few minutes. I'm paying for this."

"I'll pay you back. Put the kid on the phone."

She put Molly up to the receiver. I listened to my niece making noises like "aaahhh . . . ahhh . . . ek-ek-ek." I sang her the Texaco jingle that I remembered from my childhood: "You can trust your car to the man who wears the star, the big bright Texaco star!"

When Louise got back on the phone I told her not to cash in the flight insurance policy when it came in the mail because that would be fraud and not to tell Steven that I was okay. I didn't want him to know I was okay. I wanted to louse up his first weekend with Mary in our apartment—maybe screw up the whole relationship. I'm the first to admit that I can hold a grudge forever.

"You aren't really at a Texaco station in Michigan, are you?" Louise asked.

I told her no, I'd died on the road and gone to Texaco heaven, and I was surrounded by angels and instead of hymns they were all singing, "You can trust your car to the man who wears the star . . ."

After that, Howard, the guy in the Volkswagen, took me home and we went to bed. They're very casual about these things in Michigan. Or maybe just he was. He lived in a little place that he'd bought for nothing in a little town in the middle of nowhere. He was a math teacher, but he thought he might go into the Peace Corps. He wasn't a big talker. The strong silent type. He had a body like Superman, although he didn't have a face like Superman. He turned out to be good in bed.

I read in the *Detroit Free Press* the next morning that

my body hadn't been recovered. That was because my body was right there, eating its cornflakes. A few days later I read in the *National Enquirer* that Louise was telling everyone that I was still alive. The headline was PLANE CRASH VICTIM PHONES BELOVED SISTER FROM BEYOND THE GRAVE—A MIRACLE OR A HOAX??

I could just imagine Steven in California, sweating that one out.

The *Enquirer* made a big deal about my and Lou's early years as teenage dope fiends, making it out as if the two of us were hallucinating up a storm all the time back then, which wasn't strictly true. They distorted the hell out of all that stuff. They didn't make nearly as much fuss about how straight we were now. They also played up the fact that our parents had died in a plane crash too, although theirs had been a private plane and mine was a public plane, so to speak.

After a while the story died out of the newspapers and life went on without me. I stayed on with Howard. I had never loved anyone whom I hadn't known forever. He had a whole childhood and adolescence that I hadn't been around for. I'm not sure why he was in love with me. Perhaps because I was there. We did a lot of reading out loud and walking around in the woods and climbing trees.

Every once in a while it occurred to me that I could probably make a lot of money selling my story to somebody.

In many ways I liked this life better than my other life, except for the ache in my gut from missing good old Steven.

Then one night, after Howard had fallen asleep, I was lying there in bed switching channels and damned if I didn't stumble onto the penguin program, the same one that had made my plane crash. Soon as I saw those dopey little birds I got chills all over. I couldn't believe I was seeing them again. I had the whole thing memorized. I could hear every word the announcer said just before he said it.

"Penguins have no natural predators." I'm watching those little bozos go waddling across the ice and then pause on the brink and peer down at the water, and it's like watching my life pass before my eyes.

It reminded me of waiting in the metal-detection line and not saying good-bye to Steven. It reminded me of walking along the highway at night and sticking my thumb out just when I heard Howard's VW coming down the road. It reminded me of singing to Molly.

"We're *all* living on borrowed time," said the announcer.

No, he didn't really say that. I was just imagining it.

And there went the penguin couple, poking at each other gently with their beaks again.

"Only the strong get to mate," proclaimed the announcer. I phoned Steven. Collect. He accepted the charges.

"Hey — guess what?" I said to him. He hung up on me.

MEMO TO THE UNIVERSE

by Gwynne Garfinkle

At first Toni thought someone else's document had come through the laserjet—she almost put the piece of paper back on the tray when the words started to register and she gasped.

INTERGALACTIC MEMO
FROM: Toni Johnson

TO: The Universe (including such personages as Angie, Lilian, Bob, and the fucking oblivious Vincent Stanwick)

RE: Toni's future in the universal plan (i.e. love, health, revolution, adventure vs. eternal dreariness in the carpeted computer-laden recesses of Stanwick and Stanwick).

Perhaps we'd better start with Toni's lovers. At present they number three, although after what happened last night perhaps only two. Last night Angie saw Angela Davis (whom she considers her namesake though Angie's a few years too old to be actually named after that sister) at the local women's bookstore, packed to the gills and surrounded with multicolored activists students bookreaders and well-wishers. Afterwards Angie hurried to Toni's apartment eager to

29

share what she remembered of Angela's speech, Angela's dreadlocks, and how Angie's heart flew into her mouth when she finally reached the front of the autograph line—and when Toni opened the door there was a white guy on the sofa and Toni looked like Whitney Houston and worse yet she didn't even try and explain, Angie wouldn't have let her explain but she didn't even try, Toni just kept her in the doorway and said, "I'm sorry, Angie, I have company. You should call first next time" and it was all obviously directed at the white dude sitting on her sofa drinking wine, he was more important than Angie, being white and male.

Angie's always saying, "But Toni, that doesn't make sense. Don't you see you're contradicting yourself?" Toni bites her tongue to keep herself from quoting Walt Whitman: "Do I contradict myself? Very well, I contradict myself. I contain multitudes." Bob's forever spouting Whitman. Sometimes Toni likes it, sometimes it irritates the hell out of her, his goddamn optimistic spirit. Though why shouldn't he be optimistic—oblivious white boy? Oblivious like Vince. Jesus, she sometimes thinks, what the fuck am I doing with this white boy who might as well be Vince? Such thoughts send her (no more?) back to Angie's wiry muscled black arms, crooning Sister, crying Sister, yelling Sister!

That's where the page ended. "What the fuck?" escaped from Toni's mouth—she glanced around—goddamit, Joanne heard, Joanne was grinning. Go away, girl, just go away. She had been about to crumple the memo. Intergalactic Memo? Joanne approached, her grin slipping into a frown, her blunt blue eyes frilled with mascara searching Toni's face. "What are you doing here, Toni? You should be home in bed!"

Toni lowered the paper to her side, blank side facing out. "I was gonna take a sick day. But *he* called, said it was urgent."

Joanne shook her head. "What's so fucking urgent?" she whispered. "Can't he answer his own phones for one day so you don't get pneumonia?" She mouthed the words almost silently since they stood near Vince's office, though his door was shut.

"I'll be all right."

Joanne put the back of her hand against Toni's forehead. "You're burning up, girl. You go home at lunch, huh?"

Toni was going to say, I can't, there's too much work piled up—but that memo was hot in her hand. "Yeah, I will. I promise." She made herself smile. Your dazzling sweet smile, Lilian called it. Your shit-eating grin, Angie called it when she was being particularly "honest" one particularly difficult afternoon. "Thanks, Joanne."

The moment Joanne's long blonde hair went bouncing down the hall, Toni rushed to her computer. There, on the screen, was the document she'd meant to print—an inter-office memo she'd typed from Vince's near-illegible scrawl. She hit the print command again and ran to the printer. A page rolled out, so slowly—then another—she grabbed them and read:

Lilian loved her true and that was nice but boring. Lilian used to call her Afrekete, goddess, arms and legs wrapped around her worshipfully. They were reading Audre Lorde's Zami at the time, in Amsterdam.

Goddesses can do what they want, can't they? Goddesses are above the law. They need more than mere mortals.

Angie was more problematic. She didn't worship Toni. She called her sister. Sister-lover. And that was cool, the way she talked revolution, the way their loving was part of the struggle. Toni liked to think of herself that way, Angela Davis, the glamor of revolution. But she feared Angie saw her too clear-eyed. Would expect too much of her. Angie taught self-defense classes for women, was always involved in protests, leafletting for Black rights, lesbian rights, freedom in South Africa and the United States. She always told Toni, "When you find your real work . . ."

31

She kept their letters together, Lilian's flowery, handwritten five pagers on thin blue airmail paper ("Darling Toni, I miss you more than words can express. I dream of your breasts, wish we were in each other's arms. I would be drunk on your smell, your sweat, the honey between your legs I would sticky drink") next to Angie's forcefully scrawled notes ("Toni, thanx for showing me L.'s letter. Helps me understand your 'relationship' with her. Seems to me she's drunk on her own supposedly erotic language. You could be anyone as far as she's concerned. Not as far as I'm concerned. Love, Angie"). She did not like to contemplate how they would feel if they knew she kept their letters together. But she liked to take them from the old hatbox where she kept them under brightly colored scarves and read them all together, Lilian's gushing love and Angie's caustic comments. It was just so much more interesting this way, like living an epistolary novel. Like The Color Purple.

Of course Bob was her ace in the hole, so to speak. Angie prided herself on knowing Toni so well, loving her entire difficult self. Yet Toni knew she could never accept her sleeping with a man, a white man! He was her secret. He thought Angie was just a friend, and did not even know of Lilian's existence.

So easy to lie to her lovers, when she lied all the time at work, at her father's house, at her brother Roy's. She'd heard her father and Roy joke about bulldaggers enough years to know how they'd react. She hadn't told them about Bob either, though he'd probably be the lesser shock, being at least (she could hear them say) a man. Once she let on to Joanne about Bob. Joanne was all sympathy, saying how some friends of hers thought it was wrong to bring a kid of mixed race into this world, but she thought it didn't matter at all, so long as two people loved each other. Toni wanted to laugh in her face.

The second page ended. Toni was beginning to breathe rapidly. What could she do? What the fuck was going on?

32

Any minute now Vince was going to open that door and come out, expecting his memo. He wanted to look it over before she circulated it. She imagined circulating this memo. She started to laugh hysterically. She stepped on the laugh, hard, but it kept bouncing back up again, wouldn't squash. Dizzy and feverish and flipped out as she was, still she kept thinking, What a trip! And before she could stop herself she went back to the computer and selected the print option. She could hardly wait to get her hands on the next page.

Toni felt debased when Lilian made love to her. It wasn't that she wasn't a good lover—she was very patient, dogged, would work on her for as long as it took. She was so open, vulnerable, and this embarrassed Toni. The way she'd look at her with big open eyes, naked emotion. And Lilian was fat. Fat like her mother had been. Soft and comforting and voluptuous. Beautiful to touch and to look at, but that wasn't how Toni was supposed to think. Fat wasn't supposed to be attractive. Even Oprah lost weight. It was just disgusting, Lilian's lack of discipline. Toni didn't like people to know she slept with her. It would reflect badly on her. She didn't mind Angie knowing—small thin wiry Angie—because Angie didn't know what Lilian looked like.

When she had sex with Bob she fantasized about Lilian or Angie. When she slept with Angie she thought of Bob. With Lilian she'd fantasized sex with various women and men she knew (but would never sleep with). Thought of characters in movies and books fucking. She could rarely come without fantasy. Always there was some distance.

They all had their visions of her. Bob saw her as exotic Black chick—but not all that Black, her skin and hair light enough so she didn't seem off limits, and she was so pretty, he always said, so soft and pretty—making it with her enhanced his vision of himself as a cool, open-minded lover/ liver in the universe. Though sometimes her mask would slip, anger seep out, for instance at the fact she'd spent four years

33

at college only to become a secretary, while he, fresh out of college, got a job at his father's best friend's advertising firm. He'd grin, pale blue eyes glinting, and say, "Anger's not good for you. Don't be angry. After all, it's not my fault." To Lilian she was perfection. To Angie she was flawed, addicted to lies and white culture, not yet committed to revolution, but still worth knowing for her possibilities.

None of these versions of Toni was anything but partial. Even if you put them all together—even adding other versions (her father and brother's view of Toni as beautiful, bright young Black woman who would make some Black man a good wife; Vince's view of her as useful automaton/decorative secretary/person you could actually converse with on the rare occasions you chose to; Joanne's view of her as nice put-upon secretary who was just like a white girl really), that still left out who Toni really was.

Her dress soaking with sweat, Toni didn't hesitate to hit the print command.

She don't want to be Whitney Houston
She wants to be Bessie Smith
but what about the cost?
She don't want to be Oprah Winfrey
wants to be Angela Davis
but she's scared
Don't want to be Diana Ross
Wants to be Afrekete
wants to be
to be

Angie's so black and blatant, hair short, no makeup, strutting down the street with her pink triangle sweatshirt. Even Lilian, chocolate brown and fat in jeans, doubtless now walking the cobbled streets of Amsterdam arm in arm with a woman, or arm in arm in memory with Toni, loudly singing a Joan Armatrading song, living her life. But Toni, light-skinned,

34

slim with good breasts and hips, narrow waist, Toni with her makeup and work clothes and uncomfortable shoes, Toni feels insulated from her own life.

Maybe she'll drop dead like her mama of hypertension.
Or hype.
A Prayer for Toni's Health:
Get outa my brain white culture
get outa my bed bad dreams and hype
get outa my mouth lies
get outa my bed and brain all this phony bullshit
Amen

Amen? Toni thought. But that's not all. Don't leave me with that. What's gonna happen to me? Come on, computer goddess or whatever you are, tell me, she prayed. She went to the computer, pressed print. Nothing happened. She shut her eyes tight and prayed for a future. Suddenly she heard the printer start printing.

Toni's future:
She slits her wrists
She flies to Brazil or Kenya or Nicaragua
She murders Vince, is fossilized by fame, newspaper
photos, TV, then jail and maybe death
She murders Vince, escapes
She escapes
She wants to rip herself from her life
But how?
Into what incarnation will she goddess she ordinary
    Black woman
wish/dare/can she step?
Toni's future:
She enters her own life
She possesses her own life
She lives her own life

Okay, Toni, you want specifics? I think the best plan of action *for you is as follows:*

Vince. Standing beside her. "Uh . . . the memo . . ." she gasped, but he took the pages from her. All of them. She held her breath. Okay, I'm fired.

Not even looking at her he said, "This looks fine, but I only need two copies." He handed them back. "I'm going to lunch."

When he had gone, she looked at the pages. The Intergalactic Memo was still there. Well, one of them was crazy. Her or Vince? She looked at the last page. There was no advice, no plan for her future. Instead, at the bottom of the page it read:

THE TRUTH IS BREAKING OUT ALL OVER THE PLACE

Love,

Toni

She went to her desk, got the purple pen she used for writing to Angie, and gave the memo her signature.

DEGREE DAYS AT HOME

by Ellen Gruber Garvey

How does my landlady insinuate herself into my apartment? Why, on these snowy nights, does she lie beside me in bed, pressing her cold legs against the backs of my knees, breathing frost down my spine? How is it that even though I've changed the locks she lets me know she's there, squeezing into my bed under any number of blankets?

"It's the oil situation," my landlady says. "And besides, when I walked by, that girl on the third floor had her window wide open." She leans over me, shaking her bony finger. "Don't think I didn't see that. It was a terribly cold day, and that window with the heat just pouring out of it. Such wastefulness, and on the floor right above you, too. It never used to be like this. You should be grateful you have any heat at all after that."

"She burned something," I plead. "She was letting the smell out." It's in my lease that I have to offer my landlady excuses. I squeeze the cold pillow under the covers with me to warm it. "All I know is that there's no heat. The radiators were stone cold when I got home. They must have been off for hours."

"Och, that's a pity. I don't know what you're going to do in the middle of winter when they run out of oil."

I pull the blanket over my head, trying to find a position

37

in which both my shoulders and my toes will be covered. The landlady yanks it back to her side, pulling it around her completely. She even takes the edges that would hang free and might be enough to cover an elbow, a bit of rib. It's all tucked under her.

I cough ostentatiously. I have a fine theatrical cough which I bring out at times like this. "Could I have some of the blanket," I sniffle.

"Oh, don't tell me about your cold. I have a cold too, and at my age it can be very serious."

"But the blanket," I say. "You know I pay my rent on time."

"If you don't like it here you can move."

We often have these conversations before I drop off to sleep. I wish she'd leave me alone. I have to get up early tomorrow to pick up my proofreading work from the *Paleontology Quarterly*. I hear her murmuring far into the night, droning on above the chattering of my teeth, like the soft hum and rattle of the broken refrigerator. She wants to tell me about the laundromat downstairs that she owns, how she came to own the building and then moved out of her apartment, how she built up her business from goodwill and a bar of soap. I've heard that story before; who hasn't? I press one ear to the pillow and cover the other with my hand, but it doesn't work: she pokes her cold knuckles at the small of my back, determined that I listen to the story of the last winter her husband was alive.

It was cold then too, but the cold was different in those days, fresh and pleasant on her cheeks when she stepped away from the steam of the laundry. Back then, they were invited to appear in the *Northeast Laundry Review*. They turned it down. "We have a good life," said Joe. "What would we do with all that publicity?"

My landlady knew well enough not to believe him, knew he was only pretending not to want it. "For the girls," she told him. Their daughters' photographs, taken when they had stopped by the laundry after first communion, were framed on the wall above the first washer. To further sanctify the occasion they had posed in brilliant white dresses in front of bottles of bleach, of piles of sheets and other white wash. "Let them have a record of all we've done here. It'll be an honor."

But no, Joe insisted. "I wash my hands of it," my landlady told him. "It's your doings." The Pelletiers' laundry, across the street, was written up instead. "Good for them," said Joe. "We have all we want." But people pointed out the Pelletiers as they walked down the street. A flashy family to start out with, the Pelletiers took to bleaching up their collars and cuffs, slapping white paint on them for all my landlady knew, till those collars and cuffs turned into small glowing beacons directing customers into their shop.

Joe became sad and envious, even more so when it snowed every day for a week. No one brings in wash when it snows, but Joe couldn't escape thoughts of laundry. He shoveled in front of the store slowly and carefully; it was almost like cleaning caked detergent from the drums of the machines.

As he sat alone in the store with the silent washers, outside sounds deadened by snow, the mailman came by with the new issue of the *Laundry Review*. The Pelletiers had been given a regular column.

The storm blurred the shapes outside the storefront window. Crowds of people seemed to be hurrying to and from the Pelletiers' shop, flashing big white bundles. No one came into Joe's shop.

My landlady came in. "Take a break," she told him. "Go upstairs."

From their bedroom window, now my bedroom window, he continued to follow the snowflakes, watching as they fell a short distance, rose, and then flowed sideways on waves of invisible water. "It was like a spell came over him," says my landlady. He thought he could be like that: like snow-flakes, like soap. He climbed over the radiator onto the fire escape to float with the storm.

With the fire escape window closed behind him, how

was my landlady to have noticed anything wrong? Nothing would have been wrong, if the tenants hadn't come pounding on the door, disturbing the peace, ruining her life, to tell her about his body lying just past where he'd shoveled. It was them, and those others who came, with their poking around and measuring and climbing in and out taking pictures—they were the ones that left the fire escape window open and stole away the heat Joe had left her. As though he hadn't meant a thing by leaving it for her: they just raised the window wide open and let the heat fly out.

Ever since then, winter has been a bad time for my landlady. The sight of snow chills her; she needs warmth. First she burrows through all the laundry bags downstairs; she grabs scarves and sweaters and wraps herself in them until no more can fit and buttons fly in all directions. Each winter, customers come in asking for their clothing, their quilts. She hides in the back, refusing to return a single one.

But she's still cold. She looks at the building's thermostat, mounted above a dryer. It's not fair that tenants should live in her apartments and get all that heat while her teeth chatter and her breath turns to steam like a feeble dragon's.

She unsheathes her claws and hisses.

She sucks the heat back into herself. She sits inflated and immobile in the back of the laundromat in her nest of sweaters, surrounded by hot water tanks, with six hats on her head, wrapped in all my blankets. From this post she absorbs all the heat from the building.

I step from bed into the square of chilly light, where the sun has landed after exhausting itself on the cold radiator and frostbitten house plants, and go downstairs to complain.

"Complaining again," says my landlady's daughter, now grown and permanently stationed at the front of the laundry, beside the scale where customers lay their bundles. "She's not here right now. Wait." She knows about complainers—the ones who always lose their socks in her machines, the ones who bring in clothes too frayed for

40

dustrags and then go saying they were expensive and the dye ran and it was her fault. Laundry hypochondriacs. Sure there are people like that about their apartments too. She knows the type.

In pictures above her daughter's head, my landlady and her family pose thirty years ago among formal and symmetrical washers and dryers. But the daughter at the front desk no longer smiles and carries a little bouquet. She sneers at me.

"Look, the only reason I keep complaining is because there's still no heat."

The daughter snorts, purses her lips, and finally points: "In the back." I walk past the customers seeing their clothes off on soapy journeys. The walls are hung with instructions for the use of the machines, a rack for the return of lost keys with no keys on it, and an engraved plaque: "Cleanliness Is Next to Godliness."

My landlady sits padded and pillowy on a throne of blankets and unsorted socks. She fingers a soft fur collar draped around her neck; her eyes follow its line around her shoulder until she sees me.

"You," says my landlady. "We've had enough of your complaints. You think you want heat? You'll get heat soon enough. It never used to be like this here. It was always 'Oh, such a nice building you and Joe keep. We're so pleased you let us live here.' Then you people moved in, nothing but complaints, pounding on the door, chasing the heat out with all your complaints. It's nothing like the way we used to have it."

She plucks at her sweater buttons; her hands grasp at the nest of scarves around her.

"I don't think —" I start to say, but she shakes her head bitterly.

"There's no use to it anymore, no reason for all the hard work I do for you. You think there's not enough heat? You'll see what heat is." She stands up. Shawls, scarves, and mittens cascade to her feet as she shakes her fist. Her screams and her daughter's sneers chase me out to the office.

Now my landlady's rage will not subside. All day she broods on the golden time when she lived in the building herself with her husband and daughters, the windows fogged with heat before the day it was all thrown out and wasted, before the tenants stole it. She dials the phone with her mittened hand and reaches me at the *Paleontology Quarterly.*

"You people have ruined it. This isn't the same house where Joe and I lived. I can see plain enough what you people have done with it." It's not worth preserving among her other mementos, she's decided. I put down the phone, wrap up a bundle of galleys and manuscript, and leave the office earlier than I'd planned. I get home in time to see my landlady carry a smoky torch up the drafty, damp stairwell. Shadows waver on the walls as the torch shakes in her unsteady hand; the repellent smell of burnt hair accompanies her as strands blow into the flame.

Out on the roof, her hair streams and crackles, her sweaters snap against her in the brisk wind, the torch smolders. She can start anywhere she wants. It's hers, all of it. She paces to the front of the roof, behind the sheltering wall of the cornice. There. No; the wind is blowing the wrong way. She moves further back, considers a corner, another spot.

She passes the laundry steam vent. The smell of soap and clean wash catches her by surprise. And here are the poles that held clotheslines before the laundromat came: Mrs. Heckel's wash on the south line, Mrs. Gallagher's on the east, hers on the north. Layers of sheets hung between them every Monday. Looking west to the fiery sunset as they folded wash, rooftops once spread in layers at their feet.

Gone. But to have the white sheets downstairs dusted with ashes, shirt collars smeared with cinders, blankets soaked with the terrible smell of dead fire on them—

No. This will not bring the return of the past. It still waits in the building. She glimpses it as she shuffles down the stairway. The tenants have hidden it, stuffed it away inside the potato bins under the kitchen windows and

42

painted them shut; jammed it behind the cracked plaster and covered it with spackle; strung it on the clothesline that once linked this building to others and broken the pulleys: how will she ever find it again?

New shops have opened in the neighborhood, serving new owners of brownstones who wish to scrape six layers of elementary-school-green and boiler-room-gray paint from their mantelpieces to reveal the original onyx. Restoration, they call it, and my landlady is filled with hope. She passes window after quaint window, then stops at the shop filled with tools for restoring and refinishing Victorian radiators. She parts her shawl and brings out photographs of mine, a stately cast-iron version. The proprietor admires the elegant lines visible through the rust spots and paint bubbles. He puzzles over the inscription on the base, indistinct words followed by a date: "Pat. pend. nonrattling, 1874"? He gives her free pamphlets showing how to turn historic radiators into useful and decorative objects. Collectibles, they're called. She comes to collect my radiator.

"It's not working anyway," my landlady tells me. "Haven't you said that often enough? 'Stone cold,' you told me on the phone, like you would know how cold a stone can get. You talk to me about stones, about cold, you'll see what comes of it. I'm losing money letting you keep this radiator as long as I have. I've been around; I see what they charge. There's not many so generous as I've been. Plenty would have come and taken such a valuable piece back long ago, even without your complaining."

"But what if the heat does come on? With the radiator gone the heat can't get into the apartment."

"You think you can throw soap in my eyes, don't you, telling me the heat comes from the radiator. It comes from the boiler, I have the sense to know that. You're trying to tell me I'm stupid, aren't you, with your fancy words, sitting at that desk with all those fancy words. I know what that's all about. I've seen enough of that in my time. It'll do you no good. And standing in front of the radiator like that's not

43

going to help you. We can come for it while you're out."

But I'm not going out. Things will get much worse if I leave, and besides, I have the *Paleontology Quarterly* to proofread.

Sometimes the work is even interesting. I like reading the scholars' speculation about the placement of oil deposits; about the reasons dinosaurs, plant life, and other building blocks of organic chemistry concentrated at certain strata and were pressed into oil there, "little knowing," one professor comments, "the boon they were providing posterity."

Did some of the dinosaurs resent being sacrificed for such a purpose? Did they hope to avoid the crushing millstone of the next layer and try to arrange for fossilization instead, or deliberately rush off to the tar pits of La Brea, hoping for a type of immortality: their remains preserved whole?

Part way through my checking between manuscript and proof, I tuck my icy fingers in my pockets, distracted by the urge to go to the museum to look at the dinosaurs themselves, to be reassured that their bulk and height have not been reduced by the pettiness of the scholars' arguments. I pull a jacket on top of my thick clothing before I remember that I can't leave.

My landlady has no such problem. She can take the long, winding walk through the snow to the museum. She prefers to avoid the hall of fossilized bones, but is drawn to souvenir-stand postcards of the dinosaurs. Such delicate animals despite their size and strength; they chilled easily and lived before the invention of sweaters. How fragile their lives were, dependent on heat. Perhaps she could have kept them warm enough. But they would walk heavily, ruin floors. It would be a mistake. In the exhibit hall next to the souvenir stand she examines the Ice Age cave paintings, portraits of animals who no longer exist. Back then, they had the sense to save a record for everyone to see. The plaque on the wall describes the glacial layer that covered the continent; my landlady envisions land protected under a sheet of clear ice, preserved under the lens of a vast exhibit case.

She finds what she came for—the exhibit on heating sources through the ages: rows of fire pits, hearths, Franklin stoves, coal braziers. She admires them from different angles and reconsiders her desire for my radiator. Perhaps it is not possible after all to restore the past, but only to preserve it. She will give my radiator away to the museum, she decides. Everyone will see what her life once was. But what if the museum burns down? What if they won't let her visit the radiator? What if they ruin it by heating it up or running steam through it?

No. There is only one way to preserve it. She understands that now.

Home from the museum, in the basement below the laundromat, with flickering torchlight casting animal shapes on the rough plaster, she finds the proper lever in its hidden nook of the furnace. She presses her whole weight on it until it moves to *off*, the furnace shudders; she keeps pressing; down past *off*, the furnace quakes. The lever breaks off in her hand and she waves it aloft.

"Let the Ice Age begin," she commands. She climbs the stairs for the last time, to once more ignore my bolted door and crawl in under my layers of blankets. She lies there, heavy as a millstone, though oil will not begin to pour from our bones for many years. Around us, ferns, coleus, and ivy wither and press themselves into the surrounding stone.

FLORA'S COMPLAINT

by Kathleen J. Alcalá

One sunny morning, Flora Morales stepped out her back door to water the potted plants. It was another blazing Southern California day, and if she waited any longer, the plants would wilt in the heat. Flora sensed a shadow overhead. Shading her eyes to look up, Flora saw a dark shape looming closer and closer out of the sky. It looked like an airplane headed for the house.

"No!" she yelled. "Oh, no!" and she ran back inside, where her startled husband was watching television.

"A plane!" she yelled. "It's going to crash!"

They both ran outside to find the largest, blackest bird either of them had ever seen sitting placidly in the little fountain Flora's husband had installed earlier that summer. It was a swan, so big that it covered every inch of water on the surface of the decorative fountain. It was so black that it seemed to absorb light, and made the flowers around it appear pale.

At first Flora was frightened by its size, but it remained still, quietly dipping its red-tipped bill and preening its feathers. She walked a little closer. It gave off a smell like burnt wood. Flora's husband brought a piece of bread from the kitchen and tried to feed it, but as he approached, the swan rose up majestically and flew away over the treetops.

The next morning it was in the yard again, and every morning after that. The neighbors came to peer over the fence at the strange sight, wondering from what exotic estate it might have wandered. But it rose up in an unearthly swirl of wind when others approached. Only Flora could get near enough to feed it, and it followed her like a puppy if no one else was around.

At first, Flora thought that someone might come from a zoo or amusement park to claim the swan, but no one ever did. Each night it flew away, but was always there in the morning. Its origin remained a mystery, as deep as the black shadows cast by its outstretched wings, or the look in the depths of its smoldering red eye.

Flora took her lawn chair into the backyard in the cool evenings and watched the beautiful bird as it paddled and preened, or regarded her calmly with one blood-red eye, then the other. It made Flora's mouth set in a straight line of satisfaction. Her family was afraid of the swan and stayed away from it. The burnt smell was always there, but Flora declared that it came from flying low over chimneys.

One day Flora found her grandson lolling on the grass in the shadow of the black swan. The swan sat contentedly with its feet and wings tucked up. She ran forward clapping her hands at them, then pulled the sleepy child to his feet and shook him fiercely.

"Don't go near the swan. It might hurt you."

The black swan took flight over the rooftops. After that, Flora watched the swan more carefully to make sure that no one got closer to it than she did.

One evening, while her husband was inside watching the season premieres on television, Flora began to talk to the swan in a way that she had never talked to anyone before.

"My life has been so hard," she began.

"I have suffered so much, and no one really appreciates me."

She stared at her hands after this confession, but the swan didn't seem to mind. It sat serenely on the grass a few feet away, regarding her through half-closed eyes. She ventured to say more.

"I have raised ungrateful children," she continued. "Although I did everything in my power to make them decent, law-abiding citizens, none of them turned out right. My daughters married insolent young men with no respect for their elders, and my sons all married fallen women."

"They wear makeup," she said with distaste, "and let my granddaughters wear pants and play boys' games. The girls should learn how to cook and take care of dolls. I've tried to be friendly to those hussies, but I can tell that they don't care. All they care about is worldly goods, yet they never give me anything that's worth much, after all I've done for them."

"My daughters were never any good. I watched their every move to make sure that they grew up properly. I always punished them when they used slang or acted like boys. And yet they complained when I gave more meat to my sons so that they would grow up stronger. Men want wives who are submissive. I tried to make every one of the girls have a simple, pious spirit. Feminine. That's what men want."

The black swan shifted on the grass. The dim light from the back porch made its long shadow blend with those of the whispering flowers.

"And yet they acted like they couldn't wait to leave the house. Instead of praying in their spare time and embroidering pillowcases for their dowries, they bit their nails and pulled out their eyelashes. They acted as though I was trying to hurt them on purpose when I punished them, instead of realizing it was for their own good."

Flora hitched at her lawn chair and sighed bitterly. "Sometimes they didn't even have the decency to cover up the bruises."

"One of my daughters is even unmarried and," here she paused with embarrassment, "living alone."

"When I couldn't reach her at home one evening, she got upset because I called the police. I only have her welfare in mind."

Flora sighed again. "Decent people are home by ten. I

48

don't know who she thinks she is."

The swan seemed to nod its head in sympathy.

"Even the pastor at my old church didn't understand. He actually had the nerve to take me aside and say that some of the women, he wouldn't give me their names, had complained because I suggested that they hadn't been married nine months before their first babies were born. How dare they say anything to him, when I was just letting them know that other Christians were watching them? He said that it wasn't any of my business. If he had done his job, I wouldn't have to count."

"And then," here Flora lowered her voice to a whisper, "he had the nerve to suggest that I had . . ." Flora searched for the right phrasing "improperly touched some of the children. Who does he think he is? And who could have told him?"

By now Flora was trembling with indignation. "Imagine that man calling himself a minister of God. That's when I started going to another church."

Flora's voice turned mournful.

"He had the nerve to say, before I left, that I suffered from a sickness of the soul, and need help."

"Me!" she said, leaning towards the swan, "I who have spent every waking moment trying to enforce God's will!"

The swan ruffled and smoothed its shiny feathers.

"In fact," she added, "if I were a government official, I could make people obey the laws of God." She pondered that thought with pleasure, drumming her fingers on the aluminum arms of her chair.

"Sometimes," she said, "it's hard to see the justice in life. But I know that God has a plan."

The black swan seemed to listen patiently and attentively, resting its bill on its puffy breast as she recited her lamentations. Afterwards, Flora folded her lawn chair against a palm tree and entered the house with a great sense of calm, as though in spite of all she knew, the world was working as it should.

The years passed, and the swan became a fixture in the

Morales's back yard. Flora's husband continued to tend the flowers, but retreated to his tool shed whenever the swan came too near, as much to avoid Flora's displeasure as to avoid that fearsome beak. As a result, the formerly manicured garden began to look shaggy, while the grandchildren preferred to play in the front yard.

Flora got older, and prepared to meet her reward. She had lived a long life, and was looking forward to her eternal rest. Her children were called together from their homes all over the country. They arrived one by one at her deathbed, and Flora surveyed them with a form of satisfaction. Only one was missing.

"I have lived a good life," she said to them, "I have never tasted alcohol or touched a cigarette. I have never been in a place where people engage in immoral dancing, or handled a deck of cards. I have never even thought an improper word, or been alone with any man other than my husband."

Mr. Morales looked at his feet and shuffled them on the floor, clearing his throat.

"Because of the pain of raising ungrateful children," Flora continued in a strong voice, "I have suffered long and deep. I count each hardship as a star in my crown. On Judgment Day, which is soon if we can tell by the state of the world, the gold will be separated from the dross, and I will receive my just reward. As will you," she said, glaring at each of her grown children in turn.

At that, the last daughter arrived. Flora sat up in bed pointing and yelled,

"That dress is too short!" before she fell back dead.

When Flora opened her eyes, she was lying on a hard garden bench, her purse clutched tightly over her chest. She blinked at the unfamiliar light, not recognizing the overgrown flowerbeds, or the sharp-smelling hedges at her side.

Flora sat up, trying to recall what had happened. She had been sick, she remembered that, so sick they did not think she would live. Her sons and daughters had been called, arrangements had been made. . . . It was deadly quiet, except for the droning of insects in the overblown roses and the hedges that stretched out before her. Her feet seemed to rest on firm ground, in her same sensible navy-blue shoes, but the sky above her was a hazy, milky white, the look of late afternoon in late summer. Flora was afraid, and began to cry quietly.

Suddenly, Flora heard a raucous noise to her left and turned to confront a looming black shape.

It was her beloved swan. Flora reached out her hand to stroke it, but the swan bit her hand sharply. With a cry she jumped up, but the swan remained where it sat on the warm sidewalk. Shaken, Flora began to walk away. The swan followed at a distance, keeping one red eye or the other on her every step.

When they came to a listless fountain with a wide, low edge, and green moss growing in its cracks, Flora sat down and turned to the swan.

"Remember your fountain?" she said. "Remember how much you used to like it when we turned the hose on for you?" She splashed her hand invitingly in the tepid water, but the swan remained apart, watching her gravely.

Flora got up and began to walk again, a growing disquiet within her, but she tried to look unconcerned, fanning her hand out a little at her side so that it would dry.

After a time, they came to another fountain with benches, and Flora could make out two women sitting at the far end, talking. They wore luminous robes. As she drew closer, Flora's heart leaped as she saw her dead sister Julia, talking to a woman she faintly recognized.

"Julia?" she said uncertainly, walking up to them.

"Flora!" the woman exclaimed, and stood up and embraced her. Tears of joy streamed down their faces, for it had been many years since Julia had succumbed to cancer and passed on.

"This is la Señorita Barajas, Flora. You remember her?"

"Oh yes, Señorita. How do you do?" she said politely, and la Señorita Barajas, a tiny, white-haired woman, stood

51

up and gave Flora one of her perfectly gloved hands before pecking her lightly on the cheek.

As they calmed down, Flora turned to her sister and finally asked: "Well?"

"Well what?" asked Julia.

"Is this it?"

Julia took in her breath sharply. "What do you mean, is this it?"

Flora began again, not understanding the look in Julia's eyes. "Is this what it's all like?"

Julia was stunned. "What do you mean? What more could you want?"

She was about to say more, but faltered as the black swan stepped up to them. It stood a little too close, and regarded them each in turn with its glittering eye.

As Flora's expression turned to terror, Julia's face softened to pity. She saw Flora's clothing for the first time.

"It is different for each of us," she finally said. "We each find what we have looked for in life."

"But," said Flora, "I didn't look for this! It just came to us, while I was still alive! Why is it here? I don't understand!"

By now, the two women were moving away from Flora, the swan standing between her and them. They looked back when she called out, but did not try to answer her questions.

"We will see you again soon, Flora," her sister called out, "but we must go now."

When she tried to follow, the swan rose up on its toes, unfurled its huge black wings, and hissed in her face. Flora was really afraid of it now, and sat down on a bench and cried for some time, pulling Kleenex from her purse where she always kept a plentiful supply.

She must have fallen asleep, because Flora found herself stretched out on the chipping, wrought-iron bench. When she sat up, she was alone, but felt that she was being watched from a distance. The sky was still a milky white, and the light still that of late afternoon in August or September. Flora knew that she would find other people, other relatives, but that her shame would be almost too much to bear. The black swan would be with her always. Flora got up, straightened her dress, and began to walk through the endless garden.

EDGAR ALLAN POE IN THE BRONX
a memoir

by Lorraine Schein

Edgar Allan Poe lived on Kingsbridge Road in the borough of New York known as the Bronx, from the years 1846 to 1849, a few months before his death.

I was born in the Bronx, and lived there from the years 1950 to 1960, on Longfellow Avenue, an avenue named after a famous American poet.

My best friend P. grew up on the same block that I did, except that he lived in a building farther down the block from me. He only ate white bread sandwiches and he never learned how to ride a bicycle. Today he is a noted astrophysicist. He wrote me a valentine in third grade. It went like this:

"When you're eight I'll love
you more than I ever did before."

My other best friend, also a P., who I met in high school after we had moved to another borough, used to suffer from erratic behavior. She was tall, white and bony as a bathroom. She lived in a religious charity residence for disturbed/disturbing children, and had to take special medication. She used to threaten suicide in homeroom, shout strange things on buses and other public places, and grab onto your arm and drag you through the streets when she got very excited. We once waltzed across the steps leading to the school.

P. told me one time in those days that someone used to read her Poe stories by the East River. She said it helped to calm her down.

I visited Poe cottage that year, after it had started happening to me. Two old ladies took the tour with me. The guide showed us the bed Virginia died in, and the desk where Poe wrote. Then we went upstairs to see a short filmstrip about his life and the ladies asked the guide a question. Afterwards, he told me that he had been a philosophy student at Columbia and was now teaching an informal philosophy course, existentialism I think, in the basement of the cottage, where he lived. It seems that residence in the cottage came along with the tour job. He said that on Halloween he had heard funny noises outside. He went upstairs with a flashlight to investigate and found a group of teenagers drinking and partying. When they saw him, they ran away very quickly.

Edgar Allan Poe often liked to write with his favorite cat seated on his shoulder.

T., who was engaged to a witch who had cast a spell on him that kept him under the strictest surveillance, carried around a picture of Edgar Allan Poe in his wallet. He showed it to me once, when we were still talking to each other. She is the one who sent me to the madhouse once already, and is planning the doom of the other members of my family.

Initials instead of names were used in this piece, just to be safe. You never know who's going to read this.

One can easily imagine Edgar Allan Poe riding on a black motorcycle through the streets of the city. T. rode a black motorcycle, too.

Poe had a lady friend in Greenwich Village. According to the filmstrip, it was while he was staying at her house that he heard the raucous noise of the bells from the many churches in the area. This inspired him to write "The Bells."

This lady friend of Poe's had his illegitimate daughter.

55

Her name was Eulalie Annabel Lee Lenore Edgarette Helen Poe. She had a faint moustache. She died in 1901.

Charles Fort also lived in the Bronx.

Conversation with a psychiatrist:

"And you think I got better because of the pills?" I said. "What about Carrie? She was on pills, too, wasn't she?"

"We put her back on them after her latest attempt."

"But she couldn't have done anything anyhow because she was in the hospital, right?"

"We've had patients who've killed themselves in the hospital."

"Even while they were on medication, doctor?" I said sarcastically.

Long silence.

T. was a tortured soul. But not as tortured as I was. He looked like a cross between Aleister Crowley and Yul Brynner, and will be totally bald, like them, in a few years.

Poe believed in phrenology and cosmic forces.

Do we get the word poetry from Edgar Allan Poe? Poetry—get it? People hate poetry. Poetry is like ethics and morality in that way. Even those who profess to admire it and read it, don't, and really find it duller than a day without TV.

From the dictionary:

Poetaster—a writer of worthless verses (not one who takes delicate nibbles of Poe's poems, like a wine taster)

Poetastering—dabbling in writing worthless verses

Poeticule—same as poetaster (not to be used as an adjective, as in "How poeticule you are!" or, "How poeticule your writing is!")

Poetling—an immature or petty poet

This is all a true story; a memoir based on fact; there are only about one and a half paragraphs in here that are totally fictional.

Find that paragraph, be the first to identify it correctly in a letter to me, and win a portable electronic perpetual motion Walkman pit-and-pendulum. Or an all expenses paid trip and stay at the violent ward in the mental hospital

they put me in after I tried to kill myself (because of *her*)—
a place where I actually gained weight, because the food was
good and there was nothing much else to do but eat, like
staying in some Catskills hotel. It was a modern place, no
snake pit. A *de rigueur, au courant* place to stay for a poet.

T. was into punk music. It was the '70s. He liked the
Clash and Blondie. Because that was his nickname for *her*.

"Soon found out/I had a heart of glass . . ."
Blondie, "Heart of Glass"

They played that song all over the place that spring. I
even heard it in the hospital.

T. used to go to CBGB's and Max's all the time when he
lived in the Village. That was before he had to drop out of
school because of the spell she put on him.

The spell that made him unable to go anywhere anymore. Especially with anyone she didn't want him to see—
another woman. Especially with someone like me. Oh, he
could go to work all right. It was only in the evenings that the
anxiety got really bad, so bad he couldn't sleep, he said. It
also, for some reason, got worse when it snowed.

And if he had a date with some other woman, even if he
did manage to leave the house in spite of the anxiety,
something would happen that night to prevent the date.
Every time, he told me. Just like the night we were supposed
to go out and I got a call from him an hour before we were
to meet. He was in a freak minor collision with another car
on the highway—an accident. We couldn't go out.

It happened every time, he later said to me. But, of
course, it was no accident.

What she did to me. Not that I think all pagans are bad.
Even after what happened to me, I know there are still good
pagans. Some of my best friends are pagans. It's just that I
know that she will go unpunished, because we don't believe
in black magic anymore. The people of ancient times were
not so stupid and superstitious as we think. They believed
in bad witches and they burned or buried them way down

deep. Who knows what other things they understood and believed which we do not, what other wisdom they had that we don't know of, or don't believe in.

Today she wouldn't even be sent to a witchcraft rehabilitation group, or Satanists Anonymous.

She had sent him an inverted silver cross to wear. She always wore black, he told me. And she liked lightning, and watching thunder storms.

"One way/or another/I'm gonna find you/I'm going to getcha, getcha, getcha, getcha . . ." Blondie

I didn't believe in witches. Neither did he. Until we were both convinced; until we figured out what was happening.

She didn't even live in New York, for God's sake. And I don't mean she lived in New Jersey, like him. She was a goddamn Midwest blonde Wisconsin witch. The type men always dream about, especially a nice New York Jewish man like T. The type that comes to New York to become a model or hooker or actress. He had met her by accident in a Chicago train station during a vacation from law school. Between trains or something.

That was when he had lived in the Village and been an N.Y.U. law student. But he had had to drop out soon after. The anxiety had started. So he went to see a shrink—and then another, and another—but of course none of them helped. Because by that time he was wearing her cross.

She called him once a week, sometimes more, at the office where we both worked.

"Why are you afraid?" I heard him say to her over the phone. "What are they going to do to you—put you in jail?" She also made him send her money by mail. "I can't send more—I can't afford it," he told her once during one of these calls. She had all the power, all the control.

She sat there in Wisconsin, this modern wicked witch of the West, from Witch-consin, as I had begun to think of her, and she could control him and everything else from hundreds of miles away, without looking up from doing her nails. That was the size of the power she had.

How she made him suffer for her love. But don't get me wrong—though he wanted to break the spell and suffered terribly, he was crazy about her. Whether this was really his infatuation or just that imposed on him by the spell was hard to tell. But I think it was really the spell—because he said the sex they had was—er, supernatural. It figures—that was what the essence of her power really was. Sex is always stronger than love—isn't it? In spite of what we've been taught. It is. Try and have a Platonic relationship with someone you're attracted to and you'll see. Sex is power and literally magic in the hands of a witch like her. It was control. So what, I think now, is love? Love is only a perception maybe, a way of looking at things that may be quite superficial.

Try explaining to a psychiatrist that you were put under an evil spell by a jealous black magic witch who lived in Wisconsin, who was the girlfriend of a man you had gotten to know at work, and *that's* why you had tried to kill yourself. Just try.

Easier to write poetry, even.

There are no witchcraft survivor groups as far as I know. Not then, and not now.

I include below now some writing and dialogue taken from the notes I kept while I was in the mental hospital:

The newest patient, a darkly handsome piratical-looking man with a beard and moustache, white bandages on his wrists. A very tired look in his eyes, yet a vehement, staccato, intense way of talking:

"Here—want to see what I did?" he says when I meet him in the day room. He pushes the bandages off one wrist. Underneath, dried blood from the scar, black dark-crusted lava on the scars across the insides of his wrists.

"I did it wrong," he tells me fiercely, admitting failure. "If you slash your wrists horizontally, like most people do, you miss cutting the major artery. You have to do it *vertically*, that's the way to do it, you lose more blood that

59

way."

A small calm-faced woman with soft green eyes and a gentle Scottish burr to her voice. She said to me she was here because she had once slit her tongue, and then recently had tried to drink a bottle of cleaning fluid, and so had to be re-hospitalized. "God didn't put you here on this Earth to suffer," she says to me later, reassuringly.

"I didn't want to hurt myself," says the teenaged boy, who's spent most of his life in here because of his tendencies. "I just felt as if I had to do something, so I picked up the knife and fork. I just wanted to *bend* them, you know, and the night nurse grabbed me and threw me back into the isolation room."

There's mystery here, an unsolved mystery in these voices, that I can still hear, years later. And the psychiatrists cannot perceive it, see life as the only cure.

And me? It's as if I was a radio *she* had turned on very high, to some eerie frequency—the life force itself, but turned up to an excruciating hyperawareness, as if time itself was passing through my body, except it wasn't a pain that centered in the body, it was somehow centered in the corporeality of my mind, my consciousness, as if that had somehow been pressed into an ontological Iron Maiden, but instead of nails there was this weird, agonizing energy flow, like something gone out of control, something that usually stayed outside of this universe, millions of incorporeal infinitely sharp pins pressed against my very living awareness, pin-piercings of time itself, impossible to explain, impossible to bear very long, though long enough to constitute torture. . . .

Until I couldn't take it any longer, was convinced about what it was at last, after wasting all that time and money on shrinks, and months having passed, and no drugs having helped, I knew then it was really true. T. realized the truth by then, too. There was no cure, no one would believe it, it wouldn't succumb to the chants and rituals I had gotten from the books on magic from the occult shops I had turned to in my desperation. It was too powerful, she was, there wouldn't be a cure for another couple of thousand years at least, in the future, though maybe there had been a cure a couple of thousand years ago in the past.

So I had to take matters into my own hands, which I did, a knife, with which I tried to slash my wrists, but I was too squeamish of blood, so I tried the oven, but kneeling there was an uncomfortable position, and I didn't want to bake to death (how to turn on the gas without turning on the heat? S. Plath had managed it, but she was more domestic). So the last thing I remember was walking calmly out the door, to try to place myself under some kindly car on the highway. . . .

Which people tell me is what I did, or tried to do, for I have no memory of what happened after. I very vaguely remember the ambulance, and waking up, thrashing wildly, strapped to the bed in the hospital, and then being transferred to the mental hospital, where blessedly, amazingly, miraculously, the bizarre black energy feeling was gone, gone, as abruptly as it had started, when I woke up in the morning on the first day of my stay in the violent ward.

Poe, his pale, fine, chalky complexion set off by the dark embers of his eyes, his moustache slightly crooked, slightly comical, his tie unevenly knotted, as befits a poet. He looks a little like Chaplin, a Chaplin of death, of melancholy.

And now it's all over, tucked away safely in the long ago past. Though it still isn't over in my memory. I used to wonder what happened to T. and his witch. I am sure he was unable to break the spell, that he is now married to her, living somewhere out in the Midwest heartland, that they have a *great* sex life, of course, and little baby witches. And she never has a problem getting him to take out the garbage, not with her powers.

But in life there are no pat endings; you mostly never find out what happened—not even a postcard. Yet I know this is what must have happened, evil triumphing as always, evil the true great ruling power of this world, not good, as we've been taught. Evil, the animating energy that fuels the universe, that surges in lightning, and is its current.

And the resulting effect on me, all these years later? I'm afraid to watch *Twilight Zone* on TV, or even hear its theme music. I've become more of an atheist than an agnostic. I hate blonde women. I put down psychiatrists every chance I get. I get nervous at the mention of Poe's name. I don't have a cheerful, All-American outlook on life. The sight of lightning, or the color black, fashionable as it is and *de rigueur* for wearing in the East Village, unless you're a rabbi and come by it naturally, makes me even more nervous. As some pagans now do. . . .

But hey! Don't get me wrong! Some of my best friends, as I've said, are still pagans.

Edgar Allan Poe died in a Baltimore hospital of the D.T.'s, delirious and talking constantly to imaginary objects on the walls.

I read an article the other week in the *New York Times* magazine section about the survivors of traumatic experiences, like holocausts, political torture, etc. The worst thing for them, after they've survived the experience, is to confide it to someone and not be believed. That's what the article said.

Well, you don't believe any of this is true, right? Well, I say to hell with you then, dear reader. I don't believe in *you*. Go to my birthplace in the Bronx and *stay* there forever till the Red Death stalks you and stabs you, and the raw wet sticky blood is scrawled over your body like subway graffiti. Go to Poe cottage in Poe Park and look for the black cat still buried there. Listen to the bells bells bells ringing all over Manhattan and the Bronx of my childhood, all over the city of New York, all over downtown Manhattan, the bells of my indelible past, the memories still ringing inside my head, forever more, forever.

Can't you hear them, can't you tell I'm telling the truth?

THE MIRACLE OF SANTA MAIA

by Kathleen de Azevedo

The smooth voice rippled from the back table at the *Boa Magia*. "You want to end up like *Senhorita* Birdy there? One of her breasts got unceremoniously removed by an amorous diamond smuggler on his way to Rio."

Jackie slammed her mug down on the bar and Birdy wiped up the small splash of beer.

The seated gentleman, with lush white hair, crossed his long legs, letting his foot gently stroke the air and blew an "O" of smoke with the tip of his tongue. "Women should not be in this part of Brazil. 'It's a jungle out there.'" He laughed at his own joke.

"I'm glad it's a jungle. I'm doing a photo essay on jaguars of the Mato Grosso."

Henrique Gonsalves snuffed out his cigarette. "Why you want to take pictures of jaguars? The people here are more intriguing. Birdy will take off her shirt if you ask."

Jackie knew the scientific name for this kind of guy. *Weirdus come-on-icus.* "I came here to photograph animals, not—female chests."

Henrique slipped his crossed legs underneath the table. "Good."

She combed her fingers through her short black hair, turned and glanced at him. So. Did he have light brown skin,

63

or maybe just a tan? How about his eyes, nordic ice blue or fluid-baby innocent? Which? He softened, reached into his wallet for a cruzado. "I'll leave an extra tip for Birdy, all right? For tolerating me."

"Good. You do that." Jackie rested the beer mug on her lips.

"Jaguars, eh?" He strolled up to the bar, tossed a bill on counter, then his car keys, scooting them toward her. "I can show you a jaguar, the likes of which . . ."

". . . I've never seen." Jackie laughed.

"Yes," he said.

Jackie continued drinking. How safe was a woman? Just outside, a mother meandered down the street with a baby tucked under her arm like a parcel.

He fingered his car keys. "I'm old enough to be your father, and I drive a 1965 combi van that probably runs slower than you could walk."

She picked up her camera and they left the *Boa Magia*.

The van rattled and scraped its undergut as he drove the combi too fast down a clay road. The matted jungle grew inward, dense, confusing, as grey mist lurked in and out of moss veils suspended from hidden limbs. Her head spun from the beer she drank.

They were near the Urubu River, a dark river named after the black vulture of the region, a river that washed away old villages and miraculously washed up new ones onto shore, "each village more wicked than the last," he told her.

A jaguar skin hung stretched, impaled on two sharpened stakes of sugar cane. Jackie almost jumped out of the moving van. "Who in the hell are killing those animals!"

"These—delightful natives ahead," he stepped on the gas.

A small mob of shouting copper-skinned people in rags charged out from behind trees and hurled rocks at them.

"Be careful dammit." Jackie held onto the dashboard.

"*Caboclos* here aren't used to traffic."

A stone smacked the windshield. Jackie ducked.

64

"Scared?"

No. She dropped her forehead to her knee as he barreled on.

They stopped at the main square, which he called the *Praca*, and pulled up in front of a battered church, its steeple crumbled into adobe rubble. Jackie jumped out of the van. God, what a filthy place. Empty except for a small pack of emaciated dogs sleeping against the trunk of a lone tree in the middle of the square—IF such a yellow half-dead thing could be called a tree. More like—a claw of a monster trying to leave its underground home.

"Charming, but where's this jaguar you wanted to show me, huh?"

"In the church." He wiped the sweat off his face with a handkerchief. "I'll wait for you out here."

She unzipped her bag and took out the camera. Then she snapped on the flash attachment. "This better be good," she muttered. And she slipped into the church.

Inside, the only thing she could see was a circle of glowing red votive cups, then a narrow beam of sunlight streaming from a gash in the roof, and then—a towering statue of an extraordinary—(Jackie touched the tops of pews to guide her down the aisle)—woman, or—the upper half was a woman, mouth screaming, cursing, arms flung upward grabbing for God's divine throat but—from the waist down, her powerful belly and legs—her elegant black spotted golden fur—was a jaguar.

Jackie stepped up to the altar for a closer look. It was not a woman-beast—it was a woman in a beast. A woman lodged inside the throat of a giant cat.

Her father looked up from his medical journal. "What do you want, Jack?"

Jackie's chin came up to his large desk. "I know how babies get born. They get born from your MOUTH."

He leaned back in his chair, and looked at her as if she were a patient. "You know what would happen if one gave birth from the mouth? The jaws would rip apart, the tongue would be jammed into the esophagus, the lungs would explode. You'd die, Jackie. Jesus." He continued reading. She shuddered.

Seized by a photographer's possession, Jackie kissed her camera for luck and snapped picture after picture. At a low angle, a picture of the gold paws; then up into the pulpit for a high angle shot of the statue's red ruby nipples. She ran down again and knelt on the floor for a spectacular shot of the martyr's long human hair. The last flash exploded, and Jackie sank back on her heels, exhausted. The heavy camera dangled from her neck. *Saecula saeculorum.* Perspiration rolled down her back.

She stumbled outside. Henrique was sitting on the church steps looking off onto the road. She sat beside him and dumped the camera into her case.

"What'd you think?" Henrique said, not looking at her.

"Who is she?"

"*Santa Maia Engoleira*—Saint Maia the Swallowed One." He squeezed his fist as if he were trying to break open his knuckles. "She performed miracles."

"She didn't do too well for herself, did she?"

"Miracles are good solutions to things if we could all be so lucky."

Jackie grabbed her case and started for the combi.

He reached over and hooked her camera strap with his little finger. "May I take a picture of you?"

"Just drive me back to the hotel. I need to hire an animal tracker."

"Just one picture," he gently grazed her arm.

She unzipped her case and thrust the camera at him. "Don't make me pose. And I won't take off my glasses."

He took the camera, aimed it at her and began snapping pictures, slowly approaching her as he talked. "It's been a while since I've encountered a woman like you. What's your name?"

"Jackie."

"Henrique Gonsalves."

Henrique was taking outdoor pictures with the flash still attached; the photos of her would come out flat, but she

66

didn't care. She'd look like her father in his brilliant doctor lab coat, all white and light.

"Father. When I look through my camera, I see my soul. Or it's the animal's soul. I'm not sure which."

"Jackie. What you see is not their soul. What you see is tissue, heart, and a lot of blood. No soul."

Henrique handed the camera back to her. "Jackie. I could show you animals here—birds and monkeys, which no one has ever seen. There's a jaguar here that's so big it could—" He cut himself off.

"—could swallow a woman whole?" She laughed as she put away her camera.

Henrique climbed into the front seat of the van and waited for her.

Her father dumped the dying coleus in the garbage, the one the nurse forgot to water. "I gave you $500 for college tuition. Not to buy a camera."

"I want to photograph animals. They're becoming extinct."

"They will become extinct. With or without you."

They drove further down the red clay road and pulled up in front of a sprawling white villa, inlaid with large wood timbers. Surrounding the villa was a high, vicious-looking barbed wire fence. "My home," he said.

"You're joking." The front yard was ablaze with colorful orchids growing out of control, but the high wire fence stood controlled, clean and silver-nailed, and snapped intruding flies with shots of electricity.

Henrique tapped out a combination into the panel of buttons next to the gate. Jackie drew back.

"What's wrong?" he said.

"How can you live like this?"

He looked up at the alarm wire strung above the gate. "Smugglers." He shoved open the gate. "Come."

"I can't. Looks like a prison."

Henrique pointed to a small latch behind the panel of buttons. "You can't be locked in here, you know. Turn this latch and can let yourself out. An accommodation not normally found in prisons." He chuckled as he walked over to unlock the front door of his house. "My dear woman," he called, "my back yard is full of wild animals worth a life-long subscription to *National Geographic*. I don't know how badly you want pictures."

The nurse who forgot to water the coleus rushed in, and rambled on about some emergency in the next room, then left. Her father stared at the camera as he buttoned up his lab coat. "You mock me."

In the dining room he rolled open an entire wall of glass and presented his wilderness at her service. She stepped from the dining room onto the porch and leaned her elbows on the high flat railing. This edge of the earth opened up into the jungle stretching for miles, dropping down into a grey misty gorge, and then in the distance, more trees, more valleys. Two green birds flew a dazzling arc above her head, displaying the gold underside of their wings, and sailed up into the lush canopy.

"*Passaros estrelas,*" he said, "star birds they call them here. Every wildlife photographer in the world would subsist on mud for a hundred years to get a look at birds like these."

"I would. They're beautiful."

A maid brought out a tray with two icy drinks. Henrique handed Jackie a glass. "Are you married?"

She gulped the woody-tasting rum. Five years ago, her college professor husband ran off with a young girl who corrected his papers. "He left me."

Henrique removed her eyeglasses, brushed aside her bangs and kissed her cheek. "This is a bad place to die alone."

"Don't talk that way and give me my glasses."

This man with eyes like the ocean many miles deep, this jungle-sailor! She *could* stay here, she could bask in this paradise for days, camera to her lips, kissing it for luck, but still —

She sat on the bench and faced his back yard. "Tell me more about Santa Maia."

"I told you what I know." He took a swallow of rum.

"How do they worship her? Do they pray?"

"I doubt it."

"Do they have a festival?"

"Yes." He paused. "Once a year."

"When?"

He shattered his glass against the porch railing. A group of screaming monkeys took a suicidal nose dive from the top of the canopy, and seemed to disappear into the forest below.

She snatched up her camera case. No thanks, no ride, I'll walk the ten miles back to the hotel if I have to. I'll find out about the festival, about Santa Maia, about everything.

"Don't go," he called, but it was too late. Jackie stormed through the house, out the front door and through the front gate, setting off the shrieking burglar alarm. He doubled over and pressed his hands against his ears.

She'd been trudging in the mid-afternoon heat for thirty minutes without a sign of the *Praca*. Maybe this escape was a mistake. Exhausted, she couldn't lift her two-ton camera up to her eyes now if an animal posed in front of her and wagged its tail.

A jaguar ripped through the bushes chasing some sort of flesh, then froze not more than ten feet away from her. Her heart and stomach collided, her pulse banged away. The cat's golden fur shimmered like polished metal and its spots looked like embedded chips of ebony. Through the bushes she could see the cat's tail thrashing . . . thrashing. . . .

"Mein Gott, Mein Gott," someone whispered. *"Hilfe!"*

She drew up her camera case and eased the snap open. "Don't move!" she whispered back.

She followed her father into the examining room where the emergency was and shut the door behind her. She could see the patient's toes, curled and pointed under the white sheet. Her father and two nurses clustered around the patient's head. He turned to her. "Well, take a picture of this."

The great gold beast drew back from its prey, glided through the green, and bounded onto the road in front of her. Her camera, still in the case, slipped off her shoulder

69

and dropped to her feet. It stared at her and she stared back and—what a gorgeous animal! Then it fled.

She found Henrique clinging to the trunk of a tree. "I'll take you home," she said.

Jackie put Henrique to bed and poured him a glass of water. "You speak German."

He crossed his eyes, *"Ich liebe dich*, Jackie," and fell asleep instantly like a kid. She unbuttoned her khaki blouse and dropped it off her shoulders, letting the slow moving ceiling fan cool her skin; then she stood by the window and watched the furious red day melt into blue jungle night. Next thing she knew, her cheek touched a cotton pillowcase and she fell asleep.

By seven o'clock the next morning, the heat of the day already sizzled through the window. She cupped her hands over her eyes and rolled away from the glaring sun. He was in bed next to her—asleep. Outside a pair of spying cat eyes seemed to float, wide-eyed.

In the examining room, her eye caught a row of beakers filled with green fluid, and floating inside, refracted metal, knives, piercing things, and in another, something soft, bobbing . . .

She grabbed her camera with one hand and slipped on her shirt with the other as she ran to the sliding glass door in the dining room. The huge jaguar lingered on the porch, dancing on its hind legs, beckoning, ready. She flipped open the lock. Ready.

The golden cat led her through the back yard and finally, onto a trail that traversed the side of the steep gorge. Trembling, Jackie inched along the trail, flat against the sheer rock. Easy enough for the cat, it had nine lives! Rooted vines shrouded the face of the granite. For a moment, the cat vanished among the maze of vines, then emerged at the top of the gorge—and waited for her?? Jackie took a deep breath, and clutched from vine to vine as she scrambled her way up the steep ravine to the top. The jaguar enticed her through thorn thickets, and she followed on her hands and knees until finally, finally, they reached an amazing termite hill.

Yes (she sucked the small bleeding cuts on her hand), these were the termite sculptures she read about, and this one was twice as tall as she! These voracious insects could demolish whole trees, and chew away ventilation shafts so large that people used them for storage, even for cooking.

Her father pressed his knuckles on the examining table as a nurse lifted a sheet up and over the dead patient's head. He turned his head and caught her with her camera to her chin. His voice cracked. "Pretty, huh?"

The jaguar pounced against the hill, dug in its front claws, and stretched. "Oh baby, stay there," she murmured, pressing wildly on the shutter release. The animal clawed further up the hill slinking and posing. Fantastic!

Through the telephoto something caught Jackie's eye. Bricks were built into a large hollow of the termite castle.

The jaguar leaped away from the hill dragging a clump of loose moss between its teeth. Jackie lowered her camera. A rusty iron door was hinged onto the brick. Must've been a bread oven. She went over and yanked open the door, reached inside the oven and pulled out a handful of strange grey coarse ash. The sickening grey stuff fell through her fingers; the jaguar roared and retreated into the forest.

The autopsy. Watch. Her father forced a scalpel into her hand. But she would not dissect. Her father grabbed her wrist and pulled her toward the table, facing a smooth belly. She said, "I heard that Nazis planted cats inside human beings."

Her father snatched the scalpel from her hand.

"It's not the same thing, Jack. I try to save lives. And I work pretty damn hard at it, too."

"It makes me sick."

The Carnival of Santa Maia is held when the twelfth moon of the year is full of coconut milk. That's what a man told her several weeks later as he pumped gas into the jeep she rented to return for the celebration. She wouldn't be stranded this time.

71

When Jackie arrived at the *Praca*, the moon was filled to its outer shell. Torches flickered in the blue jungle night. The hushed crowd which had filled the *Praca* was swaying to the raspy, reed-like sound of bone flutes. From the shadowy jungle emerged dancers in jaguar skins and headdresses of *passaros estrelas* feathers. These strange catlike dancers sang pagan hosannas, whirled long sugar canes in the air as they stalked the Carnival crowd. Then, with the thud of a drum, the dancers broke into the crowd and beat people's knees with the canes until sweet juice bled from the pulp. In the middle of this, someone laughed and pointed to Jackie's knees. "Oba! What pale-looking American legs!" The dancers with the canes got horribly interested in her knees.

Luckily for her, the church door flung open for the procession to start. Six men bore a litter carrying the now decorated statue of Santa Maia. The statue was tangled in orchids; dozens of red-cupped votive candles emitted strange white smoke. Now and then, one of the orchids would catch fire.

What a shot! Jackie pushed through the swirling crowd, trying to reach that yellow half-dead tree in the *Praca*. She'd have to climb the first branches at least to shoot over the feathers and long canes. *"Santa Maia nos garde!"* they chanted, "Santa Maia protect us!"

"Excuse me . . . excuse me . . ." Finally she reached the tree. She grasped the lower branch and tried to get her footing—

A group of boys ran toward her, carrying a makeshift figure that wore a mildewed, bootblack Nazi uniform, with that lethal spider prominent on the arm band. "Move, *Dona*, get down!" They nudged Jackie aside and scrambled up onto a thick branch midway up the stunted tree. She watched from below. They hung the figure in effigy and swung it in front of her face, laughing.

Her father dragged her back to the dead one. "Look at it!" The dead one seemed to cling to her face, clutching and kissing; "GET IT AWAY FROM ME!" she yelled.

A gunshot snapped like a whip. Shoulders flinched. A second gunshot blasted a hole through the statue of Santa Maia. Its wood body split, tumbled to the ground and burst into flames. The crowd surged toward their protective forest canopy. Jackie dove under the tree for cover.

A vehicle backfired.

Was that the sound of a van speeding away? Jackie looked up. The torches had burnt out, it was too dark to see. A whirlwind of dust rose and fell, scattering particles of red glass. The burning wood statue of Santa Maia flickered. Jackie stared into its flames until her eyes watered.

She held her breath, took the scalpel and made a clean incision. The white skin fell open revealing, shiny, flickering, deep reds and purples.

A great gold jaguar rose from the statue's dying flame, its jaws cracking and popping as it swallowed a copper-skinned girl. The young saint calmly fingered her long neck, yet tears rolled down her cheeks and collected on the corners of her mouth as she sang a *saecula saeculorum* lullaby. Jackie crawled up to the saint and rubbed her hot copper skin, swollen against the jaguar's teeth. The orchids woven in the girl's hair exhaled perfume from their pure white mouths.

"Does it hurt?" Jackie whispered and gathered the young girl into her arms, trying to pull her out of the jaguar. Perfumed liquid splashed around Jackie's neck. Then Santa Maia pushed her away, slamming her against the half-dead tree.

The white membranes, suspended and caught like white lace, the small plump heart nestled between two swelling sponges, and organs, layers upon layers, folding open like petals; it all fit so comfortably inside a beautiful human eggshell.

The saint slid into the jaguar's throat like a wax candle and slipped away. Now only long strands of black hair hung from the jaguar's teeth. Jackie spat out a piece of red glass on her own hand. Had she been eating the stuff? Had she swallowed any?

The only fire left was the pink blush that now grew in the sky.

In the movies, Nazis appear in the action scenes and fade into black and white fuzzy photographs. This was no movie. Jackie ran all the way back to Henrique's villa. "HENRIQUE!" she screamed into the hall. He could be anywhere, still carrying the gun. She rushed into the dining room and threw open the sliding door. He sat facing his painfully beautiful back yard.

She stepped onto the porch. "I saw her. I don't believe it."

Henrique managed to laugh. "Don't believe it? People didn't believe Nazi Germany until there were *pictures* of it. Now they look all over the world for Heinrich Dorfman. Not Henrique Gonsalves."

"I hope they find you."

He spoke rapid-fire. "I gave this village their patron saint. When I came here, the people *wanted* me to rule them! They said, 'Henrique, you are like a *lobo branca*—a white wolf, in the land of the jaguar.' But this Maia stood up in front of the church and tried to turn the town against me."

He pulled something out of his pocket. "I fed her to a jaguar. But she didn't die. Out of spite. She lived inside the half-gagging animal and became a saint." He placed the tip of a silver pistol on his lower lip. "But you know what happens to—fallen dictators."

The gleam from the metal burned her eyes. She forced her eyes open.

"Jackie. Tell me not to do it."

No.

"Stop me, Jackie! *Ich liebe Dich!*"

"Jackie, look! You need to look at what you're doing!"

"I can't anymore!" She laid down the scalpel and cried.

The camera hanging around her neck seemed to choke her. He glanced at her. She wouldn't. Wouldn't stop him.

He shoved the barrel into his mouth, pulled the trigger and blew away the top of his master-mind. His tall body

74

landed hard on the porch. She raised the camera to her eye and whizzed through half a roll of film. HEINRICH DORF-MAN SHOOTS HIMSELF AT HOME IN BRAZIL.

She lowered her camera.

Her father threw up his hands. "Why do you cry at the sight of blood? Can't you at least faint like other people?"

Just then, the grand gold jaguar leaped onto the porch. It scared her, but it was oh so beautiful, its belly extended, exalted, it glowed like the sun. And Heinrich Dorfman, jungle sailor, sailed away in a gruesome sea of spilt blood.

She cradled the camera in her hand, flipped it over, popped open the cover and pulled the film off its spindle.

The last time Jackie had seen her father, he sat on the front steps and leaned his head gently on a pillar. He was tracing a V formation of birds flying south with the tip of his finger. "How do they know what they hell they're doing, Jack?"

Jackie lifted her head and heard a beautiful high-pitched sound, the sound of howling birds, crooning monkeys, trees and blue jungle nights. She and the golden jaguar faced each other. An orchid seemed to fall out of its mouth, but she knew it couldn't have.

"It's inside them, Dad."

THE MONUMENT

by Lianne Elizabeth Mercer

Mabel Henderson was born with curiosity and a cowlick. Mabel's papa, Uzziah, handled both with what tools he had: spit and his thumb, and frequent reminders to Mabel that one day he was going to "put this town on the map." Looking at the purple "X" that marked the town's location on the four-color, Rand-McNally relief map on the dining room wall, Mabel wondered why it needed to be put on the map twice.

When she was seven she clutched her Kewpie doll, shoved open mammoth oak doors, and sneaked into the lace-curtained parlor that smelled of dusty leather and dried apples. She lifted open the immense family Bible to a carefully hand-lettered page between Malachi and Matthew, and read to Kewpie the account of the town's founding.

Her grandfather, Jeremiah, had discovered the town-site on a warm summer day at 1:53 p.m. when he flung his axe at a tree and shouted, "This is it!" The axe had felled the tree, which had felled Jeremiah. In their gratitude, the settlers named after him the little village that sprang up on the high banks where the bubbling creek met the sluggish river. They had also offered Uzziah, sixteen at the time, his choice of land upon which to build a house and bury Jeremiah.

On a promontory across the river from the village, Uzziah had chosen a site rampant with honeysuckle, cedar, and sumac. The combination of the river's currents and the prevailing westerly winds provided a perfect climate for growth. By Mabel's eighth year, thirty-three trees crowded the apple orchard; pansies and nasturtiums bloomed lavishly in the yard. The house had grown to three stories not including the fruit cellar, and it contained thirteen rooms, seven closets, and five porches. Mabel was five-foot-five and weighed a hundred forty-two.

Uzziah's wives, his mother, and his children did not reap the rewards of nature's nourishing nook. Mabel early on recognized their frailty and fed them fried nasturtium blossoms and doll-sized teacups full of Jeremiah's home brew, the recipe for which she had found in Micah II when she was ten.

Yet, one by one, they died.

When her first stepmother, Helena, died of a bee sting while chopping honeysuckle near the river, Mabel bawled in the circle of Uzziah's arms. She blubbered and she sobbed and blew her nose on Uzziah's sleeve, then looked to him for comfort. There was none. A solitary tear track ran from the inner corner of his right eye across his cheek and disappeared into the hair above his ear. His black and glittering eyes stared across the river, and his lips were drawn into a thin line.

Mabel's stomach felt as though she had swallowed a rock. She squirmed and took Uzziah's hand in her wet ones. "Don't worry, Papa. You'll still put this town on the map."

He spit on his thumb and squashed her cowlick, then looked down at her. "And you will help me. But crying saps your strength and dilutes your beauty, my Amabilis. Come, my beautiful one, take this shovel and help me dig the grave."

Mabel became adept at adding and subtracting places at table. More than her brothers, stepmothers, and sisters, Mabel treasured her dolls: Kewpie, By-Lo Baby, Shirley Temple, and Annette, Cecile, Emily, Marie, and Yvonne

77

Dionne. They remained at table longer. Mabel felt keenly the villagers' disapproval of Uzziah's usurping an ever-larger portion of the back yard for a burial ground. But she had broad shoulders, thanks to digging, planting, and swimming to town at least once a day to visit the library or the bakery.

Uzziah encouraged Mabel in her pursuit of books and hot cross buns.

"My Amabilis," Uzziah began one day as they sat at a table on the back porch with Annette, et al. (they had just cleared a two-foot swath around Helena's tombstone), "our family has always been set apart from the village."

"I've been wanting to talk to you about that, Papa."

"What do you wish to know?"

"The children laugh at me because we have so many people buried in our back yard. They say it's not natural."

"They are jealous, my beautiful one, jealous because they must lump their dead unceremoniously in a common plot."

"But, just once, could we not bury . . ."

"Say no more. You are running this into the ground, Mabel. You are smarter than that. One day you will take your place as grand dame of the village."

"I don't know what that means, Papa."

"It means that you will inherit the bog, the gravel pit, and the pulpwood forests. It means that you must keep your resources private and share them wisely. Do not give to those who come begging."

Mabel pressed her cowlick down with her thumb.

"If I am to make such grand decisions, Papa, shouldn't I know a great deal about what transpires in the village?"

"It goes without saying, my Amabilis. You must keep a journal. It also goes without saying that the village will want to know a great deal about you."

"What must I tell them?"

"Only what you wish them to know." Uzziah licked hot-cross-bun frosting from his fingers, then mashed on Mabel's cowlick. "And even that they will twist into sticky stories such as your still having doll tea parties at fourteen."

"But Annette listens, and Shirley understands, and Yvonne consoles."

"What do you talk with them about, Mabel?"

"Boys, Papa."

Uzziah drained the brew from the delicate sand-and-sea-colored, translucent doll cup. "Have I told you that it is the monument I am going to build that will put this town on the map?"

Mabel poured Uzziah another cupful while he stared sternly at Annette, Cecile, Emily, Marie, and Yvonne. They slid down in their seats. Mabel made a mental note to look up "monument" at the library and to buy some rubber seat cushions and a journal at the five-and-ten.

"You're dripping on the rug," said Lottie Lomax, books on one arm and Warty Sullivan on the other.

"It will dry." Mabel shook droplets from her hair, then smoothed her cowlick. "Are you laughing at me?"

"No," Lottie giggled.

"Ancient history," Warty grinned, pinching Lottie on her behind. "Beasts with two backs."

"Did they come before or after dinosaurs?" Mabel asked.

"Egypt," Warty said as he led a laughing Lottie down a narrow aisle labeled "Myths: Eros-Hippocrates."

Mabel busied herself at the dictionary. Opening it to "M," she traced her finger past "monstrous" and "montage" to "monument: a structure erected as a memorial; an outstanding and enduring achievement."

Mabel turned back to "E": "Egypt: a country of northeastern Africa, bounded on the north by the Mediterranean Sea and on the east by the Red Sea, where the ancients embalmed human beings and animals after their deaths."

Finally, Mabel flipped to "B." She traced her finger past "bazooka," "beacon," and "bear."

An hour and twenty cents later, Mabel was paddling

home holding a sack of hot cross buns and a Big Chief firmly between her large, square, split, slightly protruding front teeth.

"Well, well, if it isn't the beaver," Rita Mae Hansen said, drifting past Mabel at midstream.

"I don't like you calling me names, and I don't like you following me everywhere I go," Mabel said around the sack. With one breast stroke she reached Rita Mae and dunked her.

Rita Mae spluttered to the surface. "I always did think that beavers had some merit," she said, treading water and spouting words. "They are industrious swimmers, work well with wood, and live cozily insulated in their homes."

Mabel did a lazy crawl around Rita Mae.

"You heard what Lottie and Warty said, didn't you?"

"Yes."

"I'm going to form a club," Mabel said.

"What for?"

"To investigate things."

"Beasts with two backs?" Rita Mae asked.

"And monuments," Mabel shifted the sack. "And maybe even Egypt. Have you ever kissed anyone?"

"Just Hal, the cute kid at the hardware store. I went to the storeroom with him, looking for nails and screws for my father."

"Do you know that a person's mouth has more germs than a dog's?" Mabel asked.

"You won't ever have babies if you don't kiss," Rita Mae said, paddling after Mabel.

"That isn't so." Mabel turned over to float and put the sack and the Big Chief on her chest. "The Bible says you have to know one another."

"I know Hal, and knowing doesn't do it because I don't have a baby."

"I think you have to lie together as well."

"Does getting your mouth washed out with soap hinder you?"

"I think we'd better plan on spending a lot of time at the

library," Mabel said.

"And at the bakery?" Rita Mae asked, eyeing the sack.

"Yes," Mabel said.

"Amabilis, I am glad to see that you have found a friend," Uzziah said to Mabel three months later. They had spent the day transplanting *Convalaria majalis* around the headstones of Ira and Jingo, the Siamese twins who had died of frustration at the age of four because they hadn't been able to decide which way to circumnavigate a cedar tree. "What do you and Rita Mae do for fun?"

"We have built a footbridge across the river, Papa," Mabel said. "We go to the library. We go to matinees on Saturdays, to see the Cisco Kid and to eat buttered popcorn and Milk Duds. We discuss things."

"What things?" Uzziah asked, removing By-Lo Baby from his chair and tossing her into her brass bed. He sat down while Mabel filled his teacup with brew.

"Beasts, mainly; mummies, some," Mabel replied. She filled Cecile et al.'s cups, then lay By-Lo straight and covered her with a quilt she had made herself. She sat down, dipped her finger in her cup, and smoothed her cowlick.

"Is it not important, my beautiful one, to develop a mind which can have intercourse on many subjects? It is not wise to limit yourself. Note that in your journal."

"Yes, Papa," Mabel said.

"It *is* limiting to continue these tea parties, Mabel."

"No, Papa," Mabel said.

"You have a friend, now, and you have me."

"And I have my journal, Papa," Mabel said.

"Have I told you that I have decided that the monument should be of an historical figure?"

"Yes, Papa," Mabel said.

"He ejaculates his seed into her," Mabel began, seven months, two weeks, and three days later, after she had poured libations all around, except for By-Lo, who had taken to sleeping constantly. It was sunset. Mabel and Rita

Mae wore their voile dresses, their black patent leather shoes, and their white gloves.

"After he puts his worm into her hole," Rita Mae said.

"I didn't see that written anywhere."

"Hal told me."

"Did Hal show you?"

"He said I was too fat."

"Fat doesn't matter; everyone does it the same way."

"Except missionaries," Rita Mae said. "They have a way all their own."

"That may be," Mabel agreed. "Reverend Roberts has seven children more than anyone else."

"He's fatter than I am. Do you think he'd let me watch?"

"That's not done, Rita Mae."

"They did it in ancient Egypt, Mabel. Maybe old Miss Morris will give us a demonstration."

"You mean like Mrs. Ricks does custard?"

"No, I guess not. Maybe we're pushed into it, like when Hal shoved me into the pond without a life jacket."

"Exactly."

"I wanted to kill him."

"I think we're after a different feeling," Mabel said, refilling everyone's cup except Kewpie's, who could only tolerate one.

"True," Rita Mae said. "Married people don't kill each other."

"Not true. Remember last year when Sergeant Billy Whatley found Old Man Amherst suffocated in the sauerkraut, and drove up in the police car with the sirens going, and he hollered at Hazel to surrender, and she hollered back he was welcome to come in and have some sauerkraut and sausage, and that the flavor had never been better? He never did arrest her; he just kept coming and eating and ended up wearing a uniform two sizes larger. That filled up two pages in my Big Chief and I write small."

"Hazel smiled at me the other day," Rita Mae said.

"Maybe it's because she doesn't have to make the beast with two backs any more," Mabel said.

"Maybe she's making it with someone she likes better."

"You mean, she enjoys it?"

"There was a footnote that mentioned fun."

"So it can be done, then, married or not."

"I believe that's where bastards come from."

"Marriage?"

"The absence of marriage."

"Perhaps Papa can put it in proper perspective," Mabel said.

Uzziah choked chug-a-lugging the contents of the teacup.

"Ah, my little beauty," he said in a sandpapery voice. "Stand up and turn slowly."

Mabel held her cowlick down and turned.

Uzziah stroked his chin. His hand covered his mouth and Mabel couldn't read his lips.

"Is it not like the riddle of the Sphinx, Amabilis? One day it will be revealed to you."

"Has it been revealed to you?"

Uzziah swilled small sips around in his mouth, swallowed noisily and licked his lips.

"Of course, but I can't tell it."

"Does the Bible forbid it?"

"No."

"Papa, I have read one thousand three hundred and sixty-two books," Mabel said. "I can understand it if you will tell me. I want to put it in my journal."

"It cannot be told. It cannot be read. It must be experienced, Mabel."

"When will I experience it, Papa?"

"Exactly when you are ready, and you must be brave." Uzziah held out his cup.

Mabel filled the cup again. "Why?"

"The first time, with your mother, she cried out."

"Did she say it hurt or did she like it?"

"She soaked in a hot tub for an hour each morning and evening for a week afterward," Uzziah said. "Nine months later you were born. Two weeks after that, she looked me in the eye and died."

"Why, Papa?"

"I never knew, Mabel."

Over the gurgling sounds of Uzziah chug-a-lugging, Mabel said, "Clarence Hodspepper delivered the shrubs you ordered."

"Good. Tomorrow we can set them in rows between the stones. Have I told you that the historical figure will be Jeremiah?" Uzziah continued in a thick voice. "I will need your knowledge about wood. Several oak logs will be delivered next week, and we will choose the most felicitous."

"That won't take long, will it, Papa?"

"Have I told you that I want you to help me carve it?"

"Yes, Papa."

"Have I told you that you must remove the footbridge between now and next week, because you have built it in the best landing place for the logs?"

"Papa said that he couldn't tell me but that I would find out at the right time," Mabel told Rita Mae as they dog-paddled beside the footbridge, dismantling it under the watchful eyes of Yvonne and Cecile.

"Uzziah is hedging," Rita Mae said.

Mabel dunked her.

Yvonne fell into the water past Cecile's outstretched hand.

"Come back!" Mabel shouted, then dived beneath the surface. At first in the darkness she could see only Rita Mae's plump white legs, rhythmically pumping among the weeds. Then, past the startled eyes of trout, Mabel saw Yvonne's small foot spinning away in the current. As she stroked toward her, Mabel hit her shin on a cypress knee.

Blood billowing around her, Mabel erupted from the maroon water like a fleshy geyser. "She's gone!"

Rita Mae thrashed and spluttered beside her. "Uzziah doesn't want you to grow up," she said.

Mabel dunked her again.

84

Rita Mae surfaced six feet away.

"Yvonne is drowned and Papa thinks I'm grown up enough to help him with his life work," Mabel bawled.

"He's using oak instead of pine," Rita Mae said.

"It will last longer."

"It will take longer."

Shivering and dripping and bleeding and sniffing, Mabel hauled herself and Cecile hand over hand up the rope that minutes before had anchored the footbridge to the cedar trees. Rita Mae handed her the boards one by one. Beneath Cecile's mournful eyes, Mabel stacked them under the reddening sumac leaves.

Three years later, two months prior to the senior prom, Mabel's shin had only a small, jagged scar, she had filled four journals, and Uzziah had barely begun to carve Jeremiah.

Uzziah had been particular about which log best personified Jeremiah. He let them weather for eighteen months to see if any would crack. None did. He finally selected one that was taller than the others but smaller near the top. "Daddy had skinny shoulders," Uzziah told Mabel. "But powerful. He could heave an axe a hundred feet."

Jeremiah had a long nose, too, and lips that were ajar over his split front teeth.

"I never knew if he was smiling or not," Uzziah said to Mabel one night as he sanded Jeremiah's ears.

"He looks sad," Mabel said, making tiny cross-hatchings on his cheeks.

"It's because he was cut down in the prime of life."

"Papa, I don't have a date for the senior prom," Mabel said.

"Why not?"

"Because I don't know boys the way Lottie does, or even the way Rita Mae knows Hal."

Uzziah sanded faster. "Is it not so that there will be a right time to know boys?"

"The time is getting short if I'm to know any before the

prom." Mabel shifted from one foot to the other in the thick-soled shoes she'd begun to wear to keep slivers out of her feet. Her fingers flew over Jeremiah's cheeks with the small chisel pecking and biting.

Into the sawdust and flying chips of wood, Uzziah spoke. "Have I told you that Jeremiah will carry an axe?"

Within the week, while Hopalong Cassidy galloped through the rocks after the bad guys, Frank Morse plopped down next to Mabel. She knew him to be one of the boys who occasionally did odd jobs for Uzziah. She thought he might change seats after his eyes adjusted to the dark, but he did not. Frank wiped tricklets of river water from the arm of the seat, offered her some of his popcorn and gulped, "Hello." Mabel whispered "Hello" back.

Three weeks later, Frank held Mabel's damp hand, gulped popcorn, and offered her an invitation to the senior prom. Mabel shouted, "Yes!" Roy Rogers crouched on a fake fence and harmonized with the Sons of the Pioneers.

"I'm glad that you can go, at least," Rita Mae said, tipping up her fourth cup of brew. She had already had three hot cross buns. Beside her, Shirley frowned. Beyond them, a few feet from the porch, Jeremiah's head loomed from the oak log. Rita Mae had just found out that Hal was taking Alyce Ann to the prom. "But I do think it strange that you've never seen Frank in the daylight."

"I see him in the hall on Wednesdays at two. He's tall and thin and has big ears."

"What does he say to you?"

Mabel flipped through her journal pages. "He tells me that Roy Rogers is right never to kiss the girl. He tells me that we will travel to the prom by canoe and pickup truck."

"That's not much." Rita Mae had another hot cross bun and turned Shirley's frown to the wall.

"He listens to me."

"What do you say?"

"I tell him about Jeremiah's ears and about Yvonne

being lost at sea."

"What does Uzziah say?"

"Papa doesn't say anything. He bought me a new dress. It's the color of spring sumac and has rhinestone buttons. Papa bought me some new lick 'um for my cowlick."

They watched Uzziah, who absently brushed his hand with sandpaper as he brooded at the river from a clump of quivering honeysuckle just past Florence's stone. Florence had run away from home when she was eight. The stone marked no grave, because she had never been seen again.

A loud crash beside them caused Mabel and Rita Mae to jump. Next to the overturned teapot in the middle of the table sat a large grey cat, licking a puddle of brew from the polished oak surface.

Rita Mae flung her arms at the cat. "Vamoose!"

"Shoo, cat!" Mabel shouted.

"It's broken the teapot," Rita Mae cried.

Mabel patted Rita Mae awkwardly on her arm. "There's another five gallons in the basement, and six more teapots."

"That's not why I'm crying!" Rita Mae wailed.

"Hush! Crying makes Papa nervous."

Rita Mae picked up the spout, two pieces of the lid, and a hot cross bun and heaved them toward Uzziah. As they whizzed past his head and splashed into the river, he turned slowly and stared at Rita Mae and Mabel, until Rita Mae's sobbing and hiccoughing ebbed and subsided. Then he returned to Jeremiah and started chipping away at his chin.

After it finished licking up the puddle, the grey cat jumped from the table and disappeared into the Queen Anne's Lace beyond Granny's grave. Granny had died peeling apples in the rocker, stiffened before anyone had discovered her, and had been buried sitting up. She had no marker, just a mound.

Mabel went to the fruit cellar for another teapot, which she filled with brew. On the way back she noted in her journal that there were five teapots left.

The Sunday after the prom, Mabel hung her dress

inside a sateen wardrobe bag. She buttoned each of the seven rhinestone buttons, fastened the belt, zipped the bag shut, and hung it in the closet. She put her shoes and gloves into a small box, tied the lid down, put the box on the floor beneath the wardrobe bag, and shut the closet door.

"You promised you'd tell me all about it," Rita Mae said, red-eyed and cross-legged on the bed.

"We danced in dark corners," Mabel said.

"That's good."

"My cowlick tickled his chin and he sneezed."

"That's bad."

"I couldn't see anyone else."

"Not even Hal and Alyce Ann?"

"No. Finally, the band played Auld Lang Syne while Clarence shinnied up the basketball net and let six hundred balloons go. I brought you one."

Mabel handed Rita Mae the balloon. It was soft and punchy and half-full of air.

"I was in gym class once with Lottie," Rita Mae said. "She looked just like that when she took off her bra."

"I saw her stuff in two hankies once at the library, in the aisle where the books are that tell you how to repair home defects with materials you have around the house."

"Did Frank touch yours?"

"No."

They had their dusk teacupsful with Shirley and Marie, et al., then Rita Mae took her balloon home. Mabel sat in the yard with Jeremiah, watching the sky turn violet past his jutting chin and writing in her journal. The grey cat stepped through the pansies. It curled its tail around its paws and lapped up the brew from a small saucer near the table leg. Mabel did not know whether Uzziah would approve, but tonight he was in town checking a pulpwood-loading schedule.

At the sound of a booming splash, the grey cat vanished into the pansies. Mabel hid behind a cedar tree near the bank, then slowly pulled the honeysuckle aside. Frank stood in the water up to his armpits, slowly shaking droplets from his hair.

"There is something I must tell you," he said. "Where can we talk?"

"Right here." Mabel kicked off her shoes and waded into the water. She had to swim the last few feet since she was so much shorter than Frank. She floated next to him and watched thunderheads sail the sky while he cleared his throat. The sounds bounced off the water.

"First, will you meet me at the matinee on Saturday? It's a Gene Autry."

"Yes."

"Second, your father paid me to take you to the prom."

Thunderheads grumbled above Mabel as she sank beneath the water and hung there. Through the water, clouds took the shape of dolls and Jeremiah and beasts. Her chest got tight. She rose.

"Why?"

Words darted out of Frank like water beetles and zigzagged between him and Mabel.

Mabel watched them. "Wanted what's best for you" raced "Mother's sick and I need the money." "Love" narrowly missed "Army."

"Army?" Mabel felt the river suck at her arms. She raised her eyes to purple clouds and rain.

"I'm leaving in a month," Frank said, crawling around her in ever-narrowing circles. He stopped in front of her.

"Do you know about the beast with two backs?" she asked.

Frank did a surface dive. Mabel saw the soles of his feet flash in the wet magenta twilight, then felt him pass between her legs. He surfaced at the pier and clambered out. His words came softly, like moths whispering.

"Uzziah told me not to touch you."

Mabel heard the slap slap of wet soles on the pavement. Then there was silence.

After Uzziah had sanded away part of Jeremiah's chin the next night, Mabel asked him if he had told Frank not to

89

touch her.

"Of course," Uzziah answered. "Hold the chisel right here, we're going to begin his chest."

"Papa, I was the only girl at the prom who didn't get even a goodnight kiss."

"The heart has its own knowledge, my Amabilis. Do I not know that for a fact? Have I not buried three wives and seven children? God has his plans and they will be revealed in good time."

"What does that have to do with a goodnight kiss?"

"Kisses lead to touches and to beastly heartache, my beautiful one," Uzziah said, tapping the chisel with a hammer. "You've got to keep the rhythm, Mabel. Oh, I nearly forgot, I have been meaning to tell you what a good job you're doing controlling your cowlick."

Mabel met Frank at the matinee the next four Saturdays. On the last one before he was to leave, he walked her back to the pier at the foot of Main Street. Behind a clump of sumac, near the river's edge, where the water swirled in a little whirlpool that was filled with pollywogs each spring, he kissed her.

Mabel was startled at the narrow hardness of Frank's lips and the sudden exhalation of Frank's Milk-Dud-y breath into her mouth. Mabel felt her arms tremble on Frank's back and felt her heart knock against her ribs so hard she felt lopsided and believed that she was falling. Mabel tried to clutch handfuls of Frank's plaid shirt stretched tight across his shoulders.

Failing, she shoved him away.

"Why did you do that?"

"I think I'm going to be sick."

"Is this the first time you ever kissed anyone, Mabel?"

"Yes, Frank."

"Me, too. Did you like it?"

"Yes. I don't know."

"Do you want to do it again?"

"No, Frank."

"Oh please, Mabel."

"No."

Frank took her hand in his. "Please. We can learn about the beast with two backs together, Mabel."

Mabel dived into the water. She surfaced in midstream and squinted at Frank. He stood with his arms akimbo. In the late-afternoon sunlight he looked like Jeremiah.

"You are a tease, Mabel!" Frank yelled as she stroked for her bank.

"You are sending me away with a broken heart!" Frank hollered over the croaking frogs who hopped in the shallows where Mabel rested on her hands and knees, gasping for breath.

"I'm going to write to you, Mabel!" Frank's words shook like the sumac leaves as Uzziah pushed through them.

"What's all this noise?" Uzziah stood above her, oak chips and sawdust in rippling patterns on his gabardine trousers, his knee bare beneath a tri-cornered rip.

"It is the sound of a heart breaking, Papa."

"Frank will get over it, my Amabilis. Come, I am having difficulty with one of Jeremiah's ribs."

Mabel received thirteen letters from Frank and recorded each one in her journal, underlining the parts where he said he respected her and would show her how much when he came home on furlough. She wrote to Frank seven times, no, eight if she counted the package of taffy apples she sent him on Halloween. Mabel told Frank that Jeremiah's chest was stalled, that geese were flying south in long lonely Vs, and that she and a few other young women were growing vegetables for victory.

The fourteenth letter was from Frank's colonel. He wrote that Frank had listed Mabel as the person to notify "in case." And since Frank had stood in front of a bazooka at the wrong time, there was a need to notify. Would she care to come to Egypt to claim the remains?

No, she would not. Could not. She was exhausted from digging up the iris bulbs, dividing and then replanting them in the beds that bordered the house. She was in the midst of recording the results of her attempts to improve the quality of her vegetables by watering only with a 75 percent solution of brew.

And there was no way she could leave Uzziah at this critical point. Rita Mae held the chisel for an hour once last month when a shipment of sugar had come in at the grocery store and Mabel had had to stand in line for an hour to get ten pounds. When she returned, Uzziah told her that Rita Mae didn't know the right angles.

In four months, Mabel received a small wooden box from the colonel. Sand fell out when she lifted the lid. Nestled in the newspaper-lined box, in a scorched uniform pocket, was Frank's ear plus a note from the colonel stating that the ear and the pocket were all that were found. A small advertisement on one of the pages offered 10 percent off for a mail-order course in mummification.

Five months later, between trips to the library and to the post office, Mabel had swum to town twice a day and had filled 77 more journal pages with her cramped writing. In her closet, she built three shelves above the wardrobe bag. One was for journals and Frank's ear, and one was for bottles of oil of cedar and palm wine she had had sent from Egypt, as well as boxes of flesh-dissolving natron plus powder of myrrh and cassia. The third was for anticipated monthly copies of *The Mid-State Alchemist* and *The-Book-of-the-Dead Digest*, to which she had just subscribed for life.

"I'm going to build a pyramid in the back yard, Papa," Mabel told Uzziah. She showed him Frank's ear, which she had prepared as instructed and now kept in a pyramid-shaped box.

"Don't disturb Mandy. I promised her on her death bed that I'd let her rest in peace forever. After all, she did give me four children in three-and-a-half years."

"The pyramid will be between the orchard and Hamilton, Papa." Hamilton had bet that he could swim the river seven times in succession without lifting his head to breathe, and he had lost. Uzziah had retrieved his body at the dam a mile and a half downstream.

"I'll still need you to hold the chisel," Uzziah said.

"I'm going to build a pyramid in the back yard, Rita Mae," Mabel said. She showed Frank's ear to her and to Cecile et al.

"I have something to show you," Rita Mae said.

She dived into the river, was gone for forty-five minutes and returned wet and out of breath. From her pocket she took a gold statue eight inches high and placed it on the table next to Frank's ear.

"My mother's cousin's father's brother-in-law was with Howard Carter when he entered King Tut's tomb in '22. He mailed this to us just before he died," Rita Mae explained.

"Does the statue still have a curse on it?"

"Mother removed it."

Mabel put the statue to bed with By-Lo.

At the hardware store, the bridegroom of less than a year, Hal, had recently been promoted to assistant cashier. Nonetheless, he himself made eleven trips to the storeroom for Mabel's lumber. She watched Rita Mae watch Hal's receding, sweaty back and protruding, belted paunch. Mabel told Rita Mae that they could not use either screws or nails, according to page 124 of volume 62 of *The Book-of-the-Dead Digest,* because metal altered the vibrations. Rock was appropriate, of course, but it wouldn't float. They would use wood pegged air tight.

It took Mabel and Rita Mae two months to swim the lumber across the river and another two months to stack it next to Josephine's small marker, the one with the apple on it. Josephine had liked to sit in the apple tree outside her window, and one night during a storm the tree had been struck by lightning. Uzziah and Mabel had found her the next morning on the ground surrounded by four dozen apples. Uzziah and Mabel had buried her, then made applesauce.

Kewpie, Shirley, Rita Mae, and Uzziah toasted Mabel

with a cup of brew on May Day '45, the day she placed the first board. Mabel accepted their applause and good wishes and enlisted the aid of the ladies of the garden club. The ladies planted trees, senna, and shrubs of the genus *Commiphora*. One, who owned a typewriter, wrote weekly requests to a pharmacy in Omaha which sold natron by the pound. Mabel set aside a bed near her window where another lady planted catnip. Mabel wanted to treat the grey cat who, once building commenced, appeared each evening at dusk to stroll the day's work, fashioning a furry blessing with its feet. Mabel copied carefully in her journal the recipe for palm wine produced by a third lady, who said it had been in her family for 31 generations. Mabel told Frank's ear that the honeysuckle grew best in the pyramid's shadow.

Mabel and Rita Mae lugged the tea table onto the small section of completed floor in the summer of '47. Uzziah brought Jeremiah to the party and commemorated the event by finishing his chest.

"I know where the twelfth rib fits now," he announced after three cups of brew and numerous delicate tappings and soundings. He complimented Mabel on her handling of the chisel. She smiled, smoothed her prom dress, and couldn't wait to tell Frank's ear. The grey cat licked its saucer clean, then lapped up everyone's spills. Jeremiah's cup was emptied while the others were applauding.

In '50, Mabel awoke one morning and could not remember what Frank's lips had tasted like. She licked hers. She shut her eyes and concentrated. She opened them and reread each page of her last nine journals. At noon she still tasted only the night.

"If I try not to think of it, it will return," Mabel said to the ear.

The grey cat who sat outside on the broken branch that had been Josephine's narrowed its eyes.

"Doing the opposite fools what you want into appearing."

The grey cat washed its face.

"Today I complete the floor. It's been slow because we've had to shave a quarter inch from the south edge of each board. You see, the ground has shifted in the west and the floor is warped."

The grey cat purred.

Mabel suffered from vertigo. Three feet off the ground, she wobbled like a weathervane. Rita Mae refused to climb, so Mabel worked out a rhythm: Rita Mae planed a board; Mabel climbed the ladder carrying the board on her shoulders; Mabel fit the board into place; Rita Mae handed her the pegs; Mabel pegged the board; Mabel clung to the ladder with a vise-like grip; Rita Mae pried her down; Kewpie, et al., scrambled to avoid being squashed; Mabel collapsed into the nearest vacant chair; Rita Mae poured Mabel a brew; Mabel drank the brew. Sometimes, to recover more quickly, Mabel drank another.

The higher the pyramid, the longer the recovery time. Near the end of '54, Mabel suffered from a recovery ratio of nine to one. But she was still organized.

On Mondays, she policed Rita Mae and the ladies of the club while they chopped honeysuckle. Daily it sent tendrils to explore the rising boards; hourly the tiny branches insinuated themselves into cracks Mabel could barely see; weekly the slender stalks resisted being yanked out by Rita Mae, then transformed into aromatic syrup in a boiling, bubbling vat near the river.

Tuesday mornings, Mabel gossiped at Charlene's beauty shop while she had her hair done. Tuesday evenings, Mabel repeated the gossip to Frank's ear. On Wednesdays, in a scrawling hand, she journaled the village news, such as Doc Sullivan's donation of a new wing at the library and Lizzie Schwartz's nocturnal strolls with her cat in search of stories. Thursdays, Mabel brewed and distilled in the basement. And on Fridays she chiseled. Uzziah was having trouble with the axe handle: it kept falling from Jeremiah's wooden fingers. Once it narrowly missed Uzziah.

The pyramid was completed one Indian Summer day in '60. Mabel moved the bottles of oil of cedar and palm wine, and the boxes of myrrh and cassia and natron into a chest she had built especially for them. She placed Frank's ear in a vase she had ordered from a Montana university anthropologist who made copies of his more spectacular finds and sold them through the mail. A small door facing the river was the pyramid's only entry. The boards had been fitted together and sanded and pegged air tight.

Yet there was a breeze. Tiny particles of sand appeared in low drifts on the floor. And there was light, a diffuse grey light that expanded and contracted with Mabel's breathing. It focused where it would: on the sheen of Uzziah's hairy forearm, on the tilt of Shirley's head as she sipped, on Frank's ear, on the tint of Mabel's dress, or on the shiny spines of Mabel's journals, all twenty-six of them aligned on a shelf in the southeast corner.

Mabel and Emilie and Uzziah agreed that the brew tasted better inside the pyramid. They agreed that it was drier, even that close to the river. So dry that Mabel's skin tingled and was relieved only by a drop or two of oil of cedar. The oil softened Rita Mae, polished Uzziah, and brought into sharp relief the grain of the axe handle in Jeremiah's thin fingers. Annette, Cecile, Emilie, and Marie grew tan though they never set foot outside.

In '63 Mabel did her first beast, a squirrel. She was pleased with it and sat it in the high chair where Kewpie used to sit. Its tail moved back and forth like a brushy pendulum.

"Less myrrh and more palm wine," Mabel told Uzziah, noting the new proportion in her thirty-seventh journal.

"Hold that chisel more to the right. Is it not that Jeremiah's hips keep moving? It's quite distracting."

"I haven't noticed it, Papa. Papa, when I was in town the other day, the mayor asked me when the monument would be ready."

"Soon, my Amabilis. Have I told you that you become more lovely with each decade?"

Mabel smiled through her split front teeth.

"There is about you now the look of untouched marble, cool and elegant."

"Thank you, Papa," Mabel said, noting it in her journal.

By '75, Mabel's skin had lost much of its suppleness. Only with great effort could she touch her fingers together to tie the bow on Shirley's hat. She could barely journal that Clarence had requested her recipe for Arabian Peach Salad. She apologized to Frank's ear because she had forgotten how his touch felt. She no longer wore her sturdy shoes; the soles of her feet had become like leather. Her cowlick rose from the center of her part like a unicorn's horn.

That fall she did a German Shepherd, the one which had harassed the grey cat. None of its parts moved. But in the winter, when the temperature hovered at the freezing point and ice formed in the reeds near the riverbank, from deep in its throat the dog emitted a sighing sound part way between a bark and a howl.

"Doing that dog was a mistake, Mabel," Rita Mae said.

"Why?"

"Because it's nearly driven away the ladies of the club. Haven't you noticed that they only come when I come and leave when I leave?"

"I have noticed that their wake threatens to inundate the pansies. And I have noted in my journal, on page fifty-seven of the one-hundred-seventh volume, that they are not taking care of the honeysuckle properly. It has completely usurped the east side of the pyramid."

"It's because of the morning sun, Mabel."

"It's because they've become lazy and indolent, Rita Mae."

"I notice that Uzziah finally finished Jeremiah's fly."

"Papa had difficulty keeping the buttons buttoned. He borrowed By-Lo's quilt to keep Jeremiah decent."

"You never have time to swim any more, Mabel."

"Papa is beginning Jeremiah's great toe on Tuesday. He'll be done soon. Then I will have time to do all the things I used to do. What were they, Rita Mae?"

On an October day in '84, when the sky was woven of bright blue, Uzziah finished the statue of Jeremiah. Mabel invited the entire town to celebrate. But the only people who came were Doc, who was Mayor; Hal, who was curious; the grey cat, who never passed up free brew; and the ladies of the club, who were awed and inspired but never left Rita Mae's side. Shirley and Kewpie retired to join By-Lo before the fifth toast. Doc left after praising Jeremiah and promising to send a barge within the week to transport the monument to the town square. Hal left in a different way: he passed out beneath the table with his arms around Annette and a smile on his face.

"Ah, my Amabilis, is this not what I have dreamed of all these years?" Uzziah said to Mabel in a hoarse voice that sounded trapped in his throat. "Have I told you that you have done me proud? I am so stiff I can hardly move. It must be because I have had to stand on my head these past few months to finish Jeremiah's feet. I shall just lie here and contemplate how I have put this town on the map."

Mabel placed a pillow beneath Uzziah's head.

"Let the old coot sleep and we'll celebrate with a swim," Rita Mae said, setting her cup down with a crash that made the grey cat and the ladies of the club jump.

"All right. I'll just tell Frank's ear where I'm going."

"You used to want to have fun, Mabel," Rita Mae said, paddling naked into the moon's reflection in the middle of the river. "You used to eat hot cross buns. But now all you do is journal and chisel and brew and chop."

"I must do those things."

"You've become a bore, Mabel."

"I used to want to do other things, Rita Mae. Look, I'm taking off my clothes, even though duty dictates clothes. Is it not so that I will one day be the grand dame of the village?" Mabel splashed into the river near Rita Mae. Four ladies of

98

the club followed.

"So what, Mabel?" A white blob, Rita Mae sank beneath the surface and sent back bubbles.

"I've told Frank's ear of the resources I will have to share wisely," Mabel shouted into the water. "Have I told you?"

"I believe I'll see if old Hal doesn't want to come for a swim." Rita Mae's mouth and nose and cheeks and breasts bobbed like the rotten apples Mabel used to heave into the river. With their backs turned, the ladies trod water.

"You're not listening, Rita Mae."

"I'm hearing just fine, Mabel. Do you know you haven't asked about the beast with two backs in forty years? *I* still want to know. Hal! Wake up and get out here!"

"I tell Frank's ear that it's becoming less and less important."

Rita Mae struck out for the bank. The ladies gasped and headed in the opposite direction.

"Rita Mae, I must make a note of what Doc said about the barge. What did he say? Do you remember? Did he name a day?"

Mabel paddled in Rita Mae's wake, then overtook her. Hand over calloused hand, she pulled herself up on the honeysuckle vine. Even in the moonlight the peak of the pyramid was barely visible. She sighed. It was time to forego journaling and talking and spend more time chopping.

Suddenly there was a loud crashing sound and the noises of an animal grunting and groaning.

"Oh, it's you," Hal said lurching through the vines. Mabel felt his breath hot on her bare chest as he passed. "Rita Mae? Where are you, Rita Mae, honey?" Hal hollered.

Mabel heard a splash. She heard Rita Mae laugh. She heard Hal snort. She shut her ears, hurried to the pyramid, stepped inside and shut the door against the vines. Sand clung to her wet feet.

"Papa?" Mabel said. "Papa?"

Moonlight formed a chiaroscuro of faces and geometric shapes. A dozen circles of china eyes watched her. Jeremiah's

trapezoid-shaped thighs ended in shadowy knees. A triangle, the grey cat sat near the teapot. The 163 journals
gleamed on the rectangular shelves.

Mabel couldn't find Frank's ear.

"Papa?" Mabel whispered. "Papa?"

The swish of the grey cat's tail answered.

Mabel padded toward Uzziah and knelt next to him in
the soft sand. She touched his cold skin.

"Oh, Papa!" Mabel cried. "You have finished your life's
work, and now I am the grand dame and to whom shall I give
my resources?"

Mabel dropped to her hands and knees to listen for his
reply. The wind leaking in at the door onto her bare thighs
made her shiver. Her cowlick brushed against Uzziah's
shirt. His stiff arm banged down and pinned Mabel to him.
His buttons scraped her nipples.

"Papa!" Mabel screamed.

She pushed at Uzziah's chest but it didn't move. She
tried to slither beneath the tight circle of his arms, but
Jeremiah blocked her. The sand stung her back. She shut
her eyes against the tetrahedron of the gleaming axe blade
above her.

"Papa!" Mabel's heart exploded against her ribs. She
reached up and around Uzziah, clutched at the shirt stretched
tight across his shoulders, gasped, felt hot, felt Uzziah hard
against her, and heard the sounds of laughter tinkling like
far-away bells. Expectant. Pleased, like the ripples of the
river, inviting her to swim.

"Papa," Mabel moaned, while Emilie and the grey cat
smiled their crescent cheshire smiles.

Mabel felt warm, like when she chopped honeysuckle.

Mabel felt hot, like when she opened the box with
Frank's ear in it. The laughter became taps.

Mabel promised herself that she would tell Frank's ear
about how sounds changed, and she would journal about
how the monument had been created, about how . . .

In the pearly dawn the grey cat stalked between

100

rhomboid purrs and triangles of light. It leaped over the beast at Jeremiah's feet. It meowed. No one moved to fill its saucer. The tail of the squirrel and the sigh of the dog broke the stillness. The cat squeezed its eyes shut, then squeezed out the door and picked its way through the vines to the riverbank. It rode a log to the far side, leaped off at Main Street, trotted past a barge moored there, went west two blocks and north one, then padded into the feed store. It slinked to the clock, where it was snatched up into loving, worried arms.

"Naughty kitty. Out all night again. What did you see?"

BOTTLES

by Alcina Lubitch Domecq
(Translated from the Spanish by Ilan Stavans)

Mom was taken away, I don't know exactly where. Dad says
she is in a nice place, where they take good care of her. I miss
her . . . , although I understand. Dad says she suffered from
a sickening love for bottles. First she started to buy them in
the supermarket. All sorts of bottles—plastic and crystal,
small and big. Everything had to be packed in a bottle—
noodle soup, lemon juice, bathroom soap, pencils. She just
wouldn't buy something that wasn't in one. Dad complained.
Sometimes that was the reason why we wouldn't have toilet
paper, or there wouldn't be any salt. And Mom used to kiss
the bottles all day long. She polished them with great
affection, talked to them, and at times I remember her
saying she was going to eat one. You could open a kitchen
cabinet and find a million bottles. A million. I hated them,
and so did my sister. I mean, why store the dirty linen in a
huge bottle, the size of a garbage can? Dad says Mom didn't
know anything about logic. I remember one night, after
dinner, when Mom apologized and left in a hurry. An hour
later she returned with a box full of wine. Dad asked what
had got into her. She said she had been at the liquor store
and immediately started to empty every single bottle in the
toilet. All the wine was dumped. She just needed the bottles.

102

Dad and I and my sister just sat there, on the living room couch, watching Mom wash and kiss those ugly wine bottles. I think my sister began to cry. But Mom didn't care. Then Dad called the police but they didn't do a thing. Weeks later, we pretended to have forgotten everything. It was then that Mom began screaming that she was pregnant, like when my sister was born. She was shouting that a tiny plastic bottle was living inside her stomach. She said she was having pain. She was vomiting and was pale. She cried a lot. Dad called an ambulance and Mom was taken to the hospital. There the doctors made X-rays and checked her over. Nothing was wrong. They just couldn't find the tiny plastic bottle. But for days she kept insisting that it was living inside her, growing, that's what she used to say to me and my sister. Not to Dad anymore because he wouldn't listen to her, he just wouldn't listen. I miss Mom . . . She was taken away a month later, after the event with the statue in the living room. You see, one afternoon she decided that the tiny bottle wasn't in her stomach anymore. Now she felt bad because something was going to happen to her. Like a prophecy. She was feeling that something was coming upon her. And next morning, before me and my sister left for school, we found Mom near the couch, standing in the living room. She was vertical, standing straight. She couldn't walk around. Like in a cell. I asked her why she wouldn't move, why she wouldn't go to the kitchen or to my room. Mom answered that she couldn't because she was trapped in a bottle, a gigantic one. We could see her and she could see us too, but according to Mom nobody could touch her body because there was glass surrounding it. Actually, I touched her and I never felt any glass. Neither did Dad or my sister. But Mom insisted that she couldn't feel us. For days she stayed in that position, and after some time I was able to picture the big bottle. Mom was like a spider you catch in the backyard and suffocate in a Tupperware. That's when the ambulance came for the second time. I wasn't home, but Dad was. He was there when they took her away. I was at school, although I knew what was happening. That same day we threw away all the bottles in a dump nearby. The neighbors were staring at us but we didn't care. It felt good, very good.

IN UNISON, SOFTLY

by Mary Rosenblum

Lea dropped the pickup's tailgate and lifted down the burlapped tree. She'd gotten a good deal on the laceleaf maple. The Farbers would be pleased. Never let it be said that Green Visions Landscaping didn't do well by its clients. Her braid swung forward over her shoulder as she dumped the maple onto the grass and spread a plastic tarp for the dirt.

Humming, she carved a perfect hole into the thick, green turf. It paid to dig a big hole, even if it took more work. The roots could spread and the tree would do better. Dumping a last shovelful of dirt onto the neat pile on the tarp, she reached for the bag of compost she'd brought along.

Someone was humming along with her.

The soft, wordless song rose and fell in a minor key, twisting back on itself in endless variations. It was almost the melody she had been humming, as if she'd unconsciously followed the invisible singer's lead. Lea frowned. The humming sounded soft and close, but there was no one in the yard. Down the block, a small boy pedaled a tricycle up and down the sidewalk under his mother's watchful eye, but they were too far away.

Lea tracked the sound, her eyes half-closed. They

105

snapped open as she found herself staring at the small maple beside the hole.

No. It was a trick of acoustics. Lea tugged at her braid and stepped sideways a few paces. The humming still came from the maple. There were no words, no breathiness, nothing but a thread of pure, clear sound. The hairs began to rise on the backs of Lea's arms.

Somebody was playing a prank. Lips tight, Lea pulled off one leather work glove, fished her jackknife out of her pocket and cut the twine that bound the burlap. She wasn't dumb. You could do a lot with a couple of speakers and a home computer. With a grunt, she lifted the heavy root ball clear of the folds of burlap and began to straighten the cramped roots. The tree gave a silvery trill that might have been laughter.

Trees did not laugh. Lea dumped the sack of compost into the hole and plunked the tree down on top of the mound. It trilled again as she began to work soil in between the roots. Lea began to sing loudly. It didn't help. She could hear more humming now, mellow contraltos in close harmony.

Stubbornly, Lea began to fill in the hole. Contraltos? Maybe a family of ventriloquists lived on the block. Maybe they had a warped sense of humor. Lea gritted her teeth, wondering how they'd like a face full of compost.

By the time she firmed the last of the soil into place, she had placed the contraltos. The rhodies. They hummed softly in her ear as she fumbled between their twisted stems to connect her hose to the leaking faucet. She could hear a descant now, like a thousand tiny, silver voices. It was coming from the grass beneath her feet.

This had to be some smart-ass kid playing electronic games. Lea closed her eyes, her breakfast lumping in her stomach. If she caught him, he was history. She gave the maple a quick watering and coiled her hose. To hell with the edging. She'd do the Boutros yard and come back later. She tossed the hose into the truck bed and swung into the cab.

Before heading off to the Boutros's she circled the

106

block, squinting into bushes and driveways. The preschool-
er and his mother had vanished and the block was empty.
The singing seemed to follow her, whispering at the edges of
the rock music on the radio. Lea turned the volume up and
hung onto her anger. It kept trying to dissolve into fear.

All the way to Dr. Boutros's house, she kept thinking
about her grandmother. *Shush, child, I'm listening to the
angels,* Granny would whisper when Lea asked for juice or
a story. When had she started noticing the looks on people's
faces? Crazy Terese. That's what they called her in Rojas.

Her head ached from the radio by the time Lea pulled
into the Boutros's big circular driveway. It had been a kid,
playing a joke. It had to be. Lea turned off the engine and sat
frozen behind the wheel.

A vast chorus of wordless melody filled the air, drowning
out the street noises. Lea put her head down on the steering
wheel. "Oh God," she groaned. What was happening to her?

The rest of the day was awful. Weeping birches harmonized in rich tenors, overlaid by a spritely chorus of salvia
and coral bells. Roses mused gently and tall lilies shouted
like trumpets. The whole blended into a cacophony that
made Lea want to cover her ears and scream. It was so noisy
that she didn't even hear Dr. Boutros come up behind her
to ask her about planting some daphne around the pool.
When he finally tapped her on the shoulder, Lea jumped and
sprayed fungicide on his suit.

He wasn't pleased.

Worst of all, the plants *screamed* when she cut them.
Every time the sharp pruning shears nipped off a branch,
the shrub or tree gave out a silvery note of agony that made
Lea shudder. Even the grass wailed as she cut it and the roar
of the mower couldn't drown it out.

I am not going crazy, she told herself over and over.
There had to be a rational explanation for all this and it had
nothing whatever to do with her grandmother's Alzheimer's.

If it had been Alzheimer's. No one had ever called it
that.

At three o'clock, Lea heaved the lawnmower into the

truck bed, tossed the rake in after it and called it a day. The singing had grown into a deafening chorus. It sounded as if every tree, shrub and geranium in the entire city had joined in. Lea turned the radio up as loud as it would go. I am not crazy, she chanted like a mantra. I'm not.

On the way home, a cop pulled her over for speeding and gave her a nasty lecture, because her radio had drowned out his siren when he first tried to pull her over. Lea started silently at the cracked steering wheel as he scolded. The close-harmony bass from a line of old elms nearly drowned the cop's words, but the ticket he handed her was real and $50 expensive.

At home, Lea parked the truck crookedly behind Celia's little Honda and fled into the house.

"You're home early." Celia looked up from her flute. School papers littered the sofa beside her. "Anything wrong?"

"No. Please don't play that tonight." Lea stomped into the kitchen and fished a beer from the refrigerator. On the kitchen counter, Celia's African violets trilled sweetly. Lea grabbed a second beer.

"What happened? You wreck the truck?" Celia followed her into the kitchen and leaned her hips against the counter. "One beer at a time please, unless *you* want to go to the store." She lifted the second beer out of Celia's hand and twisted off the cap.

"I . . ." The words stuck in Lea's throat. Hey Celia, did you know that plants sing? And scream? "I'm hearing noises." Lea glared down the neck of her beer bottle.

"Hey, you're really upset." Celia ran her hand impatiently through her short, blonde hair, then reached out to touch Lea's arm. "What kind of noises, Lea?"

"Just noises." Lea shook off Celia's hand and looked at her sideways. Celia knew about Granny.

"Maybe you have tinnitus." Celia frowned. "It's a ringing in the ears from noise damage. Factory workers get it and kids, after too many rock concerts. Maybe the lawnmower did it?"

"That's it," Lea yelped. "That has to be it." She grabbed

Celia by the shoulders and did a little dance.

"Hey, you're getting beer down my back." Celia rolled her eyes and disengaged herself. "Since you're back in a good mood, you cook dinner. I haven't even started on the tests. Why do I give essay questions anyway?"

Dinner turned into a disaster. The carrots sang a low, earthy note of distress as Lea sliced them. Tinnitus. A simple medical condition. It became her new mantra as she tossed the carrots back into the vegetable drawer and opened a can of soup. Celia sighed at sandwiches and soup, but she didn't complain.

She wouldn't, Lea thought grumpily. Celia didn't complain about much. Not out loud, anyway. Lea hunched at her place, stirring her soup and listening to Celia's violets. Doubt was growing inside her like an ugly weed and she needed to be angry at someone.

When Celia started to play her flute, Lea snarled at her and retreated to her chair, clamping her headphones over her ears. The music shut out the house plants.

Tinnitus.

"Coming to bed?" Celia stopped behind her chair to massage Lea's neck. "God, your muscles are tight."

"I'm not sleepy," Lea said. It worried her that she didn't seem to have the tinnitus with the headphones on.

"OK." Celia sounded puzzled and a little hurt. "See you in the morning."

"Yeah." Lea could barely hear Celia over the thundering music coming over the headphones.

After Celia disappeared into the bedroom, she opened another beer and changed records, trying to ignore the violets. She wanted to tell Celia, wanted to lean her head on Celia's shoulder. She wanted Celia to stroke her hair, tell her what an idiot she was and how everything was really all right.

Everything wasn't all right. Mother had looked at Granny with that ugly shadow in her eyes and she had been Granny's daughter. Sometimes, that shadow had still been there when she looked at Lea, as if Granny's craziness had rubbed off somehow.

Had it?

Oh shut up, Lea told herself wearily, but the old memories wouldn't stop replaying themselves inside her aching skull.

Finally, she fell asleep in the chair.

The doctor's office was almost quiet. A sickly dracaena whined to itself in the corner, but that was the only plant. She listened to its sad plaint, trying not to wonder exactly what *had* been wrong with Granny Terese. Lea remembered her as gentle and distant, a quiet, almost-not-there presence in a childhood full of rocks and sun and the few town kids near her own age. Crazy Terese, the older kids had called her. Lea had gotten a front tooth knocked loose when she punched Carlos for saying that.

Lea opened a magazine and tried to lose herself in an article about skiing.

"So what exactly do you hear?" inquired the doctor when she finally got to see him. He had a long, bony face and looked skeptical.

He sounded bored. "Ringing," Lea said flatly. "All the time." She wasn't stupid.

"I see."

He looked into her ears and down her throat, gave her a complete physical and drew two tubes of blood. Lea fidgeted impatiently. Finally, he told her to put her clothes back on and disappeared. Lea dressed and the nurse ushered her into the doctor's cluttered office.

"Barring laboratory results to the contrary," he said. "You're quite healthy." He steepled his fingers beneath his chin. "You must understand that tinnitus involves damage to the auditory nerve. I can refer you to a neurologist if you're worried about a brain tumor, but there is no cure for nerve damage, I'm afraid. All we can offer is something to help you sleep." Even his smile looked skeptical.

Sleeping pills? Lea stared at him numbly. The whole bloody world was full of noise and he talked sleeping pills?

She stomped past the astonished nurse and out of the office.

She toughed it out in the gardening business for two more weeks. She told herself it was tinnitus, but the plants were making the weird music. No doubt about it. The shrubs and flowers crooned with pleasure when she fertilized them or watered. They screamed with pain when they were cut. Trees were the worst. They groaned for hours after she pruned them.

They're just plants, she told herself over and over. Chlorophyll. Cellulose and cambium. It didn't help. Nor did earplugs or a Walkman turned up loud. After the first week, she was waking up with nightmares, picking fights with Celia and drinking a six-pack after work every day.

"All right, it's time to talk," Celia said one night after work. "You've been locked up in a simmering rage for days now." She blocked Lea's path to the refrigerator.

Lea looked into Celia's worried face, struggling with her feelings.

They think I'm crazy, Granny Terese used to whisper in her ear. *Just because they can't hear the angels.* No one talked to Crazy Terese—not really. Not even Mother.

"Lea, come on." Celia grabbed her by the shoulders. "This can't go on, kid. Sometimes you've got to share the load."

"I hear . . ." Lea took a deep breath, wavering. "I hear the plants." The words tumbled out. "Trees, shrubs, even grass. They sing—they sing all the time and they scream when you cut them."

It was there in Celia's eyes—just for a moment, but it was there. The shadow. The ugly, awful shadow that meant you are out in the cold, on the fringes, not really one of us normal people, too bad.

"You hear . . . singing?" Celia's face smoothed to a calm mask. "What makes you think it's the plants you're hearing?"

"Oh, stop sounding like a TV shrink." Lea jerked herself roughly away from Celia's hands. The shadow had turned her clear blue eyes to muddy gray. "Just let me alone." Tears made the words catch in her throat.

"Lea?" Celia's voice sounded shrill and anxious as she followed Lea into the living room. "Have you talked to a doctor?"

She meant a shrink. "Hey, I was kidding." Feeling cornered, Lea faced her, pasting a smile on her lips. "It's just the job that's getting me down. That's all." The wisteria outside the open window hummed a lilting refrain. "I was pulling your leg because I'm in a bad mood." She flopped into the chair and reached for the headphones.

"I'm not sure I believe you." Arms crossed, Celia stared down at her. Confusion, irritation and hurt moved across her face like cloud shadows. "What's going on with you?"

"Nothing." Lea turned on the music. "Just leave me alone." She looked away before she had to see the hurt win out in Celia's face.

Celia tried to bring up singing plants a few times. Lea's dismissals grew so curt that she finally quit. Lea might have been more affected by her wounded silence if the plants hadn't been making so much noise. She spent most of her free time under the headphones, anyway.

Lea told herself that she was glad Celia had decided to let her alone at last, but there was an ache in her chest that wouldn't go away.

She had wanted Celia to believe her. Oh God, she wanted *someone* to believe her.

She wanted to believe herself.

Dr. Boutros added the final straw when he demanded that Lea prune the huge boxwood hedge that ran along two sides of their enormous lot. The box wailed its agony in a hundred piercing voices that cut right through the "1812 Overture" thundering over her Walkman. Lea cringed with every chop of the heavy shears. Halfway through, she vomited her lunch onto a pile of clippings and threw her shears into the middle of the yard.

112

They bounced once on the edge of the driveway and shattered the windshield of Dr. Boutros's Lincoln just as he was coming out of the house. Scratch one client. Scratch the whole damn business. Lea took his tirade stolidly. She couldn't hear him very well over the hedge's crying and she really didn't care.

Celia came home while Lea was loading the truck. She dumped books and papers onto the hood in a jumbled pile. "Where do you think you're going?" Her face looked sharp-edged and bleak, but not really surprised.

"Antarctica." Lea hoisted a box of records into the truck bed. "Actually, I thought I'd go stay with my folks for a while." She didn't look at Celia. "I left most of my furniture. Keep it for me, will you? Or sell it, I don't care." She tossed a duffle bag on top of the records.

"Just like that?" Celia's voice shook. "Six years together and you just load up and go? You've shut me out of your life all of a sudden and you won't even tell me why." Her fist slammed down on the hood with a crash that made them both jump. "You owe me a *why,*" she yelled. "Damn it, you owe me *that* much."

Lea stared at Celia's clenched fist. Celia never lost control. "Green Visions is dead," she said tonelessly. "Dad'll give me a job in the store."

"I can loan you money. You can get another job."

"I don't like to be in debt . . ."

"Is that so?" Celia stood stiff and still in front of the truck's grill, as if she was waiting to be run over. "Or is it that you're just afraid of obligations. You always have to do everything yourself—keep everything to yourself. You're not independent, Lea. You just don't want to make any commitments." Celia swept her papers into her arms. "So take off," she said. "Goodbye."

Stunned, Lea watched Celia march up the steps and into the house. The door slammed behind her. I gave you a chance, Lea thought. You betrayed me. She flipped a plastic tarp over the load, nursing a resentment that kept wanting to die.

Too late now, anyway. The pansies along the driveway hummed a bright melody as she climbed into the truck. The engine caught with a roar and she backed down the driveway fast.

She didn't start crying until she was on the freeway, heading south.

It was a long and melodic drive to Rojas. Roadside blackberries and ripening wheat sang to her all across the state. The mountains were a rich chorus of bass and tenor voices—until she hit the logging operation.

The tree voices were almost human in their anguish. The terrible, groaning screams pursued her down the road. Shaking, Lea pulled over as soon as she was out of range of the sound. The weathered stumps sticking up out of the logged-over slopes made her think of severed limbs. It took her a half hour to stop shaking.

Plants can't feel, she told herself as she drove south. The words sounded thin and unconvincing after the deep-throated anguish of the trees. What would the vegetarians do if they knew? She tried to laugh, but it stuck in her throat. It didn't seem very funny. Nothing seemed funny.

The voices thinned out as she drove south into the desert and Lea began to feel a little bit better. In the thirsty heat, even the sagebrush sounded subdued. She didn't have to concentrate at all to hear the bored kid at the pumps when she stopped for gas, south of Phoenix.

The dingy little house baking on Rojas's main street looked familiar and strange at the same time. Lea struggled to keep her heart out of her stomach. She had never planned to come back here. Not to live. Coming back meant failure. You didn't stay in Rojas because you wanted to.

Her mother knew that. Her greeting was tinged with resignation and a dark hint of worry. Dad's welcome was warm and tearful. He breathed alcohol fumes in her face as he hugged her and called her his girl.

Lea simply felt tired. When she slammed the truck

door, yellow dust slid down the green paint. The front fence enclosed stony soil and two tired yuccas that murmured softly. The hot wind lifted her hair and she could actually hear the hiss of windblown sand across the pavement. I can live here, she thought and felt no enthusiasm at the prospect. In this hot, desiccated world, Celia was a memory like a dream of rain. "It's nice to be home," she said with false cheer.

It was quiet, anyway.

Rojas hadn't changed. There were more Mexican faces in the stores and the white faces looked more hopeless and stolidly resigned than she remembered, but otherwise it was the same dead town. Anyone who could leave had done so. Lea settled like a stone into the bottomless pool of heat and boredom. She went to work in her father's store—her nightmare as a teenager chafing to escape. The sloppy books, casual inventory and unpaid accounts were appalling, but they gave her something to focus on.

Excitement in Rojas was booze, videos and the fourth-rate Cinema House. Her evenings dragged. Dad was out cold by eight and Mom sat in front of the TV mending or just sitting. Her eyes were dull and opaque as stones and any gift of conversation that she had ever had she had lost before Lea was old enough to remember. Granny Terese's ghost haunted the little house, peering over Lea's shoulder, whispering about angels. Lea threw herself into reorganizing the store because there was nothing else to do except wait for the mail.

She stopped waiting for it after three weeks. Nothing arrived except a few bills, forwarded by the post office. It was just as well Celia didn't write, she told herself. A clean break was always easiest. At least she could hear people speak, she told herself. Down here, the singing was tolerable. No one had to know.

You should get out more, her mother said every once in a while. Go into Phoenix for a movie. She said it automatically, as if she was simply speaking lines. She didn't expect Lea to go, hadn't pried too hard into the reasons for Lea's return. Dad had taken it for granted in a beery belief that Lea had come home because this *was* home.

Mother knew better, but she didn't ask. Lea and her mother moved around each other in the house, connected by a bond of silence that had an oddly conspiratorial feel to it, as if they shared a guilty secret. They talked enough, but not about real things—not about Lea's life or Celia or the reason she had come back. They didn't talk about Granny Terese, either.

It was her father who babbled and pried and made grandiose, unreal plans for the future of the hardware store.

Her mother was waiting for her to ask, Lea realized finally. It was the way she never mentioned Granny Terese at all that gave her away. It took Lea a long time to get around to asking. First, she had to stop waiting for Celia's letters. Then, she had to settle into her dusty niche, like a dog turning around three times before going to sleep.

Actually, she was afraid.

One interminable month after she had arrived, she asked the question that she had been avoiding and anticipating with fear and hope.

"What was wrong with Granny Terese?" Elbows on the scarred table where she had finger-painted with her preschool oatmeal while Granny listened to her angels, she stirred her cooling coffee with a forefinger.

"Use a spoon." Her mother plunked one down on the table. "Why do you ask?" She had just finished the lunch dishes. Now she stood in front of the filled dishrack.

Lea watched her rearrange the chipped blue-flowered china with tiny, musical clinks. Her mother's hands were rough and cracked from a lifetime of dishes and dry air. They moved lightly and nervously across the clean dishes as if her mother was taking comfort from the familiar touch of household things. Lea tried to remember her mother touching her with those rough hands, but all she could remember was Granny pulling the sheet up to her chin with her long, white fingers. *Listen to the angels*, she'd croon. *They'll sing you to sleep.*

"Granny heard angel voices," Lea said with a sudden confidence and dread. "Tell me about her angels."

"Angels." Her mother's voice sounded thick and slow, like clotting blood. "I don't think she ever told anyone where she came from. She was pregnant when she showed up in Rojas, you know. Or maybe you don't know. It was a scandal in those days, but people gave her jobs—clothes to wash and that sort of thing. I guess they felt sorry—her crazy and all." She gave a small, bitter laugh. "They told me the whole story when it was old enough to feel like nostalgia. It's ugly, growing up on pity."

Lea stared at her mother's bony back, throat tight, remembering the whispers, Carlos, her skinned knuckles and loose tooth. The thin shoulders twitched once, as if her mother was about to cry.

"I didn't mean to get pregnant ever," she said huskily. "Your Dad's folks were pretty nice about us getting married, but I was scared. Scared that I'd end up like her or that my child . . ." She broke off suddenly.

Or my child. Lea shoved her chair back. Suddenly, the dim kitchen felt oppressive, stuffy with memories and old angers. She had to get out. The screen door slammed closed behind her, snapping like a hungry mouth, and Lea resisted the urge to run. The house crouched behind her, sagging on its concrete-block foundations, waiting to swallow her down.

Her mother knew and didn't want to know.

Was that why she had worked so hard in the store while Lea was growing up? Had she buried herself in the store because she had seen Granny Terese in Lea? She was afraid of me, Lea thought bitterly. She kicked a rock, watched it skitter along the dusty pavement like a frightened lizard. She felt hurt and angry—and that surprised her a little. Lea couldn't remember ever feeling very strongly about her mother one way or another, yet here was this grief and anger twisting around inside of her. She kicked the rock again.

Do you hear the angels, Lea baby? Do you hear them singing? Did you do this to me, Granny? Lea walked west,

117

out of town, away from the blacktopped highway and the tired, peeling buildings of Rojas. Genes were strange things. They could transmit eye color and schizophrenia. Fear was a strange thing, too—a knifeblade to sever two generations of mother and daughter. A lizard flicked across a rock, quick as a whip, and a laugh that might have been a sob caught in Lea's throat.

I can't stay here, she thought. There was nothing here that could help her. Her grandmother had heard something and now, so did she. End of story. Lea walked faster, sweat sticking her cotton shirt to her back. She could move into Phoenix and get a job in an office.

Sure. Offices had indoor plants. Phoenix had parks and trees—but that wasn't it, entirely. Phoenix would be as much a desert as Rojas, plants or no. How do you tell a new friend that the geranium on the table is distracting you? A barrel cactus sang in a thirsty bass and a hawk circled her, waiting for any small rodents stupid enough to run.

The dusty road she had followed bent north to run along the lip of a shallow draw. An outcrop of weathered red rock thrust through the thin soil at the curve. Rocks were the earth's bones. Rocks didn't sing, thank God. Lea wedged herself into a crack of shade and looked for the hawk. He had gone. She leaned against the cool stone and closed her eyes against the empty sky. Perched on this splinter of bone, Lea felt like a castaway on a tiny island. All around her stretched an empty sea of sound. There were no ships on her horizon. None.

A prickly pear trilled at the foot of the rock and Lea opened her eyes. Castaway or not, it was time to go home. Mom would have dinner ready. After the silent meal, she had to go over and total out the cash register. Dad would have been too drunk to do it when he closed the store.

Lea bent to slap yellow dust out of her jeans when a movement caught her eye. Someone was walking out along the road. Her hand paused in midair as she squinted against the glare of the setting sun. The swinging stride looked familiar and the yellow light turned the stranger's hair into a nimbus of gold around her head.

"Celia?" Lea took a quick step forward and stopped.

Her legs wanted to run—to carry her across rocks and sand so that her arms could lock around Celia and whirl her through the dust.

What had changed? Lea held herself stiff and still. Nothing, really. Oh God, why had she come all the way down here?

"Didn't you see the car?" Celia walked up to her. She was carrying a new-looking nylon daypack and her tennis shoes raised small puffs of dust. "I was parked across the street from your house. I lost the house number, so I had to go asking." She came to a stop about ten feet from Lea, hands shoved into the pockets of her jeans as if she didn't know what else to do with them.

"You should wear boots," Lea said. "There's snakes all over the place."

"I was looking."

They looked at each other across ten feet of empty space.

"I got Mrs. Wentworth to let me out of the lease," Celia said at last. "I couldn't stay there."

"I'm sorry." This was crazy. "Why did you come down here?" Lea burst out. Now she'd have to bring her home, introduce her, answer the questions that were asked and sit at the dinner table while Celia asked her mother oh-so-delicately if Lea was All Right. "Why didn't you just write?"

"I had to ask you something." Celia was looking at her steadily, but her face was pale. "I had to see your face when you answered."

"Ask me what?"

"Are the plants really singing?"

Lea blinked. She hadn't really expected it—not something so direct. Dust coated Celia's strained, white face like a dirty tan. Say no, Lea thought. Send her on her way and get the whole mess over with. She opened her mouth, closed it.

If she did that, she'd be running away, just like her

mother had run. She'd be turning her back on Celia because Celia might not really believe her. Because if she didn't send her away, Celia would comfort her. She might start to depend on Celia and then she would be vulnerable.

That was commitment.

Am I afraid of that? Lea looked into Celia's tense face. What is she really asking me? Lea took a long, slow breath. "The plants really sing," she said. "I got it from my grandmother. I think she heard the plants sing, too." She was trembling, as if she was terrified. "Maybe she was from another planet or a mutation or something." She tried to make it a joke, but her voice quavered.

Celia nodded very slowly. She shrugged the daypack off her shoulder and sat down on the rock beside Lea. "I'm sorry," she said, looking at Lea from the corners of her eyes. "Has it been really bad?"

"Yes." Lea looked down at her clasped hands, still not sure what was happening.

"What do they sound like?"

It wasn't a challenge or a demand for proof. Lea chewed on her lip. Celia sounded almost . . . wistful. Feeling suddenly shy, Lea whistled a few bars of the prickly pear's thready melody.

"That's beautiful," Celia said softly. "It sounds like the desert—sort of dry and patient."

Beautiful? Lea frowned down at the spiny ovals of the pear. She had never thought of the plants' singing as beautiful—or as anything but pain and hardship. It was true that out here, she could pick out the individual melodies. She whistled along with a creosote bush's lilting soprano.

"Wait a minute." Celia shrugged the daypack off her shoulders. She pulled her beloved flute out of it. "Do that again, will you?" This time, the thin, silvery notes of the flute blended in soft unison with the creosote bush and Lea's whistling.

It wasn't bad. Lea broke off and listened to the flute and the plants. A patch of Mexican poppy provided a blurry harmony. It sounded . . . pretty. The lump in her throat hurt.

"Just like that, huh?" Lea leaned forward, fists on her knees. "You believe me just like that?"

"No." Celia laid the flute down across her lap. "Sometimes, I'm going to wake up in the middle of the night and wonder about us both." Her smile was crooked. "I would have listened—or I think I would have. You didn't give me a chance."

"I know." Lea picked up Celia's flute. Her reflection in the barrel looked warped and strange. "My mother ran away from angel voices and I tried to run away, too."

"I took a job in Little Mesa. It's not too bad a drive from Rojas. It's a one-room school. I didn't know there were any left."

"I don't want to spend my life here." Lea handed the flute back to Celia and their fingers touched, warm on the cool metal.

"So we'll figure something out." Celia smiled at last, a genuine smile with no hint of a shadow in it. "Together, OK?"

"OK." Lea leaned lightly against Celia's shoulder. She felt warm in the cooling air. Granny had had no one to tell— except Lea. Maybe that's what had made her so strange and distant. "Maybe I can talk to my mother about Granny's angels." Maybe not, but she could try. "I'm glad you didn't let me run away," she said softly.

They sat side by side in the cooling dusk and Lea taught Celia the Joshua tree's plaintive voice.

OLD NIGHT

by Stephanie T. Hoppe

It wasn't going to work. I remember the moment I realized that—my eyes fixed on the back of the driver's erect head, on her blond, short-cropped hair that was so meticulously ordered. She stared sternly, unswervingly ahead, but I had only to lean forward, reach out my hand, make some slight motion to attract her attention. Tell her to turn back. That I'd changed my mind and wanted to return to the station.

I never moved. The car swept on. I told myself it didn't matter, I could face it out. A few days, a week—what could it amount to? An experience, one way or another, and then done.

Now I wonder. I remember how I sat there, how I sank deep in the velvet upholstery like one entrapped, even ensorcelled. That word is not too much to say. Already then it must have been too late.

We rushed through the forest. Dim, greenish recesses opened ever onward, the car moving so smoothly it might have been rather the ancient trees that slid past us in their swift, silent ranks. So silent. So still. Not a leaf moved. It felt unnatural at the time. Nor, in fact, was the forest natural. I had read that the very landforms of this region were artificial, the work of human hands and minds.

The trees fell away. As we turned a curve in the drive,

the view opened upon a wide, graceful country full of li,
In the foreground, out of its surrounding plain of st(
terracing, the great pale, pillared structure rose up, shimmering and insubstantial-looking for all its enormity.

The car came to a halt. Someone opened the door. I
stepped out upon the gravel roadway at the foot of a flight
of stairs, climbed them to the terrace, followed the avenue
marked by rows of orange trees in stone tubs. The scent of
orange blossoms wafted on the still afternoon air like a
glamour of the light. People strolled about. I caught snatches
of conversation. Two young women passed me, dressed for
tennis and laughing. I regained my assurance. Here was
just a hotel, however grand. People like any others, like me.
How not?

But I wondered—from the very start, I remember, I
wondered.

By then I'd been bumming around Europe for over a
year. On no budget at all, hand to mouth, any way I could
manage. Just to be there. To see for myself. Then I won that
pot at Monte Carlo and decided to spend it on one big splash,
at a grand hotel. I wanted to see everything this old continent had to offer, and if there was a special place frequented
by some other, older strain of European, why, I wanted to
see that also. Monte didn't amount to much, no more than
Vegas, really, the same tinsel and plastic. But this place—
I could see already this hotel was something different.

I failed, though, to see what was right in front of me. I
ran smack into her—a large, bulky person in black. I must
somehow have taken her for the shadows that swelled
surprisingly dark and solid behind the tubbed oranges. I
blinked and jumped, taken aback by the face thrust close to
mine, the sharp, yellow eyes sunk deep in fleshy cheeks
streaked with crimson: a head like a fallen eagle's, crowned
in waves of bedraggled feathers. Her clothes hung like
plumage also, dark all-covering draperies. She carried them
well. Fallen she might be, but she was still an eagle. Nor was
she a member of the hotel staff, however formal her dress in
daytime, but some grand, eccentric personage—dowager

123

perhaps. Precisely the sort of thing I had come to see. I nodded and then supposed she would think me overly familiar. I expected no answer, but her gaze fixed on mine with some intensity.

"So young," she said, her voice deep and grating. "Carefree. American, no doubt—"

I waited—to be polite.

"What I could tell you—" The jowls shook. The eyes lost focus but then sharpened on me once more. "Would you listen? Take precautions . . . as one must. Go to sleep before night."

"Go to sleep—!" From very startlement I started to repeat her words. Then I grew out of reason angry. "Why? And what of the night life?" I demanded. "What this hotel is famed for—"

The bleary eyes gazed through and beyond me. "With night," the deep voice rumbled on. "With night—" Again she paused, but yet again, nodding to herself, went on. "I think you'll find, with night, things . . . change."

I pressed my lips together tightly, refusing to answer. Still nodding, the old dowager lurched into motion, creaking somewhere in her structure, noises that put me in mind of steel stays and whalebone. But it might have been her own bones and joints. The real thing, I told myself. What I came for. I wouldn't mind hearing her story.

First I must get settled. I went in and looked around for whatever passed in this place for the reception desk. I was unprepared for the casualness of arrangements, but neither then nor ever did I find any lack or inefficiency.

A slender woman, dressed also in black, but circumspectly, came up to greet me on behalf of the management: I was expected, my rooms ready. A porter entered from the terrace with my battered backpack, bearing it for all the world as if it were the natural and appropriate luggage for guests here. As it and we converged on the grand staircase that formed the central feature of the large entrance hall, a flicker of movement drew my gaze on toward an archway opening into another room that must run back at a right

124

angle. I glimpsed ranks of white-clothed tables. And that battle-ax of a dowager who had accosted me on the terrace, scuttling around the corner out of sight.

Would she dine so early?—having reached an age where the claims of digestion outranked those of society? Did she follow her own advice and retire early to bed also? I would leave her to it! I went after my guide up the broad flights of stairs, debouching upon a second story scarcely less lofty than the hall downstairs. Up a second flight, where lay our destination, the grandeur continued undiminished.

"This way."

She opened tall double doors with a ceremonious flourish upon a scene that briefly struck me speechless, just the space, the large, high rooms, richly furnished and ornamented, gleaming in the reddening light through the west-facing windows. I stepped over a low threshold onto a balcony ingeniously fitted into the exterior ornamentation of the building, high enough that I had a considerable vantage. As far as I could see must be the pleasure grounds of the hotel, circled by the forest I had driven through. A bright magical landscape—I could think it another world! For some moments I quite lost myself in contemplation.

I came back in to find the contents of my pack laid out for me. Guessing the others would dress formally for dinner, I wished I had been less hasty in my journey, come better prepared. There was nothing for it now. I soon settled—I had really no choice—on the corduroy pantsuit that had seemed so elegant when I tried it on in a boutique in Saint-Tropez. I buttoned up a white shirt, pulled on the trousers and studied the result in the mirror. I remember noting that the costume had at least the merit of self-effacement, with the deep blue-black color of the soft, unreflecting fabric. I was as ready as I could be, and it was time to go down.

That glittering place I came down into!—bright-colored gowns and jewels set off against starched white linen and black broadcloth, crystal and silver shining. I tried to take it all in while the waiter led me to my place. Before my eyes, the scene changed. I stared about me in shock as all thinned

125

and paled. The faces of my fellow guests, the women's bare breasts and shoulders went quite gray. In an instant, their voices and gestures turned horribly flat—

The sensation disappeared as quickly as it had come on. The midsummer sun, setting late this far north, had burst forth with a last bright blaze, mocking all it touched. Already the waiters were pulling heavy drapes across the windows.

The room brightened again with its proper light. Wine was brought and poured. The voices around me swelled rich and full. I reached for my glass and then my fork. I ate, and found the food marvelous, even exceeding its reputation.

Strains of music came faintly across the outer hall. People rose. Joining them, I was caught behind a group pausing to speak to others still sitting over their wine. I waited, feeling no hurry—struck up a conversation with a man on the fringe of the group. Then I saw her.

So close she was, I had to step back to avoid crushing the skirts of her gown. I marveled that I had not noticed her approach—with that wide-skirted gown she wore, blood-red satin that glistened and shed the lamplight in streams like fire. Out of the full, shining folds of her dress, she rose up like a white flower from its calyx, her breasts quite bare, her white shoulders and long slender neck bare of any adornment. Her skin had that fine fragile texture of the north, very pale, but shining, as with the heat of her blood. She was like a glittering jewel or a flame, quivering slightly, barely perceptibly but continuously.

I could not take my eyes from her. She turned her head, shedding a harder glitter from diamonds nestled in her dark hair, and only then did I see her face full, and that she was not, after all, either young or beautiful, not in any strict sense. Her features did not quite go with each other: the mouth rather large, her eyes set too close and very deep. A moment we stood close in the press. I muttered something— an apology; her gaze crossed mine without response, indifferent or unseeing, and she passed on without a word, others making way for her as I had done.

By the time I reached the hall, she was already far down the length of it, recognizable only by the fiery flicker of her gown. That held my eye, as also the attention of those around me: I realized they were speaking of her.

"Marchesa—" one man said to another, in a tone of voice that could, in that moment, have been mine.

I know for myself the allure that can be felt for a woman. In my time I have loved women as well as men. Nor had it escaped my notice that among this company were women wearing tuxedos, and that not all of the persons in ball gowns were women. I supposed I should have expected it—in this place devoted to pleasure there was also frank admission of the full range pleasure takes; and here, too, might remain the more open mores of an older time.

But this—what I felt now was nothing so obvious or easy as sexual allure. Marchesa—sprung from some different race, a lineage of arrogant marcher lords whose blood even today burns with a strange heat?

Did I half guess even then what line was hers, how old it was, what borderland they watched?

Now, I can't say. Nor does it matter, now. Of course I followed her. I stalked her through the crowded ballroom like a hunter bent on a kill, tracking the lines of conversation and social intercourse. I could make my way through some circles, but hers—it was something apart even to old intimates of that place. It seemed impervious to entry: not a member of her set, none of whom looked on their own to be anything out of the ordinary or in any way commensurate with her, had any acquaintance, or would allow any, outside their own company.

I acknowledged temporary defeat and moved on through the palm arcade into the casino. Gambling had brought me here. I could not rightly refuse to hazard my pile on the gambling here. I played high, and that was excitement to engage me for a time, wins and losses—enough of the former and not too many of the latter but that I both could and must continue. When later I lifted my gaze from the table, I was surprised to find *her* seated across from me, facing my direction but with no sign of seeing me. I drew myself up, feeling nettled, and addressed her so she could not mistake.

"You'll grant me luck, will you?"

Even then I couldn't say she saw me; she said nothing, but she turned one hand upward in a languid gesture. I nodded, to make there seem to be something just by my perception of it; and played on. I won steadily. In fact, I found I couldn't lose. I gambled against myself, actively seeking loss if it was the more elusive.

Nothing availed. I could only win. I would have to give it up. I looked for her again, in some anger, but she was gone. Some other woman sat in her chair, no one I cared to know.

In fact, I had been some while. The hour had grown late, and the music had ceased in the ballroom. I could feel the vacancy there, and it spread through the casino also. The gamblers' numbers had thinned to those possessed or desperate, the ugly facts so plain on their faces that I started away in distaste.

To bed. But my path was blocked. *She* stood in the doorway, filling it with the spreading folds of her wide-skirted gown. Quivering slightly, not seeing me—her own being seemed to occupy all her attention and energy, so none ran upon anything exterior to her. A man came up to her from the room beyond, one of her set. He bent close to her, his face so unmemorably anonymous as hardly to seem the face of an actual individual. I couldn't hear that she answered him, but she took his arm when he offered it, and they moved off.

The route they took was my own, across the great hall, empty now but for shadows descending from the carved heights and swelling over groupings of furniture. We mounted the first flight of stairs. They turned off down a corridor. My rooms lay up another flight. I started to turn, then turned back.

She glanced over her shoulder, in my direction if not at me, though there was no one there save me. I felt her gesture as a goad, and without thinking, I stepped into that corridor down which she and her escort now moved rather quickly.

Though I hurried, they continued to outdistance me. I broke into a run, and the corridor seemed only to lengthen. Then, quite abruptly, I arrived at an intersection where the corridor met another that ran transversely. Through the bay of the window opposite, I saw a formal shrubbery of high, clipped hedges, whose long lines ran like a continuation of the hotel corridors. Seen from above, they lay obviously purposeless, leading nowhere, giving on nothing save each other, a maze of hallways within hallways, quite empty.

At my side—I had not realized: she stood beside me. She was shorter than I, by several inches, really quite a small woman, for I am not myself all that large. She turned, as if to look at me only sidelong, a gesture somehow sly, even offensive, and . . . irresistible. I wanted—well, *her*, of course. Along with—everything.

He was also there, her escort, standing between us. But he was nothing. I held a knife in my hands now, a curved shining blade at least a foot long. I threatened him with it, meaning no ill to him, but to be quit of distraction and interference.

He stood his ground, and I struck. I reached across the space where he had been, reaching for her. There she stood, quite within my reach, and yet I seemed unable . . .

I felt confused. Was she not real? Was *I* not bodily present? Was nothing that I perceived in fact happening? What had I done . . . I half remembered. I would have my prize at least! I set my hand upon her bare breast, my hand blurred . . . darkness stained her paleness—

What I had done! But she was mine now, or would be. I bent closer. I couldn't see her eyes—the light was dim or deceptive—she must see me! She spoke softly. I turned my head, straining to hear.

No, that mutter came from farther off, down the corridor, the way we had come.

We: she and I and the one who lay at our feet, bloodied and motionless, dead by my hand. As I looked back toward the knot of persons in black and white coming down the hall, I saw what was real.

I had killed a man. Here came his friends to avenge him. Or, even if they were strangers, persons who would take his part against me. All civilized persons would take the victim's part. I would find every hand raised against me.

I panicked. Who would not, on comprehending so swift a metamorphosis from luxury and ease to outlaw?

I ran. My pulse and breath roared so I could not hear to judge the pursuit. I dared not look back or slow up, but strained ahead to the shadowed distances of corridor, to see where it would turn or lead.

There came no turnings. The corridor ran on undeviating, without side access, I saw the end. I soon came so near I could no longer doubt that blank end wall that barred escape.

I searched frantically, side to side. Closed doors ran in ranks, dark and locked against me, a mockery of entrance. The end closed in where I must be cornered and caught.

Still my feet carried me onward. They swerved to one side, my hand closed on a doorknob. The knob turned. The door swung aside. I leapt through the opening, one last bounding pace and a halt, closed the door behind me and was enclosed in darkness. Standing with my back to the door, I struggled to quiet my breath, strained to see what was. Furniture: a sitting room like my own, silent and vacant. To my left, a door stood ajar upon the silent bedroom, where bulked a canopied bed.

Noise sounded in the corridor, voices questioning, loud and self-important; hunting. Doors opened and closed, ever nearer. In one bound I was across the room into the doorway to the bedroom. But I had neglected to lock the outer door. Looking back as it opened, I saw a thin shaft of light fall where I had stood. Tensed to leap onward, I now heard a noise ahead, from within the room, which I had taken to be empty.

Someone lay in the bed—indeed, a large person—lying sleeping, snorting softly with unhurried breath. I felt a start of recognition, something of the silhouetted shape, or perhaps a quality to the sound even in that unconscious snore.

130

Yet I continued also to feel that sense of vacancy, of absence. My head swam. It was the dowager, she who had warned me. She was there—and not there. What was she? *What did she know?*

But I had no time—a voice sounded in the outer doorway, questioning peremptorily. Panic flushed me from my cover in shadows. I sprang across the room, past the bed to the long window, through it to the balcony. I was over the carved stone railing and lowering myself hand over hand along the projections of the ornamental stonework. Rushed, I lost my grip—I slipped and fell to the terrace below, only the height of one story, but a very high story. The fall knocked the breath from me so I lay paralyzed it seemed an eternity.

Then I was up, running across the broad barren expanse of the stone terrace. I took a flight of stairs in two long bounds. Gravel spattered under my feet. And again silence—I ran on grass. Somewhere there was shouting. Of a sudden I thought I was still indoors, hemmed close in a corridor between two walls, high but strangely indistinct.

The shrubbery, I told myself: the formal shrubbery of the west garden. My own pounding blood made the rhythmic sound I took for quick-marching feet. I was past sense. I threw myself at the enclosing walls, hammered myself against their prickling restraint, tearing at the branches with bleeding hands; no escape, not that way. I fled inward.

The world came up again, gray and tentative, but real, I thought. As I was. I knew by the pain when I moved, all my body bruised and aching. My skin felt as if I had been flayed. I lay quietly, wondering where I was—out of doors, lying upon cold ground. As the light increased, the dark wall above me took on particularity, black prickling branches, the yew hedge. I looked myself over; the almost new pantsuit I had bought in that boutique in Saint-Tropez was in tatters, one knee wetly stained. Blood. The blood of a man I killed —

In a flash I relived the whole. I had killed. There were witnesses to the deed, the marchesa herself for one, and those down the hall would have seen enough to corroborate her story—the undeniable outcome outweighing all impossibilities I could assert.

Where so much was impossible, what matter any fact? All night I had run, and never come beyond the garden I had seen from the hotel window.

Daylight relentlessly grew. Birds burst into song, mocking me with their mindless natural existence: living by instinct, unknowing of good or evil or the drives and illusions that bulk larger than all else to my kind. I was what I was. I must exert myself. Take stock of my situation. Take action.

In my flight I had reached anyway the outer boundary of the formal gardens. The hotel itself lay behind me, hidden from view by the high yews. What I looked upon was a more remote section of the grounds, a sort of wilderness, a grassy glade snaking deep under enormous trees twined with blossoming lianas. Several persons walked along the edge of the glade, approaching where I lay. They strode briskly, in step, almost as if marching, men or mannish-looking women, each carrying a long slender case slung by a strap over one shoulder. They were hunters carrying guns. Hunting me.

I realized I had been coming to accept the notion of guilt, of capture, confinement and punishment. I had assumed that despite what I had done I could yet take some benefit of the civilization I had outraged, that mine would be the rights and privileges that in these days accrue to even an admitted murderer. To be hunted down like a wild beast— that was a very different matter.

And yet, was it not what I should have expected? I remembered the scraps of conversation I had overheard in the ballroom and the casino, references to the marchesa and her set, what had been said and the more that had been implied. The whole came clear to me: how such remnants of ancient nobility would have ways all their own that antedated the modern order. They would acknowledge no kinship with me. If I trespassed upon them, killed one of theirs, they would not turn me over to police or judge. They would deal with me in their own way . . . hunt me down . . . Fear greater

132

than any yet seized me, stopped up my breath and held me immobile.

The three approached more nearly, the path they followed curving toward the hedge under which I lay, a distance finally of no more than a dozen paces. They could not have failed to see me had they even glanced in my direction.

They did not. Talking among themselves, all their attention on each other, they came abreast of me and passed me by. They passed on into a patch of bright sunlight, and I saw them more clearly. It was not hunting attire they wore, but ordinary sporting clothes. The long bags slung from their shoulders held no rifles, but golf clubs. I remembered the layout of the hotel grounds I had seen on a map provided in my room: to one side of the wilderness lay a golf course.

The golfers were gone, their commonplace conversation blending into the rustle and chatter of early morning, an ordinary day in which anyone's hunting was preposterous. As was also the notion of my having killed a man I didn't even know or attempted to ravish a woman.

The night's doings fell away from me. I even managed a shaky laugh as I sat up and tried to straighten my rumpled clothes. Their ruin was a matter of fact! But I supposed the staff at this hotel could take it in stride. Getting to my feet, I brushed away bits of hedge clippings and dirt. I rubbed at the muddy mark on my knee. Bloodstain indeed! I must get to my room and cleaned up, if possible without making any worse fool of myself than I had already done.

How I ached in every joint! and smarted with every movement of damp stiff fabric against my skin. I set out, grimly refusing to allow myself to limp, skirted the shrubbery though it meant a longer route . . . reluctant even by daylight to trust myself to the maze-like confusion. I came around to the back of the hotel and slunk up a flight of stairs to the terrace, heading for an unobtrusive side door.

I began to think I was to have luck on my side. It was still early. A family, parents and small children, strolled toward the far end of the terrace, but otherwise I saw no one.

A grouping of tables set for breakfast under a row of tubbed oranges stood empty. I strode out more boldly upon the terrace.

A sound like a shot rang out behind me and I spun about. There: at the last table, half-hidden under a tree, a massive figure smoothed the new-turned page of a newspaper. Rheumy, yellow eyes gazed over the upper edge of the paper, blinking into the sun behind me.

"Oh! You startled me—"

The yellow eyes blinked and gazed, their expression unreadable.

"I—"

But I had recalled my appearance. I turned and fled, indoors, upstairs along the spacious airy corridors flooded with the morning light. I gained my room to find a set of my own clothes laid out on the bed, the bath drawn and steaming. Gratefully I went through the motions prepared for me, descended to breakfast, answered greetings from persons I had apparently met the previous evening. Later I played tennis; lunched; rode with some others I met then, down bridle paths in the green forest. Returning in the late afternoon, we joined a dozen others on the terrace for an aperitif.

Conversation lagged as the light slanted and lengthened and took on deep hues of red and purple. The party broke up, some going up to change for dinner, those who were left gathering in smaller, separate groups. Sitting somewhat apart, I felt an odd, nervous stirring as the sun dropped behind the bulk of the building and cool shadow flowed over me. I ordered another drink.

A limousine drove up smartly, halted to disgorge its passengers at the foot of the broad stairs to the terrace. While I idly watched, four or five persons emerged from the car. Then came a woman in red. I rose to my feet. The party approached the stairs below me. I heard the women commenting in high, artificial tones on what seemed to have been a visit to an acquaintance in the neighborhood. I could not distinguish which was the voice of the woman in red. I wondered if I would know *her* voice.

This woman wore a wide-brimmed summer hat that hid her face. Her dress was quite simple, a street-length silk jersey such as anyone might wear. She could be anyone. She turned slightly as she reached the terrace and I caught a glimpse of her face, the close-set eyes; the vacant, rather stupid expression.

She passed with her party into the hotel. I could see through the open doorway that the lights were on in the hall and the dining room. The hour grew late. People were already coming down to dinner. I sat down again, shivering, alone on the terrace.

It seemed a long time I sat there, but the sky was still pearly with sunset when finally I got to my feet. I didn't go in even then. With only the clothes on my back, I turned and walked down the terrace stairs, across the graveled drive and the lawns that ran down to the already darkened forest. It was no use, of course. Running. I suppose I knew at the time.

Now it's been years. My luck's held, as the world would say. Everything I've turned my hand to has flourished. I say it with despair.

Not that it matters to me. To me only the nights matter, where she is. Where I am with her. With what I do to be with her.

As I believe anyone would do—I don't wonder at that. But why *me*? That's the question I ask myself, and her. She never answers. And I—

I sometimes think of the rheumy-eyed dowager, she who warned me with those cryptic words. Was it warning, I wonder—or promise?

HEARTS OF SAND

by Conda V. Douglas

Waves of sand blew in gusts across the road, like animals on the hunt, searching. Mora pulled at the shirt stuck to her back and regretted her allergy to the sun that kept her fully clothed. Even this early, heart roiled the air and dust devils scurried. It seemed as if the sand bit at the corners of her eyes, obscuring her vision.

Flashes of the nightmare, frozen like paintings, came to her as she drove. The boy's face flared sudden in her mind as she pressed down on the accelerator. His face was marked by—the image disappeared. Realizing how fast she was driving, Mora willed away the dream and forced herself to concentrate on negotiating the turnoff to the museum.

Ahead she saw the lean-to built by a Navajo for the summer tourist trade. Mora prepared to wave. Every day for the past three weeks she had waved at the elderly woman who sat by a loom, her rugs spread like skirts around her. Always the woman watched, impassive, like a stone carving of the traditional Navajo, never acknowledging the Anglo. Today the woman wasn't there, the bundles of sticks with wood supports vacant of all her bright loomed color.

Mora rubbed the sides of her hands against the hot steering wheel. The heat coursed into the ache deep in each palm. Desire to paint had moved her to come onto the Navajo reservation, to sit for hours and imitate the sandpaintings, pouring sand through fingers till her hand shook. She despised her pallid copies, and wondered how she ever believed she could capture the desert in her paintings.

She frowned at the faint lines where a sixth finger had been amputated off each hand shortly after her birth. Those long absent fingers surely could not be the source of the ache? She had read that in some cultures sixth fingers were signs of grace and never amputated. To her, the anomaly had never been anything but shameful. Still, would those missing fingers have functioned like the others?

Mora tried imagining her hands as they existed before the surgeon's touch. She felt as if she struggled half-awake, no longer wishing to dream, yet afraid to open her eyes.

As she drove into the museum parking lot, she saw the flashing lights of the police cars and an ambulance. Mora resisted her impulse to turn around and leave. Instead, she parked and walked across the lot, her feet kicking up tiny dust devils.

Within the museum was a confusion of milling bodies, flashing lights and heavily accented voices. Attention focused on a tumbled heap on the floor, covered by a sheet. From one corner protruded a familiar worn boot. Turning her face to the wall, Mora leaned against it, willing away the nausea.

"You're late again," came the scolding nasal voice of the museum director. A gawking vulture of a man, as always he wore a ridiculous, outdated pince-nez, now askew on his nose. "And now," he said, pointing at a demonstration sandpainting done loose on the floor, "look at this mess!"

Someone had tracked through the loose sand, destroying the intricate design. Mora trailed a finger through a red coral line and her hand flared with pain. She clutched a fistful of sand until the cramp faded.

"Hey, you're destroying evidence," a young Navajo policeman said. He gave her a Navajo glance, flat, low and quick, seemingly uninterested.

She looked past him to the crumpled doll form beneath the sheet, and let the sand dribble out of her hand. I should gather up the sands and scatter them to the wind, she thought, so that the evil in this place will go. The trails of blood-stained lines more permanent than sand, she knew.

The policeman, following her gaze, moved, blocking her sight of the dead man. "Who are you?" he said.

"She's my new assistant," the director answered, "she's a painter—another person who thinks she's Georgia O'Keeffe."

"Ah, she comes cheap then," the policeman said, and Mora caught the glint of humor in his eyes. "Does she have a name, this painter?"

"I'm Mora." She started to hold out her hand, then dropped it. The ache still lurked inside her palm, waiting.

"Mora," he said, giving the name a Navajo inflection. "We don't know what happened to the old man. Not yet."

"His name was Running Feather," she told him. "At least that's his tourist name. He was past running and as for the feather part—" her voice caught, trapped by the heavy bulk beneath the sheet, "—he loved grape jelly donuts. And he always saved me one, said I was too skinny, that I ought to put on more flesh, so, so—" her voice scratched, high and tinny.

The policeman reached out and shook her hand. His hand, large, dry and hot, enclosed hers in a soothing balm that helped the ache.

"I'm George," he said, "and we'll find out what happened."

"It's obvious what happened!" the director said. "Running Feather let some of his thieving friends in last night and they killed him—"

"Thieving friends?" A deep line appeared between George's eyes, a line that someday would etch itself permanently into his face.

"The old man was an ex-convict—"

"You hired a thief as a security guard?"

"Well, you know, he—"

"— came cheap. Now it looks like a price has been paid."

The director peered, a nearsighted carrion bird, at the policeman. "I'll be in my office when you are finished here," he said, then stalked off.

"I wonder why I can never remember that man's name," Mora said.

"We call him—" George said something in Navajo, then translated: "It means Maiden Aunt." He crinkled his nose and Mora smiled. "You'd better wait till we're finished here; then maybe you can see if anything's missing."

"I'll wait in the gift shop," Mora said. She glanced toward the sun streaking through the dirty window, illuminating the faded, shabby native costumes of the museum dummies. Into the window dirt two wavering lines like the letter Z had been drawn. Mora smiled at the memory.

The first time she had seen Little Boy Blue, as she nicknamed him, he had stood outside. He wore dirty overalls and nothing else, his face somber as if he carried a heavy weight of Navajo heritage. When she had gestured for him to come inside, he had scrawled the lines. After that, every day, he stood in the doorway, morosely watching the tourist parade. A few had tried to pat his head or give him money. He shrugged away from their advances and remained at his post, a silent sentinel. Where was the boy now?

She felt his absence like the pain in her hands, insistent, impatient, a deep wound waiting to open and bleed. She rubbed the scars, probing deep into the flesh, searching for a last vestige of bone. The surgeon had been thorough, nothing lurked there to trouble her.

Using her artist's sense, she scanned the room—and there, inside a display case—disturbed dust. What had been taken? She couldn't remember.

George, who was talking to another policeman, caught her glance. He hesitated, then jerked his head toward the door, as if ridding himself of a disturbing thought. She obeyed.

In the gift shop, Mrs. Harrington waited. More than plump, to support her extra poundage she wore an elaborate understructure that crackled and popped when she moved, reminding Mora of an ancient Ford truck creaking along a washed-out roadbed.

Mrs. Harrington held out a cup of coffee and a cookie, her panacea for any crisis. The coffee was always hot and the cookies homebaked and both free.

"What's happened?"

"Running Feather—"

"Dead? Heart attack?"

Mora felt as if she walked on shifting sands. Mrs. Harrington helped her to a footstool piled with rugs for sale. Sipping her coffee, Mora thought of the times she and Running Feather had retreated here when the director's peckishness drove them to this sanctuary. Inside Mrs. Harrington's pristine display cases, polished rows of silver jewelry lined up, soldiers waiting for the order to march, happy to be waging war on the tourists' pocketbooks.

Mrs. Harrington snuffled into a man's handkerchief. "I told him to quit drinking, I told him."

Mora remembered when she had found Running Feather asleep on duty and waked him and not told the director. "Wait a minute," she said, "he was supposed to be working days this week."

"Yes, but Alfred fired the night man yesterday, said R.F. could do both shifts, since he slept on the job anyway. That's Alfred, always saving a buck."

"Alfred?"

"Your boss, that's his first name. At the beginning he thought he could find his own beautyway, despite being Anglo, but—" Mrs. Harrington gestured at the gift shop window. Outside the wind tore the sand around in cutting arcs. "—this is a land of no mercy. Alfred gave up, buckled under the weight of being too alien ever to belong. He sold all the most valuable pieces, or traded them for modern."

Mora remembered what she had been told about beautyway, the complex belief of a balance between good and evil, a way to survive. She thought of how, when she tried to paint now, her vision blurred with the touch of her brush, the desert and its people too elusive. Mora stroked the harsh wool of a rug, seeking comfort there. Beneath her hand, she spotted a familiar pattern. The ache rustled in her hand.

"Who did these rugs?"

"What? Oh, Evelyn Yazzie, the old woman who looms by the roadside."

"I thought she sold her rugs there."

"Nobody buys from her. She despises Anglos and it shows. It's her grandson that hangs around here, that child should be in school—where are you going?"

Ignoring the men now loading the body onto a stretcher, Mora searched the museum case. There, an outline in the dust marked the absence of an item. A small pile of golden flecks, corn pollen perhaps, lay on the unfaded felt. She reached into the case and stroked the pollen, sifting the silky, ethereal stuff through her fingers. Then she placed her throbbing hands against the glass top of the case and pressed down, hard, forcing one pain to cover another. And she remembered—

—the boy, his calm face still, as if he holds the secrets of his people secure, standing by the doorway. She gives him half her jelly donut and he takes it, inclining his head.

"Come inside," she coaxes.

"No," he says, his mouth smeared with grape jelly. He points at the museum dummies. "Not real, not like me, not real."

—then the boy's face, as it was in her dream, dark with fever, frowning.

"Whose medicine bag does that belong to?" Mora stood, hands on hips, in front of the director's desk. He blinked at her from behind his wall of pince-nez. She glared back. Her hands burned now, blurring her thinking. "The medicine bag, with the two lines," she drew them in the air, "who owned it before?"

"Why?"

"It's gone."

"But it's worthless," the director said, "it's modern, why would—"

141

"Perhaps it isn't money the thief was after."

"I don't know." The director removed his glasses, revealing two deep red marks at either side of his nose. He rubbed at the marks, as if hoping he could fade the wear of years away. "I didn't even know Running Feather liked jelly donuts, and he's worked here for years." His shoulders collapsed, and he looked like a captive vulture with its wings clipped. "Sometimes," he said, "I feel that the wind has blown my soul away and filled me with only sand."

Mora reached out and patted his arm. Beneath the cloth she felt the wasted muscle of a desk-sitting man.

"It's all right, Alfred, we can look it up—"

"I know who it belongs to—" said George. The Navajo policeman stood leaning against the door jamb.

"—Evelyn Yazzie," Mora finished for him.

He straightened. "It's her clan. How did you know?"

"Where does she live?"

"Let George handle it, Mora, he knows better what to do," Alfred said.

Mora looked at George and held out her hands, suppliant. He nodded. "Come on," he said.

Bounding along in the police jeep over the dirt track, George told her how Running Feather died.

"Looks like when he fell he hit his head against the sharp corner of a display case. Might not have killed him, except with all his drinking—" George paused, drinking was too often the nemesis of the Navajo, "anyway, he hemorrhaged inside his head, and—" George paused again, "—and so maybe it wasn't intentional."

"She didn't know he died."

"How—"

"What do the two lines mean, on the medicine bag?"

"They represent lightning, a protection."

"Hurry," Mora said. She clutched her hands tight together, feeling the ridge of scar along each palm.

"We're there," George said, pointing at a hogan.

Built of sandstone blocks taken from the cliffs around it, the hogan blended with the mother earth, a natural

142

camouflage. The hogan had settled like an old woman hunched from the wind. The caulking had weathered away from the stone, leaving gaping holes where summer rain and winter snow found a path into the heart of the house. Soon the stone would surrender to the wind and become only sand, its true form, freed from constriction, a guest on the desert wind.

Mora was out of the jeep before it stopped rolling.

"No, wait!" George called.

A tumbleweed blew against her, its branches catching at her legs like long fingers. She stumbled, recovered and kept on running.

"No time!" she called back, knowing Navajo tradition had already been broken.

On the left of the hogan doorway, scratched into the soft stone, were two lightning lines, a child's playful vandalism. Mora pressed her hand into the scratches and felt a sharp pain radiate, as if she touched razors. She hoped she was not too late, that she did not enter a death hogan.

"Get out!" Evelyn Yazzie yelled at her. The old woman sat cross-legged in the light filtering from the round hole in the center of the hogan. Next to her skirt the medicine bag lay open and empty. In her hands she cradled a cup of steaming liquid, the contents of the medicine bag floating on top.

"Out!"

"No," Mora said, looking at the silent, huddled form beneath a blanket, next to the old woman.

"You were not invited here."

"Not by you." Mora gestured at the cup, "It won't work anymore, the tea won't heal."

"What do you know, Anglo?"

"That Running Feather died—"

"What?" Evelyn Yazzie dropped her scowl and under the lines cut by bitter anger was a handsome woman. "He only stumbled—"

"Did you look back?"

"No, he is too much of Anglo ways, him with his Anglo

job, he would have prevented me from taking this," the old woman pointed to the bag, "what was meant to be used, not locked away, behind glass, away from life."

"It is Running Feather who is away from life."

"An old man, a drunk. He tried to stop me. Why should I not take what is mine?"

Mora bent over the boy. He seemed too still, then she saw the rhythmic shifting of the tattered blanket as he breathed. She gathered him into her arms. As she lifted him the pain in her hands faded, disappeared.

"Where are you taking him—away from his grandmother? Capturing him for the Anglo?"

Mora thought of how perhaps her sixth fingers would never have worked, only crippled her, prevented her from painting. She moved toward the door. Evelyn Yazzie grasped at her skirt, clutching tight.

"And what will you tell them, stargazer?"

Mora looked at the deep grooves marring the woman's once-generous mouth.

"That not only Anglos have hearts of sand."

The old woman, defeated, dropped her protesting hands and Mora carried the boy out of the hogan to the waiting George. The boy opened his eyes to the day's light, and looking up at her, smiled, his trust blooming through the sheen of fever.

She smiled back, then noticed the golden cast of the desert sand, a patina on the earth, a painter's path. Now she knew she would sit before her easel and hand-tremble her path to her own beautyway.

THE MAN HANGED UPSIDE DOWN

by Lucy Sussex

Champagne was going up Mabille's nose, she couldn't stop it. I'll burst, she thought, I must get out of here. Around her the first night gallery faces milled—she ran from them, disregarding her bulk and her status as a critic. There was a little balcony overlooking the gallery's sculpture garden and she reached it just in time. Kicking the door shut behind her, she laughed and choked simultaneously.

It had all been so sudden. She had been following Oliver's life in art around the walls, mentally reviewing as she went. The retrospective was on the patchy side, but she couldn't say that—Oliver was a friend. At least the champagne was good, and as she took a consoling sip she noticed a showy frame enclosing a large sketch.

She could date this drawing by its elegant acerbic line, Oliver at his best. Twenty years old and never been exhibited—she would have remembered, the sketch was excellent. It was of a male nude, and she idly recalled the pretty young things who had drifted into Oliver's studio and modeled for him. He must have been in a snit with this one, the portrait was caricature. Then she intook breath and champagne, as she recognized the subject.

Philip, the prettiest of the lot, but not model but artist. He had been budding then; now he was in full career bloom,

145

rich, famous, and as thorny as in his youth, so well depicted here.

Best and worst of all, Oliver had drawn Philip sexually underendowed.

Leaning against the balustrade, she quieted, except for the odd eruptive giggle. She had work to do, and pulling out her makeup kit, she painted the laughter off her face, replacing it with media blandness. There was a knock on the glass balcony door: her producer.

"Canape went down the wrong way. I'm coming!"

Inside the gallery, she gave him the list of paintings she would review. The team from *Artsviews* program was coalescing around them.

"I'll talk for two-three minutes. Okay?"

"Name, but not a big name length. Sounds right, Mab."

Someone tickled her shoulder and she turned, to see Oliver's agent Noel.

"Where's that client of yours?"

Noel made a moue. "Ollie's feeling poorly. Apologies, dearie."

"Well, tell him I want an interview."

Filming was about to begin; the producer handed her a microphone and tactfully pulled the agent away. Lights, camera, action:

"Mabille Marty here, with this week's gallery opening, 'Lines and Faces,' perhaps more accurately 'Lines on Faces,' for this show is a retrospective, looking back over the career of Oliver Lane . . ."

When this segment was edited in the studio, film of pictures and picture-fanciers would be interpolated between the film being shot now, of Mabille the talking head. She had a visual memory, and commented on the paintings as if they, not the camera, were before her, pacing herself carefully. Her intention was to end this review with a bang.

"Highlight of the show, for me, is no. 24, 'Untitled' in the catalogue, but recognizably a study of Philip Holbrook, as he was—the portrait of the artist as a young nude!"

146

She smiled gleefully, holding the expression until filming had ended, then relaxed. It was done now: the identification would be made not only in the microcosm of an art gallery, but also in the macrocosm of telecommunications.

Both worlds would soon be treated to Philip's tempest-tantrum.

Oliver met Mabille in his studio, a familiar place, but unfamiliar now with much of its contents looted for "Lines and Faces." She watched him, as he prepared gin and tonics, and decided that he too seemed different. Oliver was still the sleek old cat, but now he had a harried look. When they sat down together with their drinks, she reached for the tape recorder, but Oliver forestalled her:

"Oh leave the little eavesdropper alone."

"Interview, Oliver."

"Later."

She realized that for the moment he would talk to her only. Leaning back in one of the big faded studio deckchairs, she waited, but he was not forthcoming. Needs prodding, she decided, and drained her glass, beaching the ice cubes at the bottom of it.

"All right then. Why the sketch?"

"You know Philip."

"Yes, but there's more to that portrait than the odium he usually trails in his wake."

Now Oliver was emptying his glass.

"It was when we parted. He'd got himself noticed, got a good agent, so he didn't need me anymore. I wasn't upset— I'd had other young men use me for my art contacts, and I'd use them back. A reciprocal contract, entered into with good cheer.

"Now with young Philip it was all gimme, no takee. I told him so, as a parting shot, and was he surprised! He thought I should be grateful to be treated like an old . . . paint rag."

"Raving egomaniac," she said.

147

"Like most artists, most male artists. The muse and machismo, it's a bad combination. Me, I never took myself that seriously, not the way Philip does. I've known you a long time, Mabille, and I don't remember you being that way either, back in the days when you were sculpting . . ."

She twitched.

"I stopped being a sculptor years ago."

"And now you're the most fearsome critic in Arttown, and you love it."

Do I? she thought. He was looking at her, reading her face, but before he could comment she sent the conversation back to its original subject.

"Oliver, I want to hear your story."

"Where was I? Oh yes . . . the door slammed behind Philip, I pulled out the charcoal and scratched that sketch."

His lips curved.

"Best likeness I ever did from memory."

"I hardly thought it was a life study."

"You mean the teensy penis?" he said, grinning now.

"Er, yes. Why that?"

"Pun. He always was a little prick."

She collapsed into giggles, rocking the deckchair—really Oliver's sketch was the best laugh she'd had in ages. Then, as she dabbed her eyes with the hem of her flowing skirt, she noticed he was stone-faced, and instantly sobered.

"If I know you, Oliver, every time Philip won an award you got out that sketch and looked at it."

He nodded, still serious.

"So why share the joke now?"

"What did you think of 'Lines and Faces'?" he asked.

She hesitated.

"I know what you said on *Artsviews*, but what did you really think?"

She sighed. "Oliver, I love you, but that wasn't much of an exhibition."

He sighed back. "Don't I know it. Noel knows it too, but retrospectives are good for the art stocks. And they have to

148

be *big*. All the collectors want their Lane in, to show the investment's sound.

"I have something that's good, irrespective of fashion—"

(That was a one-claw jab at Philip, she thought.)

"—but it's not there all the time. Put the Lanes together, and it's obvious. Were it up to me, I'd just show the top ten."

"Good aesthetics, bad economics," she said.

"That's roughly what Noel said. He came in here shouting: 'Cough up dearie, I want to see the lot—your crayon drawings at age four, the porn you did of your prettyboys, phoneside doodles, the works.' He left no sketch unturned for the show."

She'd heard that pun from him before, but nonetheless she smiled approvingly.

"And what happened when he found that sketch?"

"He snickered."

"Was he responsible for the Mexican brothel frame?"

"He said: 'To hell with good taste, this has to be noticed!'"

"Knows his publicity."

"Speak for yourself, Mabille!"

"You mean my announcement? Oliver, I'd never miss a scoop."

"I almost wish you had."

She opened her mouth wide: "Why?"

"Philip's not nice . . . angry."

"I'm not afraid of him." He stared into his glass, exasperating her. "Oliver, don't be a scaredy-cat. Philip's got you the publicity *nothing* can buy, and if he blusters, so what? More publicity. This is the best scandal for yonks, and I intend to make the most of it. Now can I have my interview?"

"All right," he said meekly.

Oliver cooked Mabille scrambled eggs on the studio Bunsen burner, and settled down with the gin. She left, not wishing to hear Oliver's life story yet again. In her flat, she flopped down in a chair and rang the number she had for Philip.

It was his public relations officer, the best her contacts could do for her. She got the answering machine.

Bleeep—"This is Mabille Marty, from *Artsviews*. I want to re-schedule the interview. Can you ring me? Ciao!"

As part of the media blitz for Philip's next exhibition, she had been booked for an audience next month. However, that time, while convenient for Philip, would not be for her. She needed to follow Oliver's interview with the opposing point of view, to keep the feud frying.

She closed her eyes, letting the egg and alcohol digest. After some time the phone rang, upsetting the process.

"Mabille."

"Oliver here." He was several gins down the road, by the sound of it. "I've had an int'resting phone call . . . from a stooge of Philip's. . . ."

"Stop pausing dramatically and tell me what he said."

"He was gonna beat me up!"

She soothed him for some minutes, then disengaged, having had enough of Oliver for the day. Only when the receiver was down did she take note of the emotion in his voice, at odds with, and odd, given his message.

He had sounded relieved. Very.

The next few days were hectic with Mabille's work: editing the interview with Oliver; making contacts for a serial she was preparing on corporate art buyers; inputting her columns for the computer networks; and talking to Philip's answering machine. The organization was not returning her calls.

Revenge, she thought, for the glint in my eye when I identified him. Well, I shall be difficult back.

Bleeep—"Mabille Marty again. If I don't get my interview rescheduled for next week, I shall cancel. Ciao!"

She knew the limits of her power; a non-interview with Philip would not jeopardize his public relations. However, the absence would be noticed, as if she smiled into the

Artsviews cameras with a tooth missing. Philip might bluff her, but his organization would not. His agent was negotiating sponsorship with a Japanese corporation, one Mabille wanted to include in her art buyers serial. Until the deal was finalized, Philip's people would be very nervous.

Mabille switched on her answering machine, and put on her hat to go out, being hard to get, for a change. She had an invitation to an opening by some Korean performance artists, a show to be seen at rather than see.

Mid-performance, she saw Noel.

"Enjoying the show?" she asked.

"I might, dearie, if I could understand it."

"There is a program," she said.

"I had one. Then that female with the red ochre face grabbed it and folded it into a tricorne hat. All part of the show, but . . ."

Mabille consulted her program. "That must have been the Korean witchcraft dance. She was cursed, it says."

"I'll curse her!" he replied loudly. Some of the audience turned towards them curiously and Mabille had a glimpse, in their negative space, of writhing leotarded bodies.

"How's Oliver?" she asked.

"Bizarre."

She waited.

"You remember the opening? Ollie was stuck in the loo throughout, with the collywobbles. I mean, most of my stable are shit-scared at such dos, but it's never physical."

He paused.

"He was contrary about the phone threat," said Mabille. "Almost happy."

"And when it was withdrawn he nearly wept! 'Dearie,' I said, 'did you want some handsome hunk beating you into a meatball? I never knew you were a masochist!' But he wouldn't be jollied, not until threat number two—a dirty big lawsuit."

He shrugged daintily.

"If I'd known he'd go potty, I'd never have shown that sketch of Phil Holbrook, delicious though it is . . . oh!"

A trapeze had lowered from the ceiling, dependent on it, by the knees, the red ochre girl. Her face was at the level of theirs, but inverted.

"You mention Philip Holbrook," she said.

"This part's audience-artist interaction," Mabille muttered to Noel. "Interact!" But he was glaring at the program-purloiner, so she answered for him: "Yes."

"You know him?"

Mabille nodded.

"We did dance adaptation of his horse paintings."

"With live gee-gees," Noel breathed into Mabille's ear, "or panto horses?" She dug him in the ribs. The Horse Exhibition—Philip's first "To hell with good taste, I want to be noticed" show—had featured bestiality, painted gaudily. Oliver claimed responsibility: "I tell that literal-minded sod his name means horse-lover and look what happens!"

"How interesting," Mabille said, suppressing a giggle.

"Yes. We want very much to meet the famous painter. To explore kinship of non-European artists. Asian and Australian Aboriginal: Korean and Koorie."

"Been reading his old press releases," whispered Noel, and feeling she really would laugh, Mabille pushed him away. It had been an early talking point for Philip, his wise old black grandfather. That influence had apparently been stronger than the old man's genes: to the uninformed eye, Philip looked white. He had no more melanin in him than a Southern European; nobody would have identified him otherwise, until he had.

Mischief pricked at Mabille. "Do you want Philip's phone number?"

In answer the girl somersaulted down with a thump. As Mabille recited the too-familiar sequence, the dancer dabbed fingers in her facepaint, then daubed the numbers on her leotard. She then capered away, to rejoin the troupe.

Noel was studying Mabille's program.

"The next item is a sacrifice to the rain . . . god!"

An ox was being led into the gallery, bedecked with flowers, and ridden by several performers, including the red

152

ochre girl.

"I'm getting out of here," said Mabille.

As she anticipated, when she got home, there was a message on the answering machine, from some minion of Philip's.

"Interview tomorrow, 10 p.m."

Philip knows I hate rush jobs, she thought. The sod. The next message in the recorder was from Oliver, maudlin drunk.

"Come 'n' have a drink, Mabille. Philip won't sue me." She took off her hat.

"Oh Oliver, I haven't time," she cried to the empty air, and sat down to prepare the questions for his opponent.

The interview with Philip was a contrast, not a companion piece, to her interview with Oliver. To begin with, she left the boho quarter where she and Oliver lived, and traveled to the money part of town. Philip owned a studio complex there, complete with interview room, into which she was shown on her arrival. It had a bar, shiny photos of Philip, pristine white carpet and lush chairs. She waited, sipping the drink proffered by an edgy young employee.

"Do you also do phone threats?" she asked, and he fled, either nonplussed or guilty. At 10:45 precisely, Philip entered this magazine layout, like an illustration of the low life. He was unshaven, bare-footed and -chested, clad only in tight paint-smeared jeans. The paint continued onto his torso and even onto his face. It was like warpaint, like an atavism of his tribal ancestors.

"You!" he said, curtly.

"Me what? Are you going to insult me? Words don't hurt, Philip, and if you get one of your slaves to beat me with sticks or throw stones at me, I'll get you filthy publicity."

He glared at her, attractive even in anger.

"I'll do what I want," he shouted.

"Not until the Taguchi Corporation signs your contract. I heard."

"Fat cow," he muttered. "Fat bitch. Fat faghag."

"What a thing to say to someone here to present your side of the Lane-Holbrook fracas," she said silkily.

He was startled.

"You're a mate of that . . . deadhead."

"True, but scam comes first."

In their sudden quiet the employee knocked and entered, carrying a cloth soaked in cleanser, which he handed to Philip. The artist began to massage the paint from his skin, and with it, apparently his belligerence. His muscles rippled, the relaxation almost palpable.

"For your next interview," she said cautiously, "you could get him to do that for you. Like a champion boxer being rubbed down after a fight.

"Him" blushed, but Philip was oblivious.

"A fight with an empty canvas," he said, still surly, but intrigued. At moments like these, Mabille thought, he talks like a real artist.

She put her tape recorder on the glass table between them, and he sat down opposite. The aide poured two drinks, then exited.

"Deal, Philip. I've got thirty minutes, standard interview time, right? For twenty of these minutes you can rave about your art, then for the other ten, you can say how hurt you are to be libelled in paint."

"Not hurt. It din' do anything to me."

She recalled his literal-mindedness.

"Anger isn't anything?"

"I'm fuckin' furious . . . but not made small."

He grinned rakishly.

"I'm not here to talk about the contents of your jeans," said Mabille, and quickly switched on the tape recorder.

"Now, you talk painting."

He did, she only half-listening, inured to artists, bullshit or otherwise. She asked questions like an automaton, while pondering how much to probe about Oliver. Just once, he got her full attention.

"How many paintings in the show?"

154

"Seventy-eight."

She whistled, then was puzzled. There's some significance to that number, she thought, I should know it.

"Why seventy-eight?"

"You'll find out"—with another grin.

"The theme of your show must be good, to sustain all that art," she said.

He grinned wider.

"You're fishin', but I ain't bitin'."

This is what you get with a pre-show interview, she thought: suspense. Nonetheless, she persisted.

"A good theme. The European invasion of Australia?"

He showed his teeth, not in exasperation at a correct guess, but something else.

"Why'd you say that?"

"A performance artist was talking about art and ethnicity. I think she'd read your old interviews, where you talk about your Koorie granddad. He's important to you"—Philip nodded warily—"but not to your painting. Every Holbrook show has had a European theme. Those horses were derived from the Parthenon, not . . ."

An image from an art history book had come to her mind.

" . . . the Koorie paintings of horses. I saw one once, it was huge, blocky, tail like a brush. I remember it was throwing its rider, a policeman. The composition had incredible power."

"Don't talk shit," he said flatly. "You belong to the race that shot at that artist, stole his land, and you tell *me* his art throws you! What do you know about it?"

"In aesthetic terms . . ."

"It wasn't painted so you'd like it!"

He sprang up and paced to the end of the room and back, scuffing the white carpet.

"I'm sorry," she said. "It sounded patronizing, didn't it?"

No answer.

"Mabille running off at the mouth again. I didn't mean

155

anything, I was just curious. Shouldn't have mentioned it."

He had stopped, and was looking over his shoulder at her.

"Shall we be professional?" she said, meeting his gaze. "There are five minutes left. Why don't you let rip about Oliver?"

"I might not," he said, rocking on his feet. "Why should I give you good copy? Help sell that draw-ring of me."

"It's been sold."

"Well, help sell that clapped-out old . . . He hasn't done a good picture in years. Just dead, as an artist."

"He'll never work again?" she said dangerously.

"I din' say that. But Oliver's all washed up, isn't he? Nothing but spite . . ."

Excellent copy, thought Mabille.

". . . spitting on the works of the real artists."

Within her, something gave way.

"We are all going to heaven and Van Dyke is of the company."

"Eh?" he said.

"Gainsborough's last words. I mean, the real artists get judged by time, not PR. I think Oliver's real, erratic but real. Okay, I'm biased. I should go—time's up. Have you anything else you'd like to add?"

"I'll get even," he said.

She reached out for the tape recorder and switched it off, her hands trembling. I didn't mean to get intense, she thought. What happened? Where's my professionalism?

Philip was looking in half a mind to hit her, but there was a sudden hubbub outside the interview room. The door opened, admitting the head of the aide. He looked flustered.

"There's some people want to talk art with you, sir. I've tried, but they won't go away."

Behind him, Mabille had a brief glimpse of a face, denuded of red ochre, but familiar. The Korean performance troupe had arrived. Seizing her opportunity, she grabbed the handle of the door, and pulled it wide open, using her weight to push past the lithe, incoming bodies.

"Of course Ollie's cross with you, dearie," said Noel. He put a piece of spaghetti in his mouth, slurped it up, then spoke again: "First you don't join him for drinkies—not that I blame you, he's a dull drunk—and then you publish Phil's venom."

"It was too good not to use," said Mabille, as the waiter whisked away her empty plate. Noel slurped again.

"Oh I agree! No attention is bad attention, I always say, though not to Ollie at the moment."

Mabille was playing with the bread on her side plate, ripping the soft white underbelly from the crust and kneading it.

"I have to do my job. Oliver knows that."

"Not when he's off the planet." He put down his fork, bisecting the circle of the emptied plate. "Why be surprised? You should be used to artistic temperament by now."

Mabille was looking at the lump of bread. She pushed here, prodded there, and saw it assume the shape of an Aboriginal head.

"I must rush, dearie. That was nice. Repeat sometime?"

He glanced at the bill in its silver salver, then covered it with another bill, large denomination. "There's my half," he said. "Ciao."

"Ciao," Mabille said grumpily. She waited until he was out of the door, then brought her fist down on the table.

"Artistic temperament shouldn't be reserved for artists!" she cried. There was silence in the restaurant for a minute, eyes staring at her, then the serious pleasure of eating was resumed.

Maybe they agree with me, she thought. She dropped the bread head into her shoulder bag, paid for her half of the meal, and left, oddly cheerful.

The team from *Artsviews* were huddled together, a world unto themselves, within the crowd outside Philip's exhibition.

"Holbrook shouldn't keep everybody waiting," said the

157

producer.

"He can afford to," said Mabille, "with these backers." She glanced up at the marble panelling of the Taguchi Operations Center, at the polished bronze doors sealing off the display wall.

"They mostly show their products in there," said the camera girl. "I've seen it—state of the art."

"And now it's the state of the artist," Mabille said. A crack of light appeared between the doors, slowly widened.

"Okay gang," she said. "Charge!"

By butting and elbowing, they were first through the brazen doors, but they did not stop there. Mabille saw a dais at the live center of the hall, a perfect vantage point from which to view the exhibition. She pointed—and the team ran raggedly towards the dais. They clambered onto it, then turned, looking at the paintings properly for the first time.

"Wow!"

Waves and waves of violent color streaked up the marble walls, as if barely contained by the large, rectangular canvases. Each painting was exactly the same size, producing the effect of:

"The devil's picture book! Playing cards."

"Excuse me," said a small voice, and Mabille looked down, to see an oriental girl in a silk uniform. "I sell programs here," she said expressionlessly.

They jumped down, and she looked at their press badges, then distributed gratis programs.

"Thank you," Mabille said absently, staring at the nearest paintings. One showed ten gold cups, the next nine. She ruffled through the program for the explanation.

"Not playing cards. The tarot!"

"Wow!" the producer repeated. "That's a big theme: seventy-eight cards in the greater and lesser Arcana."

"I *knew* the number meant something," said Mabille. She clutched her head: "How am I going to take it all in?"

"Challenge, Mab," said the producer. "You can do it."

"Ha!" she said, and began to walk systematically along the walls. She felt reduced to a pair of eyes, with a brain behind them, sorting, absorbing, assessing. Yet she could not wholly ignore other sensory input: people brushed against her, buzzed conversation.

"—the cost of all that canvas—"

"—no wonder he sought sponsorship, the crafty devil—"

"—that him? I thought he was black—"

"—over there, with the little Japanese guys in the Italian suits—"

"—tailoring like that has power written all over it—"

"—notice Holbrook's brushed up the old image. Nice suit, nice tie, nothing boho—"

"—come a long way from that grotty backstreet studio he had. Y'know, Philip used to cook over a Bunsen burner?"

"Dearie, I know. The studio belonged to Ollie. He was letting Phil Holbrook use it, and him."

"Noel!" she cried, seeking a break from shrieking symbolism.

"Mabille, you're bug-eyed!" He put his arm around her.

"Enjoying the show?" she asked, hoping to pump him.

"Hardly glanced at it. I came here chasing clients, although so far I've been nobbled by bores."

"How's one particular client?"

"Feeling poorly."

"Again?" she said, recalling Oliver's exhibition.

"Yes, same as last week." She hadn't seen Oliver for a fortnight, at least. "I got bored with his hypochondria, so I booked him in for a checkup."

"Oliver's never been a malade imaginaire," she said, concerned.

"He's been everything since his show."

The *Artsviews* producer suddenly darted from behind two culture-vultures in black feathers.

"Mab! Come and see this!"

"Duty calls, Noel. Ciao."

The display hall was swarming now, and they linked hands, zigzagging past human obstructions to the other end of the exhibition. The crowd was thickest around one painting, and he led her into the thick of it. As they nudged and niggled their way to the front, Mabille recognized a couple of old art lags, minor somebodies of Oliver's generation. They were grinning.

"Le Pendu," said the producer. "The most famous tarot card."

In front of her was the depiction of a man hanging upside down from a withered tree. He was painted in livid magenta, slime green and dull red, the colors of agony. They were also, Mabille recalled, the colors that had bedaubed Philip at the interview. The viewers were twisting their heads sideways, trying to see the reversion of the contorted, screaming face. Mabille did likewise, and saw it was Oliver.

She closed her eyes, but the afterimage remained, in reverse colors, floating inside her eyelids like a scene from a video nasty.

"I want to be sick," she murmured, and the producer dragged her out of the crowd of voyeurs.

"Mab, no! You can't be sick."

She leant against the wall.

"I suppose not," she said weakly. "Professionalism." But she made no move.

"Sure you're revolted," he said. "But express it some other way. Slag off the show."

"Can't. It's good, in his flashy, fashionable way."

"Do something! Oliver's your mate."

The image was fading on her retina now, and as it went, an idea came felicitously to her. She opened her eyes and stood upright.

"My Polaroid camera's in my bag, I just got it fixed." She pulled it out and handed it to him. "Can you get me photos of ten Major Arcana paintings, please.'

"Including that one?" He gestured sideways.

"Yes. I'm not going to rely on my memory tonight. During filming, I want to be prompted, on my cues, with the polaroids."

"In any order?" he asked.

"I don't care. Shuffle them so that some are upside

down." He caught on then, and laughed.

"Mab, you're a genius. What a way to trivialize the show!"

"And Philip."

He left her alone then, and she deftly hooked a glass of champagne from a passing drinks tray. Dutch courage, with what tasted like the best French wine. She had another drink, and might have had a third, had not an oriental woman in Italian tailoring approached her.

"You are Mabille Marty?"

"Of course."

"I am from Taguchi Public Relations. We would like Mr. Holbrook to say a few words on *Artsviews*.

It would look good, thought Mabille. "If he's brief," she replied.

"I bring him!" and the PR lady ducked into the crowd, returning in a few minutes with Philip. Mabille had passed quite close to him and his backers earlier, but had not spared a glance from her perusal of the paintings. Now she could appreciate his nice suit, white linen cut generously enough to accommodate a painting on its surface, should Philip so choose. The artist inside the canvas, however, looked the picture of discontent.

"Not your idea, obviously," she murmured.

"No!"—with a glare at the Taguchi employee, who took several steps back in response. In this quasi-privacy, Mabille said:

"I've seen your nasty piece of work."

"I don' care what you say about it!" He did, though— artists are so self-conscious, thought Mabille.

"Outside of Goya's black period, I've not seen anything so hateful."

"Hate-full," he mused, defiant.

"Also exciting hatred," she snapped. "Any reason you painted Oliver as Le Pendu, inver . . ."

She stopped, the answer and a mental flashback of the painting staring her in the face.

"You and your literal-mindedness! Upside-down, and

Oliver an invert!"

He smiled, and she resisted a powerful urge to box his ears.

"What do you want to say?" she asked, noticing that the PR woman had crept closer. She, not Philip, answered:

"Mr. Holbrook would like to talk about his theme."

Over the woman's head, she saw the producer atop the dais, to the obvious annoyance of the program seller, giving her the okay symbol. "You can have a couple of minutes," she said to Philip. "We're about ready to go."

The *Artsviews* team and their equipment were grouped to one side of the dais. She stood in front of the camera, Philip glowering beside her.

"Remember, two minutes," she said, between clenched teeth.

He nodded, bending towards her.

"'Member what I said to you? I got even."

So will I, she thought, and the filming began.

"Mabille Marty here, from a new art venue, the Taguchi Corporation Display Hall, site of Philip Holbrook's new show: 'Images of the Tarot.'"

She knew, from long experience, how this introduction would be treated in the *Artsviews* format. Long tracking shots of the hall would be shown, then her image would appear again, this time wide-angle, to show Philip beside her.

"We have here the artist. Welcome to *Artsviews*, Philip."

"Ta, Mabille."

"Tell me, Philip, what led you to the tarot, one of the oldest fortune-telling mediums in *European* culture? Was it the richness of its symbolism, already plundered by literature in poems like 'The Wasteland'?"

"Symbols, yeah, there's tarot poems, but seems to me the images of the tarot have never been prop'ly explored in the visual media . . ."

Again Mabille tuned him out, preparing her next speech. She wished for a moment she had a tarot handbook handy, then dismissed the thought as panicky.

The producer drew his finger slowly across his throat, a cue to Philip, who came to a neat close.

"Thank you, Philip. The question everybody must be asking is: will 'Images of the Tarot' succeed as brilliantly as past Holbrook shows? We shall consult the tarot itself, hanging on these walls, in order to answer the question. Ladies and gentlemen, I will now tell Philip Holbrook's fortune!"

Mabille was dimly aware of Philip turning, astonished, towards her, and the PR woman leading him away. She returned soon, with Philip's backers, a little group disconcertingly intent on Mabille, who ignored them. Her attention was focused on the producer, who held a Polaroid photograph in front of her eyes, an image of an image.

"Card one," she said, "which reveals the present influences upon Philip Holbrook. We have here the Emperor—"

Oh, easy!

"—a card symbolizing worldly power. What better card to represent the Taguchi Corporation?"

Another picture.

"Card two: present obstacles. This painting is Philip's depiction of the Fool, a card symbolizing lack of discipline, unrestrained excess."

Always a problem with Philip's painting, she thought, but did not voice.

"Card three: specific goals. We have here the Sun card—"

Van Gogh yellow, she mentally muttered.

"—signifying success or triumph. What else does an artist want?"

"Card number four—"

Bring some clever computer graphics in now, she thought, and show all four pictures in tarot pattern on a black background. Then enlarge the fourth painting, to fill the screen.

"—past foundation. The image is of the Magician."

Wonder if that's Philip's wise black granddad, she

thought. The fourth card always shows influences.

"Card number five: past events."

She almost gasped aloud as an image of agony, the Oliver picture, was held before her—even reduced it had impact. The Polaroid was upside down, something which from the producer's wink had not been random. Well, you miss the libel otherwise, she thought. And for added emphasis we'll follow with a close-up of the face.

"Le Pendu, the hanged man. This card has appeared reversed, showing a weak influence."

Well, Oliver never had much power over Philip.

"Card number six: future influences."

The Polaroid was of the Wheel of Fortune, a card symbolizing:

". . . luck, future, felicity."

More success for Philip, she thought. Worse luck. Where are the disaster cards? He deserves them. Several paintings later, the producer drew the Devil card, in position nine, Philip's influence on other people. That's better, she thought. Unnerving, this tarot.

"Last card, number ten, the final result."

It was the World card, which Philip had interpreted as four fleshy female nudes, holding aloft a globe. That's a painting screaming aloud: I'm heterosexual! she thought. He must have done it to dispel the doubts raised by the feud with Oliver.

"The World, representing completion, perfection, success."

More fame and fortune for Philip, she realized. How unjust.

"Mabille Marty, signing off from the opening night of 'Images of the Tarot,'" she finished, on automatic pilot. The filming ended, and she quietly collapsed onto the nearest shoulder, which happened to be the producer's.

"Well done, Mab," he said.

She waited for the furious response from Philip, but it never came, not even after the broadcast on *Artsviews*. Daily she played back her answering machine, but there were no phone threats, no messages from corporate lawyers. The explanation came, in dribbles, from her art gossips.

"—Taguchi have a sub-corp, which does sidereal horoscopes, computerized I Ching—"

"—got the idea after that impertinent little broadcast of yours—

"—manufacture tarot packs with his paintings on them—"

"—Philip powerless to stop it—"

"—makes him moolah, though—"

"—so he'd see some good in it—"

"—but it's lousy for his art stocks in the long run—" Mabille finished. "Links him with gimcrackery. I really *did* trivialize him."

Alone in her flat she leapt into the air in glee, only to come back heavily to earth at the sound of her phone ringing. It was Noel.

"Dearie, Ollie wants to see you."

"I'm forgiven?"

"You're number one on his hit parade, shafting Philip like that."

"I'll come down at once."

"Wait! He's not at the studio, he's in the hospital. I'm to escort you."

"Is it bad?"

"Yes, Mabille, very."

At the hospital, their respective shoes beat a rataplan on the polished floors.

"I could kick myself in the bum," Noel said loudly. "I was sure it was all in Ollie's mind, not his bod . . ."

They made a turn, into the AIDS wing. Oliver was in a private room, looking if not skeletal, certainly like death. Noel sat tidily on the end of the bed; Mabille walked up and kissed Oliver's sunken cheek.

"Mabille, lovely to see you. I'd offer gin and tonic, but they don't allow decadence here."

"How long have you known?" she said starkly, unable

165

to voice pleasantries in response.

"I've been AIDS-positive for some time, but the virus was a lazy little bugger. Dormant for years, then all of a sudden . . ."

The bonhomie abruptly vanished from his face. Almost simultaneously, Noel slid from the end of the bed, stiff-legged.

"Ollie, I can't believe you've been pureed!"

"Please leave," said Oliver.

"Very well, dearie," said the agent, and stalked noisily out of the room. Pureed? thought Mabille, but Oliver had put his lukewarm hand into hers, demanding attention.

"Ignore Noel, he's a skeptic. Philip did this to me."

She stared at him, thinking: mon dieu, it's affected his brain!

"Don't be silly, Oliver. AIDS virus doesn't lie dormant twenty years."

"You misunderstand me. I never got anything from Philip."

She let out a breath.

"Do you mean you've been worried sick, literally?"

"The painting did it," he said in absurdly somber tones, as if accusing a butler.

She jerked out of his grasp and paced angrily around the shiny little room.

"Oliver, you aren't making sense. Noel said you were ill before Philip's opening night, so you couldn't have had a psychosomatic reaction to Le Pendu . . ."

"I didn't need to see it," he cried. "I could feel it. From the minute Philip put brush to canvas."

She stopped short. Spotless white wall was before her eyes, a screen for a memory, of an olive brown torso smeared with red, magenta, vomit green.

"Vanity, vanity, mundane vanity," he said. "I wanted my sketch in 'Lines and Faces,' I knew it was good. I also half knew he would do this."

She sat down in the dent on the cover left by Noel.

"Oliver, begin at the beguine."

It was an old joke of his, and it relaxed him. He leaned back against his pillows, spoke without self-pity.

"It was just after he moved into the studio. I got him drunk, hoping for a libidinous reaction, but instead he got talkative. We had a wow of a conversation. In between bottles, we got onto the meaning of art, and I asked what painting meant to him. He answered in one word: power.

"Now to me art is being in love with line and form, and expressing that love in pencil on paper. I was rather shocked, and accused him of being an opportunist. Not at all, he said, it was his cultural milieu. No he didn't, it was some rough phrase, he was a real boy from the bush then."

"Roots," suggested Mabille.

"Probably." He switched back to the past again. "Trying to make sense of what he said, I asked Philip if he saw art as an escape route from the have-nots, the powerless. You've heard his working-class hero speech: family of six living in a caravan, kids lying awake at nights scared by granddad's snoring. He delivered it for the first time, probably, that night."

"Lucky you," she said drily.

"No, he said. He didn't mean the culture of the poor, he meant the culture of the blacks, his granddad's people. The family were all scared of the old man, he was a witch. Supplemented their income by doing love magic, Philip said. It worked, he claimed. I was wishing I could call on the old fellow then, get something to use on his grandson."

"I know you were besotted, I've heard many-a-time. What has all this to do with art?"

"Painting to the old man meant magic. He came from the tribes responsible for those great rock paintings in North Australia. Philip got out the postcards and showed me. I had never seen them before—they had incredible power, aesthetically. Philip said they had power in actuality. His ancestors painted the wallaby pierced with spears, so they'd have a successful hunt. They painted pregnant women, to ensure a supply of babies. They painted their enemies upside-down, to kill them. Puri-puri, it was called . . . not

167

bone, but brush pointing."

"I've seen one," she said. "A policeman, being thrown from his horse, heels over head."

"Mmn," Oliver said absently. "Funny how one symbol has different meanings in different cultures. To me, or you, an inverted figure is a homosexual, or the Hanged Man, or the Fisher King, if I recall Tom Eliot aright. To Philip, it's someone being pureed, as Noel calls it."

"For once," she said, fascinated, "Philip used a symbol from the Aboriginal culture. But he put it in a context where nobody would notice."

She remembered Philip's anger at the interview. No wonder.

There were steps on the parquet, and Noel appeared in the doorway.

"Mabille, do you believe that fairy tale?" he said crossly.

She looked from one to the other, and saw that both were pleading with her to support their respective cases.

"I don't know," she said.

Back in her flat, she went through her reference collection of art books, heaping them on the floor like sandcastles, as she searched for the image of the policeman being thrown from his horse.

She found it with the caption: "I hope you break your bloody neck!" Did he? she wondered. Oliver must believe he died, and maybe Philip does too.

He could have power, she thought. Perhaps all these years he's secretly been painting banknotes and awards with spears through them. He was certainly murderously cross with Oliver.

Alternately, Philip could have been trying to scare him . . . scare him to death, she thought. Or maybe working out his annoyance in traditional fashion, then exhibiting it. I don't know. The point is, Oliver thinks he's been a victim of puri-puri, and he's responding accordingly.

She flipped through the glossy pages again, looking at photographs of great limestone cliffs, open-air art galleries.

A rock wall is an immutable surface. If you paint a picture on it, if you paint an enemy arsy-versy, nothing much can alter the work, short of explosives. But a painting on a canvas can be moved, stolen, slashed.

She stood up and went to the phone, dodging bookpiles. Flipping through her address book, she selected the number of an art broker firm, where one of her favorite gossips worked.

"Mabille here. Do you know who bought Philip's painting of Oliver?"

"Taguchi, of course."

Mabille had, while researching her corporate art buyers serial, noted the Taguchi Corporation art curator as a likely interviewee. Several phone calls later, she found the curator was a promising young sculptor, who had exhibited in the boho quarter only last year.

"Junko! What are you doing at Taguchi? I didn't give you that bad a review, surely."

"It was a wonderful review," the voice at the other end of the line said. "But sculpture's an expensive habit—with the price of marble what it is, I had to take a day job."

"Some day job," Mabille commented several hours later, gazing around at Junko's small, but luxuriously appointed office. The same adjectives could be applied to Junko herself: she wore a suit and thorn-heeled shoes, with the same ethereal confidence as when Mabille had last seen her, at her sculpture opening, dressed in overalls and sneakers.

"I've got a great-uncle on the board of directors," she said to Mabille. "But keep that under your—very nice—hat."

In the glass and chrome lift, Mabille said:

"So the corporation had first option on Philip's show."

"As part of the contract. When the bosses saw the marketing potential in the paintings, they grabbed the rights."

She fell silent as some middle-aged Japanese men, as immaculate as she was, entered the lift. They exited at the marble and bronze foyer and the lift continued down with the two women, into the clay feet of the skyscraper.

"Here we are."

The lift door opened, to reveal a vestibule walled with grey metal, and an armed guard behind an office desk. Junko flashed their documentation, and he laboriously unsealed a dense security door for them, revealing a cavern lit by glaring neon light. It was filled with art treasure, arranged on racks, paintings in narrow protective cases and bulky irregular shapes, swathed sculptures.

"This recalls Goering's art mine," said Mabille.

"I know," said Junko. "Same impulse: power expressed via the acquisition of artistic objects."

They walked between the racks, stopping at a large sculpture, free-standing, unwrapped, on the concrete floor. Amidst the harsh functionalism of the vault, its marble and steel nakedness had an unearthly beauty.

"That I recognize," said Mabille.

"One of mine, that you highly recommended. My predecessor must have decided it was a good investment, although I suspect uncle had a hand in its purchase. I keep it out, to cheer me."

"So would I, in this salt mine," said Mabille. It depressed her, all this art, salted away, just gathering money. "Do you spend much time here?"

"Some. Nobody else does, although we had the photographers down yesterday, making copies for the Taguchi tarot packs."

"Where are they?" said Mabille, remembering her mission.

"In a moment!"

Junko took Mabille's elbow and pivoted her around, to face a stretch of grey vault wall. Hanging from it was a sketch in a red mirror frame: Oliver's libellous nude.

"I keep that out, too, because it's fine drawing. The company bought it on my advice."

"Even in here it looks good," said Mabille, pleased.

"Now," said Junko. "You want the Hanged Man."

Mabille turned to face her.

"Did I make myself clear, over the phone?"

"Loud and," said the curator. "Despite your embarrassment. Why be ashamed? We Easterners have never underestimated the spirit world."

"Even that of another culture?"

"It can't be as good as the Japanese supernatural," Junko said proudly. "We have the most gruesome ghosts. But I don't discount it, nonetheless."

"Okay. Take me to the painting."

Some five meters further, they came to a rack filled with boxes, all exactly the same size. Junko walked along it, checking numbers.

"Painting 12: that's the one."

They womanhandled the narrow rectangular box to the floor, and opened it at the top. Junko drew up the first six inches of the painting: a withered branch, with a rope tied around it.

"Yep, labeling's correct."

They dragged out the rest of the painting, lowered it to the ground, then stepped back, eyeing it. Again Mabille felt stunned by the painted violence.

"Not," said Junko, "what the directors like hanging in their boardroom. They prefer soft porn actually. This painting will stay locked away in the vault, quietly appreciating in value. In five years time, maybe, it'll be traded to some museum in a tax deal."

"Five years," said Mabille.

"Or ten, depending upon Philip's art stocks."

"Enough time for Oliver to get better, if he does. I don't know."

"But you have to do it, right? Come on!"

They each took a corner of the painting and wrestled it round, until it was inverted. Oliver now seemed to be doing an Indian rope trick, floating at the end of his tether.

"Can't say it looks better that way," said Mabille. "But, as the tarot handbook says, inverted cards have a weak or negative influence. I haven't got a puri-puri handbook, to

171

say if the curse fails when the image is reversed. I can only guess, and try it. Say cheese!"

She took out her Polaroid camera from her bag, stepped back, and took several shots of Junko, leaning elegantly against Le Pendu. Then they swapped places, Junko snapping Mabille.

"For Oliver," said Mabille. "Proof."

"For his eyes only," Junko replied sharply, unwrapping one of the new, sticky, prints. She glanced at it, assessing her image, then handed it to Mabille. "The price of marble what it is, I don't want to lose this job."

They carefully replaced the upside-down painting in the box, wrote THIS WAY UP on it in large letters, and returned it to the rack. Panting a little, they retraced their path through the vault.

"When's your next show?" asked Mabille.

"Dunno. Working full-time saps the energy."

"Don't become like me," said Mabille. Junko looked at her quizzically. "I started writing columns to pay for raw materials, and next thing I'm Mabille Marty the critic, not artist."

"You could always come back to it," said Junko. "I saw some of your clay busts once. They were good."

"Thank you," said Mabille. She mentally stored the compliment, for future relishing. They were nearing the security door now, and she noticed her camera was still in her hand, still visible to the curious eye. She quickly replaced it in her bag, to discover something else there: the bread head, forgotten since her lunch with Noel.

"You should go back," said Junko.

Mabille held the tiny sculpture on her palm and surveyed it, as a critic. It looked dry, unappetizing, aesthetically awful, but then she was rusty, as an artist.

"Maybe," she said.

172

BAPKA IN BROOKLYN

by Batya Weinbaum

I.

I have never hated the members of my immediate family as intensely as I did during the three days of my grandfather's funeral. I was relieved to feel this hatred actually. Prior to the funeral I had complained to my shrink, Doris, that all I could feel was detachment. To prove it one session I kept repeating all the things I hated about my mother.

In the short space of a 45-minute hour, I listed incident after incident unfeelingly. My recitation wore on and on about how I could never remember my mother feeding me. But Doris didn't respond. I began to admire the plump red lamp, the frilled white shade, and the green plants which decorated her somber office. Straight ahead of me (I was flat on my back) I could see rooftops of other houses filled with shrinks (we were in the Village). I offered an interpretation so Doris wouldn't get bored. "You know what, Doris? Underneath all this is a projection on my part that my mother was always furious."

"At you?"

"Yeah." I crossed and uncrossed my ankles nervously. "I don't know why or how. But that must have been why she refused to feed me."

My throat, suddenly dry, constricted. I got frightened.

173

"What do you think, Doris?" Pause. "I said, Doris . . ." I urged, getting no response, musing how my mother was too angry to feed me.

"Why do you want to know?" Doris, swishing stockings and flicking ashes from an ivory cigarette holder, finally asked me.

"I said I wished I could feel hatred for my family. For my mother. That's why I pay you, to help me do this work. But I only feel frozen when I think of her. Maybe I'll list all the things that make me melt instead. Like the sound of silverware clacking, at the cafeteria in Brooklyn where my grandfather hangs out, when I visit him. Do you think that will work?"

Doris reached over and put her cigarette out in a gold-leaf miniature saucer. "Do I think what?"

"Well, isn't that, you must have had something in mind when—" tears washed up from my throat. I stifled them, wishing I were dead.

"Why do you think I had anything in mind?" Doris tidied up for her next appointment, straightening an array of black leather account books.

"Of course you do. You're the shrink. You do your part. You're not my mother."

"Now is not a time to mourn, now is a time to rejoice," three days later said the Jewish Minister. A rabbi really, but so reform a minister he might be. He gesticulated over the front pew at my grandfather's funeral. We were in a candlelit memorial chapel on Avenue J. My grandfather lay behind him in a pine box, draped with a blue and white flag like an Israeli soldier. In the first pew over which the Jewish Minister ministered sat my brother, the Doctor, and his wife. And next to them sat my father, the Doctor, and *his* wife. On my brother's hip was perched his baby daughter. My brother's wife is German. Next to her sat my 79-year-old Orthodox aunt with her shopping bags from Macy's and Gimbel's. Before the funeral, this one had burnt all my grandfather's shoes, insisting religiously, "You grew up in the Midwest. What do you know. In Jewish we call this a ritual."

"Now is not a time to mourn, now is a time to rejoice," the Jewish Minister repeated. "After all, today we place the last vestige of ghetto mentality in the grave. With this man passes an entire generation. The last traveling salesman in an otherwise professional family. The last lady's man and gambler and pauper. No Nussensweig will ever again bet on the horses. No Nussensweig will ever again come crying to a relative for money, that is if everything goes OK." Here Jewish Minister peered over his spectacles at me. "The last man to speak English in inverted Yiddish sentences," he continued. "Today we rejoice, believe me."

I cried, my head on the lap of one of my friends.

I had also organized a crew of my grandfather's friends from Dubrow's, the neighborhood cafeteria on Kings Highway, as Jews from Brooklyn should know. My mother, horrified that such clashing, check-tweeded riffraff should barge in on the family occasion, huffed past the *shamas* and rabbi from my grandfather's local *shul,* refusing to greet them. She slid in next to Southern Belle, who stood up to pull the lace belt of her green and white seersucker fluffed skirt together tighter around her slim waist. She was the converted Texan Wife of the Jewish Minister.

The Jewish Minister goes on, once my mother is settled in his wife's thin arm. "Louie always had an intelligent question to ask of Israel, and if he didn't, he would have wanted to . . ."

"My god," I heaved, sobbing, the only one, "don't put the man down on his dying day!"

My friends and I followed the funeral procession in my beat-up car. We drove behind the limousine all the way to Mount Lebanon Cemetery, where they lowered the pine box. I felt a thud as the box hit the bottom of the grave. I pulled my dark blue shawl, purchased from the Lower East Side for the occasion, around me, tightly. Family turned and left. End of funeral. No sitting *shiva.* No tradition.

"What am I going to do?" Aghast, I asked one of my

friends.

"Maybe," one of them said, "you can sit your own *shiva*. Take over his apartment and write a novel in his neighborhood."

The one who said this had a grandmother in Sea Gate so I believed her.

"Oh, is your mother Jewish? Are you sure? We thought she was Gentile." This from Jane, in the cafeteria. "Girlfriends do things wives won't do these days. You know what I mean. You're a grown girl."

Jane, piano player at the Senior Citizen's Club, was the only woman from Dubrow's who came to my grandfather's funeral. She came wearing red lipstick and a purple knit hat over a gray wig with a gold spider pinned into it. Something sprightly and bright to pin down her fading hold on the physical.

The whole crew consists of Minnie, who has, rumor has it, practically a museum in her apartment. Her floral silk dress collection was also beautiful. Nobody from the whole crew had seen the apartment. An antique collection, from Ida I once heard. Ida has already disappeared into a convalescent home since I began my appearances at the Cafeteria. Then there was Goldie, who when I called to invite her to the funeral and to tell her about Louie's death said, "OK, sign off, sign off, I don't want to hear it."

Even the most simple of talk was—musical.

I first became a member of the Crew when after the funeral, strained and drained, I rushed over to put blood back in my veins through the red meat and spirit back through my soul with the *halvah;* words back in my mouth from the meditations I knew I would hear: old bearded fellows in blue-brimmed denim hats complaining, "When I was a man, I mean, when I was young—"

To my delight, when I burst in, there they sat in a circle. "Come on, sit down," Jane called; and Minnie, in floral dress, piped up to announce, amidst talks about whatever happened to funds appropriated for the Second Avenue

Subway, "She's with us." And Lena. My favorite, looking like a Russian peasant, strong face clear of makeup and stark white hair pulled low in a bun in back. I saw her white bun duplicated over and over in the mirrors behind her, along with the mural of Pilgrims being welcomed to America by the Indians with the gifts of harvest.

"Here, get her anything she wants," Minnie called over her shoulder to Lena's silent husband, the Listener. "Louie used to be generous to her. Anything she wants. How would a piece of gefilte fish do ya?"

"No, thanks, I—"

"What's the matter, won't that be enough?"

"No, something American, do they have fried chicken?"

"Borscht? How about a plate of borscht?" I nod. Lena goes for a borscht, punching my black and yellow ticket for me.

"My parents went, left already to Hometown. They flew out three hours after the funeral."

All around the table, brows shot up.

"I'm taking over his apartment." I try not to sniff.

"Get this girl, here, eat some of my roll. Or you can take this extra roll home with you." From white-bunned Lena. I felt like a Pilgrim on a spiritual quest for home, what with the natives feeding me.

"Let her eat the roll. Let her eat the roll. If she's a mourner, let her be a mourner, feed her," the Listener chimes in.

None of them came close to my grandfather Louie, in my mind. He had been a proud man, in a society without much respect for his struggles.

The ladies were cool in Dubrow's that first night. But after a while . . . "Listen," floral-bodiced Minnie began to tell me, "it's better he's gone. That diamond ring," she'd hint, "with three chips, you found?" Then, "How's your social life? Found any men around, dear?"

Meyer, the Listener, would say, "Says she's a writer, and she sold her first book." Jane would perk up, defensive, aware I was still around. "And why not?" She'd look up from

177

putting a finish on her lipstick. Meyer would snort. "A writer, what is a writer?" To the crew he would turn. "I'm a milkman my whole life. To the milkman, what is a writer? A writer is someone who comes in on weekends and vacations, so the milkman can go to his wife."

Jane returned to her ritual with the lipstick, something she did every time her hold out there got dim, sort of to re-cement herself to reality a bit.

Crew returns to its conversation. More felt-hatted men walk in, fresh from arguments on the boardwalk about whether Carter is another Hitler.

I decide to check out.

"Bapka, ya left your cole slaw, and pickle," Minnie calls, straightening out the sheens of her silk skirt as Lena pushes a bun pin back in. "Let her go," Lena defends. Jane shuts her compact shut with a click.

I slink home. Pulling my shawl around me, I bathe in the sounds, the only luxury, as I enter the stark white barren apartment. I sit down on a recliner my grandfather left, practically the only piece of furniture, and turn on the TV. I see my shrink Doris on a talk show, going on about conflict between generations of women. About how death often uproots deep-seated guilt for sex. Doris, in whom I had confided, focused on me and my case to draw from for detail. As she flicked her cigarette in the ivory holder into the little gold-plated saucer she had apparently carried with her, I noticed a three-chipped diamond on her finger, remarkably like the one floraled-Minnie had told me to search for in the apartment.

"I knew as soon as she took this dive," I hear from my shrink, Doris, on the TV set leaning forward menacingly and snapping shut her black leather appointment book, "she'd never be able to keep me." I turned the damn thing off, to get some sleep, and wandered down the hall and into the back bedroom in which there was a bed with a few tousled sheets on it.

I wondered to myself over sounds of babies crying, police sirens, a baritone singing, teenagers revving their

178

motorcycles, piano teachers giving lessons and piano students trying—can a small-town girl from the Midwest find happiness in one of Brooklyn's Jewish neighborhoods? As sleep suckled me, the answer came, if she's Jewish, probably yes; and I knew the old people would stay in Dubrow's til ten that night, that right then Meyer was gnarling his square knuckles together muttering, "I'm a grown man, I'm married, my children are married, they love themselves, the husband loves the wife and vice versa." He is being comforted across the table. Some things come too late in life.

The next morning, I see it. My analyst's comments had hit the *Times*. I felt at peace with my decision to leave Doris. Some analyst. She couldn't really understand how I enjoyed this neighborhood, the empty apartment. Only last night, around midnight, with kids on the street skateboarding and motorcycles gunning, I had thought of my grandfather, the old man, lying home alone. Had it been the same for him, listening to the sounds of night? Did he, too, feel not lonely—sucking in the sounds like the baritone across the way to feed him? This lessened my feelings of guilt for how little I had been to see him.

"So what do they serve, applesauce? *Oi, gutenu,*" I overheard on the Highway when I went in search of a hot biali, restless with myself in the morning. After an onion bagel, which you could watch the Israeli guys make right before your eyes, my eyes hit more of my shrink's headlines. "JEWISH SEARCH FOR ROOTS ABSURD, COVER FOR ORAL PERSONALITY CRAVING." I slunk past the newsstand in disgust, pulling the blue shawl I had worn to the funeral tighter around me for disguise, hoping I could pass for authentic in this neighborhood when I had grown up in a two-story brick house, white picket fence, imitation colonial. On the short walk between 18th Street and 15th, I saw a black woman wearing white lipstick over gold teeth and decided you could wear anything and pass in this neighborhood. Then a string of three to four Catholic teenage boys dressed in green and covered with badges darted past. I guess they were boy scouts, though at first I took them for soldiers.

I amble back to the Highway. In front of Dubrow's, I recognize one of the raggedy fellows in tweed whom my mother had not been too happy to see at the funeral. This morning he had dropped his tweed to get some sun in front of the cafeteria, revealing a neon orange T-shirt. Stooped and nearly bald, except for a white wispy fringe, he peered up at me. I took a step back and spoke to him.

"Hi, I'm Louie's granddaughter," I announce.

"What, you recognize me?" he asked. "You, of course, I know. But you, me, this I didn't know."

"Sure," I assured him. "I wanted to thank you for coming to the funeral. That meant a lot to me."

"Why, sure." He ran a tan hand over his neon orange chest, and then over the white fringe. "Listen, maybe we can go out some time," I heard. "I knew Louie for years," he hastened to inform me. "I'm Old," he went on (yah so what, I thought, so is everyone else in the Cafeteria), "Old Geezer, but you can call me Geezie." Suddenly I felt his whole body thrust too close to mine. I squinted. He winked meaningfully, and leaned back again, fondling chin. "Yah," he started. "I would have come to the grave with yas, but the other fellow I came with, he had to go." Pause. "Well, I just wanted to tell ya," Old Geezer, with white fringe, said mysteriously, "look around up there. Maybe he left some cash. The last few days he was cashing check after check in Dubrow's by the manager. He couldn't have possibly spent the money."

Clues, clues. Maybe my grandfather left a fortune. But the man Louie had been poor. Could he have won it at the races? "OK, I'll see ya," I said, stepping back, waiting for him to move away. He didn't. Old Geezie lingered to drop his eyes from the rim of a red bandana I was wearing to the v-neck where the man's white shirt I had picked up in the apartment was open to the third button. I pulled the blue shawl I had thrown over it around me and walked away, calling, "Maybe I'll see you."

What's home—it's not that it's lonely, it's just that the longer I'm out here, searching for a clue in Louie's meager possessions, the less my links to Manhattan seem real to me. And lessening my hold on what was real to me back in the city, the more my vision of Louie comes back, restimulated by seeing his possessions. I felt it all subtly begin to redirect, remold me. For example the wooden clothespin. I had picked up the nearest object to tap my own inner source of feeling. Memories came up in a rush: hooked nose, black overcoat, balding head under a black derby. The cane leaning on the slat wooden chair brought it all back to me: the way he used to hunch down to peer long distances to the ground through milky cataract glasses, after the last operation. I leaned back on the bed, letting my mind go, opening up, realizing how strange it was that Louie always dressed so formally and wondered if he always did so, or just with me. He would shed the black overcoat in the spring, I remembered, listening to the baritone singing, and don by summer a $400 blue serge suit just for a simple stroll, topped by a wide striped tie with gashes of blue and yellow and red, and tie clip of garnet. With a matching gold cufflink on a stiff pink cuff and a long gold watch chain. He, in such splendid dress attire, would rely on me to walk him to and fro from the cafeteria.

Together we'd run the gauntlet, I'd remember, getting up to fiddle with the blinds, parading past people in lawn chairs, talking. Or rather we'd float. "Yah sure," I'd hear in overtones of disbelief when the old man would stop to fumble for his keys, with me leading him; or to check to see that his newspaper was carefully folded under his arm. Or he would have to all of a sudden double-check his breast pocket for his black Moroccan wallet. I would take the opportunity of each deliberation to glance up, catch an eye, overlisten to a conversation. I shut the blinds, and walked through the TV room to scrounge around in the nearly empty kitchen. Among old bills and creditors' notes in the kitchen cabinets, I would recall how we'd move along, step by step, and heads would turn to follow, bent on determining our relationship and my, the stranger's, role. "So I says to my sister," matter-of-factly chimes in next, "I says to her, Edith," as the old man stops again, this time to carefully remove a white monogrammed handkerchief from his inner pocket.

The smooth marble stairs of Jericho Courts like sand on a beach would greet us. Civilization behind us, we'd leave it. Key prepared somewhere back on the walk, the old man would hand to me. I would open the door, and we'd move in. The coolness, oozing from the cavern we stumble into, washes us free of outdoor chatter.

Heavy metal door creaks, and slams shut. We sedately approach the row of golden mailboxes to check for dividends and bills, invitations to *bar mitzvahs* at the Plaza. Footsteps of our walk would cease to echo. We'd follow the smell of moth balls, and wonder which missus is cooking the cabbage, and approach the one flight of back stairs, each marble step worn down in the middle. Upstairs I expect heights, a fountain. Only the number B4, and a button to ring on the left side, a round peephole in the center, and a *mezuzah* on the right side of the ancient peeling door.

Mornings are when I let my unconscious up to cancel my anxious self. I seem to have time to do that out here. After falling asleep in that reverie, I awoke with a start at 5 a.m. to a baritone already practicing singing, and realize that Dan Danderson, this guy I'd been seeing in the city, was anti-Semitic, really. His father had been a literature professor back at Discover America U, attended by New York Jews in Ohio exploring the frontiers of success. His parents helped Phil Sloth (as Dan calls him) edit *Farewell, Discover A*, submitted to Dan's Dad in manuscript for the bachelor of arts degree. Phil then went on to become rich and famous, 17 novels plus movie rights later; and Dan's Dad at the age of 55 threw over his vocation of literature professor entirely to finally attempt his own novel. Clearly this seduced me when we first met. The family on the other hand is politely saying he is unemployed temporarily (and who knows what friends and family are saying about me). Dan's family doesn't know how else to comprehend that he is living in the streets of New Jersey, watching little boys in his old playground, checking out old haunts. The come-down of his old man horrifies Dan, on his way up; and the Jews did it to Dan's Dad, like the Jews killed Jesus, the Jews shot Lincoln, Jews invented auto accidents, firecrackers, and sexism.

Anyway, Dan, the good, tall, blond robust son, pink face on the way to a suntan, blue eyes popping out behind Ben Franklin glasses, wears tan khakis and striped shirts, explores virgin jungles and political revolt in the southern hemisphere, and makes a fine journalistic career reporting on details of tongues being cut out of international prisoners, and other sadistic facts. He also goes out with Jewish women to take revenge for his father—am I one of them, I wondered with a start as the baritone across the way stopped practicing his singing. The D train shook the apartment and I woke up. So, rush hour must have started, I mused to myself, time to get going and up.

I opened my eyes in the bare white apartment to see the last lone star of dawn hovering above the red brick wall directly ahead of me, and then the baritone I had heard singing staring in at me from the next apartment on the other side of Jericho Courts. I got up to bolt the window shut so he couldn't climb the fire escape between us and get in. I took a few steps from the back room up the narrow corridor and turned to face myself in the mirror in the bathroom along the hall. I look for my toothbrush, pushing around in bottles and boxes of unused samples and prescriptions. I got discouraged, slammed the mirror door of the cabinet shut and faced myself again. There I was: red bandana kerchief tied like a babushka; high forehead, snub Polish nose and high cheeks; white shirt, blue elat stone, cut-off jeans. When drowning in Jewish out here I dress in red, white, and blue to remind myself of my origins—middle American.

I headed for the Cafeteria to look for the Crew, and to put some food in my stomach. Maybe I'd see orange-neoned

Geezer. I look for his white fringe.

Sure enough, there they were waiting for me. "So how's your social life," Jane greets me, as I stop by the old man with the dark glasses who passes out the tickets. Floral-gardened Minnie enters the conversation as Jane pauses to adjust gold spider on wig. "So, you found the money, the diamonds?" I excuse myself to bother Bermann behind the counter for a bagel. Bermann's a black wavy-haired Puerto Rican who changed his name to something Jewish, hoping he'd get promoted. The Crew hears him answer me with, "I've been through this with you a hundred times, lady. No bagels 'til after 9."

Jane, touching up on lipstick: "Let her eat. She should be healthy."

Sign-off Goldie signs in: "Get a cole slaw."

Jane, closing compact: "One cole slaw? She's entitled to two cole slaws."

White-bunned Lena: "Go ahead. Get the cream cheese and pumpernickel."

The din settles down a bit.

"What did you get, briskit?" In unison they ask as I re-approach the table. I nod silently.

Floral Minnie points over to the next table. Sadly: "We used to be family like that. Now they're all gone." I turn my head to follow. I see two men, three women. Each of the former with fat cigars, pink-shirted; one of the latter in gold lamé. Louie used to tell me this woman fought with guns on her belt during the war, killing Nazis. I thought she was still carrying on the resistance until, straining, I caught a word or two I understood. ". . . then you cut . . ." "tomatoes . . ." Feeling me staring, she looked up. "What's the matter, you mind if I pass on a recipe? Your grandfather," she says, "is a gentleman."

"*Was* a gentleman," I corrected. "He's dead."

". . . *is* a gentleman." Her head turns away from me. ". . . then you cut . . . potatoes . . ."

I turn to the Crew.

"How are you, Minnie?" I ask as I put down my plate.

184

"If I were good I wouldn't have come here. I cry right up 'til I leave the apartment. I sold my diamond ring, sent $1,000 to my son's wife. She's getting her Ph.D. in psychology, after raising the children. What do I need the money for."

I pull out my chair, sit down next to her, and use the briskit to form a sandwich on the rye Bermann gave me. As I reach for the hot mustard an ice cream plops down on Jane's plate across from me. She adjusts her purple hat on gray wig, making sure the gold spider still had a place, deciding whether she would eat the ice cream. She postpones the decision by again touching up lipstick. A piece of cake falls down next. No one looks up.

"What's that?" I ask.

"What?" As a group, they remain nonplussed.

"Jane!" I pick Jane to get impatient with. "What's that?" I point to the cake.

"Marble cake." She answers, nonchalant, shutting compact shut. "Don't it look good?"

"Where did the cake come from?" I ask.

"Oh, the ice cream." She ignores the plate and pulls out the mirror to put more lipstick on again. "That's from your grandfather, Louie."

"What do you mean?"

Eyeballs roll around the table. As if to say, how could I be so dumb.

"What, didn't you see it?" In unison they finally put it to me.

"What, see what?" I look up, to see if wavy-haired Bermann had neglected a hole in the ceiling. "Didn't you see the ice cream and cake fall down?"

"No, not that. The talk show. Last night your grandfather Louie was on a talk show explaining how, after you die, you can send things down to people on earth if you want to. Things they want or need. Food, a car, an understanding. Anything. Whatsa matter? Can't you plug in a television every once in a while? Would it be such a trouble? Then you'd understand the ice cream, cake."

I take a break from my strain. I eat. I know he's dead.

He can't be on television. Much less be sending things down, I confirmed to myself over small bites. The ladies remain nonplussed. But there was the ice cream, cake. Orange-neon Geezie walks in, visor over his white fringe. Constraining my panic, I nod to him.

"Geezie," Minnie calls. "Come tell Bapka here about the talk show. She doesn't believe it."

Neon Geezie smiles, in the know. He glides over. I don't respond to him. "Well," Neon Geezie turns to Minnie after I fail to look up, "tell her to go to the aquarium. He'll be on again at 2."

Goldie: "Why? The fish wanna see it? Don't they have enough to watch on the beach?"

"No." Neon Geezie shakes his head and fondles his fringe. "They figure it'll be a tourist attraction. Build up local industry. Ya know, God in an empty chair talks to old man. Et cetera. Et cetera. Ya get the picture. Well, I'll be seein' ya ladies." He tips the black visor he had donned over his white fringe and flips the brim up again with thumb and forefinger of left hand. "Gotta catch the numbers on the races." He glides on down to join the men.

White-bunned Lena, after he leaves, and the heads of the crew rehuddle unrefereed around their table: "Yah, that'll sound good. Guy in an empty chair, God. Did anyone call Hollywood? My neighbor, she's got a son . . ."

Gold-spidered Jane: "No, *Broadway* first. *Then* they call Hollywood, if it's any good. Go see it, kid." She turns back to me after setting peasant-like Lena straight. "It'll be good. Talks about how once you're dead, you're not gone, and if you want, you can send things down to people." She pauses. "If they're good."

"God talks from an empty chair," Lena entices, "did ya hear that? Go!"

"And your Aunt," Listener adds.

"What?" I can't believe I heard.

"Some kinda Zen Monk, a Midwest psychiatrist . . . an analyst, named Doris. She yours?"

"Why?" I ask. Nobody looks me in the eye.

"Well—"

"*Oi.*" I gulp my food and go to the phone. I called Dan. If he could explore virgin jungles in Brazil, why not Brooklyn with me?

"Dan?" I press when he answers, looking out at the Crew, heart beating and panic rising. "Hello . . ." he says, then "Agnes? Marie? Renee?" when he gets no response to one name after the other on the other end of the phone. An Ambassador from the UN parades past with his wife on a session break. I overhear a debate about whether Brooklyn should be admitted to the UN as homeland for the Jews, or whether it's occupied territory. "Dan. I've got a story for you," I finally burst out on the phone. "Meet me by the aquarium at 2." "Bapka!" "How did you guess?" The aquarium, isn't that Brooklyn?" Dan asks. "Yah, Coney Island, so?" I get defensive. "Well, that's how I know. The story better be good. I'll have to get a map. I'm in Manhattan."

"Take the D train to the second-to-last stop. Forget the map."

I hang up the phone before he has time to say no.

II.

HUP TWO THREE FOUR
TELL THE PEOPLE WHAT THEY WORE
HUP TWO THREE TEN
WHY AM I SEEING A *GOY* AGAIN

I was jogging along the silver tracks thinking about why, for some reason, when I had last seen Dan, he had told me going out with a Jewish woman was like going out with a foreigner. I was behind the D train, running to catch the talk show at the aquarium, impatient to see the empty chair, God, et cetera, the Crew had told me about. I waited on the Kings Highway platform for a bit next to the black woman wearing white lipstick over gold teeth I had seen on the streets with the CYO boys. She was reading *Yeats: A Vision*. Vision Lady waved to me as I hopped off, figuring I could jog there quicker.

> HUP TWO THREE FOUR
> DON'T STOP TO PANT
> JUST BREATHE IN MORE
> HUP TWO THREE TEN
> WHY AM I SEEING A *GOY* AGAIN

Well, it seems to be in my history, I guess, I reminisce as I jog along . . .

Religion and politics were the main issues my high school boyfriend and I could never see eye to eye on. Oh yes, I remember Jake. He'd worship me, try to save me, type all my term papers for me, try to get me to quit smoking, come to dates equipped with fundamentalist pamphlets on the evils of smoking cigarettes.

But he was slower than a herd of turtles, as the guys in the hoods used to circulate about him. As the blocks ticked off, the memories peeled off. The summer before I was off to college, poor little Jake hit me with the worst invective yet: I was off to the east coast to become a LIBERAL. Well, huff, huff, maybe he was right. I puffed to myself. The movie ran right out in my mind. When I arrived on the east coast to tackle books, the first thing I found was that the east coast prep school kids had been screwing in basements since they were 12. So of course on this sex thing I felt left out. For I arrived short in that major college prerequisite, due to religious differences. Now, what does religion have to do with sex? Well (huff, huff) all I recall is how we used to park in the backwoods of Indiana in one of those beat-up tin cars with the popped lids: He called his "Jam." Once, too hot to make it to the backwoods, we took Jam to the shopping center . . . We were by the cardboard boxes that JC Penney's emptied out, and just as our mouths met, we were boldly interrupted by a beam of light.

Huff, huff, as I jogged, the memories played right out:

188

Jake, fearing God, heaven and hell, and other forms of religious experiences, sat up with a bolt and shook himself free of my arms. In the process of doing so he pushed me out of Jam's door back into the emptied boxes. "No, I'm sorry, don't do it," he called out. His teeth chattered. He seemed frightened. "God, don't take me! Please!" He adopted a military salute. "I wanna live long enough delivering papers to become a first lieutenant in the army." I guess he was afraid of death. "I'll be finer than frog's hair," he promised. "God, from now on."

"Get your maggot off a gut wagon, son," we looked up into the face of a guard. "Now get out of here, kids," he barked, and ambled on.

I stopped short in the tracks to take a breath as this memory shot off, and climbed over to the Sheepshead Bay platform. *Goys* everywhere. And I was still seeing them. East coast preppies on the platform doing a multimedia photography project on ethnic neighborhoods. Expensive cameras around their necks. Maybe, I pondered, I had left something unresolved . . . oh yes, I smiled to myself and lit out to the tracks fast, so as to avoid being photographed by outsiders, for to them I too was part of the picturesque.

There was that final summer before leaving Hometown, when my sneakers hit the track, I recalled, when Jake and I had been rolling around on the floor in front of his mother's TV set. I pushed him. "Take your pants off, quick." I could see by the moonlight the blinds let in that he had an erection, but he was still zipped. "I can't," he answers. He seemed forlorn. "Do you want me to help you? Is it stuck? Let me see," I offered.

But like a bolt of lightning, Jake stood up. I sat up, I remembered, feeling numb.

"Are you afraid your mother's coming home?" I asked him.

I straightened up my red, white, and blue skirt so it looked cheery and right, spreading the folds on the corn-cob-colored carpet.

"You told me she was staying with your sister for the

189

evening." I stared into the television set.

"It's not my mother." Poor Jake clasped his hands around either side of his head, hung down. The rays of the moonlight came through the Venetian blinds, as if to scorn him.

"What is it then?" I prodded.

Jake kept his eyes down. I sensed tears forming behind the lids. He tried to change the subject, changing the station on the television. He reached out for one of those pamphlets on the coffee table. I knew I was in no mood to discuss the evils of cigarettes.

"Making love is *natural*," I said, throwing the pamphlet on the floor behind him.

"No, you don't understand," he sobbed, and threw his face down on my red, white, and blue lap before him. My eyes were averted from the television with alarm. "We can't make love, because we can't fall in love, because we can't get married—" His tears fell harder and faster. "Because I have to marry somebody I can go to heaven with, and when we die . . ."

I had no idea what Jake was talking about, but leaned forward, and urged, "Jake, what?"

"In the pamphlet, it says—when we die, we won't be together." He sat up to dry his eyes with fists, and said, "Don't you see?" He tilted his head mournfully at me.

"No, not at all." What did death have to do with right then, jogging, I strained to recall.

"When we die, I'll go to heaven because I'm a Baptist," he told me, straightening up and looking military again, gray eyes focusing on some other planet, "and you'll go to hell because you're a *Jew*." On the last word, he broke down again.

And that's why, I reminded myself, huff, huff, feeling the drops of sweat, I arrived on the east coast a virgin, and why I'm seeing a *goy* again . . . puff, puff.

At that moment I had to stop to run in place, as the Ambassador of the UN I had seen earlier in the Cafeteria was being ushered across the tracks by other representatives of some scapegoated race. As soon as they had passed, I sped on, and on back into the recesses of my memory, into another dangerous place . . .

Still a virgin in college (hff hff) had to learn my place (pff pff) all the virgins in college (hff hff) we had an extracurricular race (pff pff) I won mine (hff hff) or came in on time (pant pant) in Mexico (pant pant) Christmas vacation (gosh I'm about to faint) I remember that time (blond-haired blue-eyed football player) pant pant (from Eastern State) gasp choke (wanted to share me with others in his commune grinnin') (didn't believe in private property, the bloke) . . .

I fell on the tracks, hurt. I hadn't wanted to sleep with the whole team.

Just as I fell on the tracks, a black limousine pulls up. A man with a sleazy grin pops his head out, as soon as it stops.

"'Scuse me, miss. Wanna ride?" he calls.

"Who, me?" He nods yes.

"What is this, some kind of a pickup?" I ask, dusting myself off.

"No, little lady," says Sleaze Grin, opening the door to get out and help me in. Inside the limo I see a pine box, guarded by an Israeli soldier. A very bent-over Chinese lady stood up, to make room for the black woman putting white lipstick on over gold teeth, still reading *Yeats: A Vision.*

"Have you read this, it's good," she asks me. I shake my head no, as Sleaze Grin leads me around to the other side. He opens the door and a bunch of preppies with expensive cameras chase out.

While I am observing this, blinking my eyes, wondering if it's a mirage, Sleaze Grin is introducing himself to me. "Barry's the name," he says, "Barry Tone."

"Oh, tell me, Mr. Tone, do you live in Jericho Courts?"

"Yes, Little Lady. I do." I recognized the singer I had felt staring at me in the morning, and the preppies from the Sheepshead stop on the tracks, the pine box from the funeral, . . . but everything was all mixed up.

"Well," I said, dropping my eyes down to watch my dirty

191

white sneaker kick a blue beer bottle around on the ground, "I don't believe I better—" "Why not?" persists Barry Tone, alias Sleaze Grin, as he leans down to brush his knuckles up against my reddened chin. "It's safe. He gestures ominously again that I should get in. "Your grandfather sent me. He doesn't want you to be late." I hesitated again. "And I also stopped to pick up this Ambassador here . . ." Ambassador tips his hat. "He's conducting a survey about Brooklyn, for the UN." "No, thanks. I'll jog." I stop him, and run off. "Hold the show, Louie," I cried, dizzy, fear mounting, not sure what was real any more, or not. I waved goodbye to the limo gang and ran right through a pack of CYO kids in green, realizing too late I was in front of a train. The limo lurched and left me. My feet flopped one after the other on the ground. I ran faster and faster. Heart pounding, all reminiscences driven down to the ground . . . harder, harder . . . faster, faster . . . I stumbled into the Talk Show and collapsed on the aquarium's stone cold ground.

III.

"Bapka!" My aunt, in black lace boots and a tan trench coat, calls to greet me.

"It's about time you showed up," Fran, the girlfriend of Louie, follows.

I turned to this cold woman.

"Hi, Fran. I didn't know you were going to be here." My eyes sped over her shoulder and collided with the scarlet eye of a gold-necked fish swimming around in one of the tanks of the aquarium.

"You look like Mark Twain in that hat!" Grandpa calls to me from straight ahead on the television, before Fran could get another critical word in. He adjusted overcoat, leaned back, and folded gloved hands over cane again.

"What hat? I'm wearing a red babushka," I turned to the television screen above the fishes and said to him. He adjusted his tie, making gashes of red stripes align diagonally with garnet tie clip.

"Well, take that off. Wipe the sweat off your face. Here," from my aunt. She was handing me a hat. She had worked in millinery 27 years. "Here's the hat I bought you to meet some nice young fellah by NYU in."

"I don't want to meet a guy by NYU, how many times have I told you . . ." I turned back to the television. I saw she was handing me my sloping sisal. The one I used to wear to Doris'. "You didn't buy me that hat." I protested madly. "I got it myself, in the Village, at the Merchant of Oyo. Besides, it'll fall off, jogging."

"There's nothing wrong with meeting a fellah by NYU," insisted Dinah innocently. "I met mine, wrong number, over the phone. Young man, I says to him, you call this wrong number one more time we'll have to get together. We did and I married him, worked as a bookkeeper in his office 27 years. There's worse ways to meet a man than that! But Bapka," her words, as her eyes, ran right through me, "Tell me something, Bapka. Jogging. Now what's that? Is that—"

"Jogging, run, boys do it—I mean," I stared into her blank eyes, devoid of recognition.

"Jogging," she says. "I don't believe that's Jewish. Louie," she turns to address the television set. "That's not Jewish, is it?"

Louie pulled out his watch as if to check. "It's OK, Dinah. The young do it. They jog. Like we used to go to the lockers at Brighton." He put his watch away.

"Dinah," I moved away from her. "Please, I came to see the show."

"Oh, you missed already a lot in the story," she admonishes me.

"Dinah, it's not a soap opera. It doesn't have a plot. It's a talk show."

"Yah, oh?" Dinah adopted a look, as if she were in the know.

Fran: "Is that all you have to say for yourself, Bapka? A dying man shouldn't have been going to the doctor by himself. You had a car. You should have driven him. And you left him in strange places."

"Fran, you know," I said pulling away from her clutch-es, "I did the best I could. After I stopped driving him when I got my job, he went by car service."

"Well, Bapka," I felt the disapproval exude. "Your excuse is no good. God willing, you left stranded a dying man."

"Besides," ignoring both the dismissal and the knowledge that if God were willing it must have been OK, "I had to leave him at the eye doctor's to go get the car that time where I parked it, at the closest meter." I wormed away, on, upward, up the aisle, closer to the television. "How else could I have," I called back sideways to Fran, "—you wanted him to walk nine blocks? He could have fallen."

Fran stays on my back. She doesn't hear me. "Nine blocks! You could have parked better than that!"

"Midtown?" I cried, coming to a halt midstride.

I found my way to a soothing cluster of old men, sidled in, trying to tune the show back in.

"You mean you want to give her a pill cause you think she's *sick*," from the empty chair on TV I hear as I plop down.

Old Geezie, among the men, flicked his black visor at me. "Some brim ya got there," Geezie grins, referring to the tricolor band around my sloping sisal.

"Yes, thank you," I answered him, "from Merchant of Oyo in the Village. I mean, from Africa. Dinah brought it for me."

"Well, yes, she's your aunt after all. She's just looking out for you." Geezie stretched his left arm out over the back of my chair and brought it down, his left hand resting behind my shoulder, too comfortably.

"Yah stay out all by yourself in the day time too?" With his free hand he fiddles with white curls on pale chest.

I nodded, yes, and then shook my head, no, falling into confusion. "Have a prune," Dinah says, to rescue me.

"I just want to watch the show, Dinah."

"My prune's better than Dubrow's prunes," Dinah persisted self-righteously. She fumbled in one of her bags and found a jar of prunes, which she held out to me. Geezie dropped his arm from the back of my chair, and stared straight ahead, watching the television.

"No, Dinah, I'm *not interested,*" I repeat.

"Very well then. Put on these clothes I got for you." She put away her jar, and pulled out a red and blue striped silk tank shirt. "You'll like these," she insisted. "I took the D train all the way to Manhattan to get them for you. I know what kind of boys you go with." A pair of white satin balloon pants appears next.

"Dinah, no—"

"Why not?" Her voice went shrill. "I saw an ad, reduced in the paper! Don't you like them?" She held the waist of her purchase to her own waist and looked down to where the golden ankle strings hung on the floor. "Me, they don't fit. Of course I could take them in." She holds them up, waist to chin.

Geezie flicked the lid of his black visor. Taking the clue from him, I said, "Very well, Dinah, if you leave me . . ."

". . . us . . ." from Geezie.

". . . alone . . ." I went right over him, "I'll take them."

"Oh so that's the story is it," she rasps at me. "I know when I'm not wanted. In our family there was never a cross word."

Dinah stumbled away with her bags, one on each hand, leaving her fancy dress clothes for me. Geezie returned his hand. I looked at my reflection on the screen—wide-brimmed hat, red and blue striped shirt, white balloon pants. Suddenly bangles appeared on my arms, and a diamond ring with three chipped pieces. For some reason she had dressed me this far (and Louie must have sent me the jewelry) but left me in dirty sneakers. The glare went down on the television set, and instead of my reflection, the face of my brother tuned in.

"Well, actually, uh, no—" my brother appeared to be giving testimony.

My brother fell on his knees. The witness stand turned into a Catholic confessional.

"Oh God, it's not that I think she's *sick*," he bawled, head in hands. His wife melted in behind him carrying babe on hip on one side, and handed him a turquoise bandana handkerchief.

"It's that I want her to shut up. She's running around telling her sex history to everybody in Brooklyn. What if she gets to me?" Wife steps back.

"Whatever do you mean?" prodded God earnestly.

". . . it wasn't my fault . . . when we were kids . . . the boys at school . . ." my brother ran on coherently. ". . . they had these *Hustler* pictures . . ."

"Yes, I've seen them," nodded God, "not bad . . ."

" . . . they told me everybody was doing it to their kid sisters . . ."

"So you did?" God prodded him.

"Yes," my brother shuddered, sobbed, using his handkerchief to wipe his brow. "I wanted in the club! I had to prove I was a man! It wasn't much to ask of her!" He was completely broken down, caved in. "Besides, I had to fuck somebody, and no one in Hometown would go with me because I was Jewish, even though Dad said Jews are just like everyone else—so who else was there? My kid sister. She's the only other person who would believe it."

God guffawed.

Southern Belle, the wife of the Jewish Minister who had performed the ceremony, appeared in green seersucker skirt and lace belt. Platinum wings sprouted on her.

"There, there," she comforted him.

"Are you a—nun? Sister?" he peered up at her.

A Zen monk in a terry cloth beach robe ran up the aisle, ominously carrying a big stick. "Brother, sister, it's all the same, from the point of view of the gobbley de guck," he said taking long strides and brandishing stick above him.

A tattooed woman with suns all over her body from the woods in Central Park runs after him. She seemed like another or future form of my aunt, here behaving as if she were attending a political speak-out. She flits in front of the monk and grabs the mike calling, "I want to speak out on

196

Borderline Personality Disorganization. This I think is a disruptive categorization." Someone calls out, "That's a thought disorder, did you go off your medication?" She ignores him. "First I organize my life around one kinda job," she goes on, "and then the government stops funding that type of organization. Then I organize my life around my loft, and the building gets coopted when the rich move in and ruin the neighborhood. Then I get put in a mental hospital and given green pills and a routine to organize myself around." She checks to see if anyone is still with her. The old men nod yes. She goes on, "And I jump the fence, I can't stand it. I escape to live in the woods. In the woods, nobody stands there and says, 'Pine cones over here, leaves over there, trees not allowed in, brooks not allowed to flow.' In the woods we are all free, and we go where we want to go." She totters, mike clutched to tattooed bared breast in enthusiasm. She begins to prance, dance, sway, pray. "Wild and free! We are all free spirits! Free the brooks! Free the animals! Free the people!" She floats to the air, hovering above the speakers. "Our society is disorganized, not us."

Applause breaks out. She lands in a huddle and grunts.

"Besides," my brother stands up and takes the mike from the tattooed lady, who cowers, "I heard about these pills in medical school." He wraps the turquoise bandana around his head, brushes himself off. "They are supposed to help the—heh heh—crazy disorganized people." He pushes Tattoo Lady away from him.

"And about when we were kids," my brother goes on, this time kicking Tattoo Lady under the table with an air of finality, "I had no indication she didn't enjoy it just as much as I did." He contemplates the crowd with satisfaction that his view would be heard. He gives Tattooed Lady one last kick, and wanders off, whistling, fondling a gold hoop earring which has appeared in one ear. His wife, abandoned on the podium after closely attending to her role of backup, looks wistfully after him.

"Bapka," Grandpa leans up to the mike, folding his

197

newspaper under his arm after the last bit. "What do you say to that?" I look down, swinging my legs back and forth, contemplating my filthy sneakers. Geezie nudges me. I sit up. "What. Oh . . . " Geezie repeats the question. "Um." I sit up straight. "I don't believe in early childhood conflict resolution. It's fun to watch though." I look back down to the ground again.

"*Oi vay is mere,*" shutting her appointment book, from Doris, as the camera zooms in to reveal my analyst on the far side of my Grandfather. "All those years of psychoanalysis," Doris despairs, "did her *no good.*" She flicks ashes into her portable ashtray. "And she had *me,* the *best* in the country to work with . . ."

"Oh, I don't know about that," from Minnie, watching the televised version in Dubrow's Cafeteria, where the whole Crew sat around a 20x24 set which the super had brought in from Louie's. Bermann had plugged it in for them.

From the screen, God, Doris, Louie, the Zen Monk, the Tattooed Lady from under the table, my Brother's Wife, Southern Belle—all look out at her in the cafeteria.

"There's my son, in Seattle . . ." she insists, speaking to them on the screen.

Bermann breaks in, from the cafeteria again.

"Lady, I been through this with you a million times. He's not the best in the profession to *everyone.* Just to you, because he's your son."

Crew, roundtable on TV, ignore him.

Show goes on.

"She's a disgrace to her family, the profession," Doris laments on the screen, and the Crew turns back to watch again.

Just then the Football Player (to whom I had recalled losing my virginity) runs in, on the television.

"What?" he asks the Jewish Minister, who just in the nick of time had appeared next to his Wife, "you mean she wasn't a virgin when I screwed her?"

"I dunno," says the Jewish Minister, trying to think of something quick. "I'll check the Kabbalah. It's not in the kosher-nonkosher rule book. At least not the updated version."

"Yah better find out, because that's what I told them, the guys on the squad from the frat house."

Southern Belle flutters in. "We thought you were from a commune, that you wanted Bapka to sleep with all of you because you didn't believe in private property." She bats her platinum eyelashes at him, and flutters her wings, waiting for the guilt to settle in.

"Well, yah," he hangs head down.

Jewish Minister proclaims he can't find anywhere in the United Hebrew pre- or post-marital rule book if someone screwed in an incestual situation is still a virgin, since the religion made no record of this phenomenon in the first place.

"When I was a Catholic," offered the monk in the beach coat, "we thought of it as original sin."

A black-and-white-striped referee in a black cap comes in and blows his silver whistle. "Let's take a commercial break," he says, "while the coach determines whether or not this is a violation."

Southern Belle agrees yes, yes, and huddles her wings around to comfort the poor, broken-down, goldilocked football player, the confused Jewish Minister, and Doris, still hitting her head muttering *vay is mere* over her lost analysand's situation. The show cuts to chair, and referee yells, "OK, Coach, 60 seconds to settle this one."

"Save my seat, Bapka," Geezie says to me, "I'm going out to the boardwalk for popcorn."

Bermann's face comes in full flush on the screen once Geezie is gone. "I just thought I'd take this opportunity to advertise myself," ladling, he announced. "I come here, shirt on my back, from Puerto Rico. Pretty soon I learn . . . Jews own all the businesses in this country."

"City. City," says Jane. *"Oi* is he mixed up." She rolls her head. "He thinks this is the *country.*" More powder on her nose. "This is *Brooklyn.*"

"So if there is any Jewish restaurant owner watching

this TV," Bermann goes on when Jane finishes, "and wants to hire me as an assistant manager . . . I'm willing to relocate, Miami, Arizona . . ."

Bermann sits down.

Camera flashes past Crew.

They wave. "So how's Seattle?" Minnie jumps up and calls out to her son through the television. "Having a dry spell?" She is pulled down by the Crew.

Talk show fades back to an announcer announcing Minnie's daughter-in-law, the clinical psychology student in Seattle, who settled it for God: Object (me) is still a virgin, since subject (I) didn't remember sex with Brother until after exhibiting virginal behavior for an extended period.

Wife left, to give Brother good news on the boardwalk.

"Want some popcorn, kid?" Geezie offers me an open bag as he slides back in.

I take the bag from him.

"Is this a talk show?"

I shove hand in, saying thanks, and munch loudly.

"That's what the Crew told me," I explained to him.

"It's a game, it's a game," says Sleaze Grin, sliding in next to Geezie to watch the television. "That's why they have refs and everything." Old Geezer pats me on the back. "Just enjoy. It's not really your life. It's television."

Just then a big man wearing a blue Portuguese fisherman's cap with a gold braid on its navy brim ambles up to the mike wearing pink polka dot socks underneath his green denim hoppers. Jewish Minister and Southern Belle step aside. He sports two guns on his hips, nice silver ones, not that he was shooting Nazis or anything, just that he liked the feeling of having something to handle if he wanted.

"Midwestern Psychiatrist #1" was engraved along the barrel of each one.

"Erm, I was wonderin' . . . might it be possible to call a guard." He fingered his gun.

He addresses God.

"And who are you?" asks God.

"Jake, m'name's Big Jake, sir," he shuffled kindly. "I

represent the Voice of Hope in this travesty."

He smiled bashfully, dropping his hands to his side.

"Yes, you're just the man we need," from God.

A warm smile spread over his face, as he basked in the recognition. "Well, sir, we need a guard," Big Jake went on.

God: "What for?"

Jake, taking a stance: "Well, sir, to take away these crazy people." I ducked to be sure he wouldn't get me.

The eye of the empty chair followed as Big Jake made a round circuitous gesture with his left hand. There was Southern Belle down at one end, adjusting her platinum blond wings as she leaned forward, comforting the Jewish Minister and Doris. Brother had already wandered off to the boardwalk, along with black-striped referee and goldilocked football player, and Wife, who had gone to inform him. Louie was still there, and Zen Monk and Tattoo Lady were arguing about who should go out to the beach for another beach chair as Tattoo Lady didn't want to sit under the table where Brother had last kicked her.

God asked, "Which ones?"

"Why, the monk in the beach robe, and the Tattooed Lady, sir. We have institutions to deal with them."

"Well, I wouldn't say," answered God, "but you're the psychiatrist, you're the best judge . . ."

"Why, thank you, sir." Big Jake took off his gold-braided cap and blushed warmly. He called the guard.

"Now, just a minute, son." Louie looks up and reaches for the mike with his white kid glove. He jumps up. Jake stops to listen to him. "Now what, just what are these people being arrested for?" Big Jake looks chagrined. "Young fellah, I ask you a question, answer me."

"Disturbin' the peace, officer," says the guard with the beam light, amblin' in. "Shucks, that's clearer than hog water."

"Now, you wait a minute, young whippersnapper," hollers Louie, holding the key to B4 to the light. "Where were you to arrest the tax collector, the landlord, the employer? They disturbed my peace immensely."

"Well," the guard hung his head down, light on low beam, "I can only go when I'm called."

"I called you plenty, and you were never around." Louie sat down, rough, returning the key to B4 to his pocket again.

"You were poor, Louie," answered the guard fiddling with the flashlight. It was now on dim. "What can I say? I work for the other people."

"The phone company man, the guy who turned off my electricity, the . . ."

"OK, OK, Louie, we got the point," says God. "We'll arrest only one."

Monk and Lady stand back to back, arms crossed, each determined not to be the one.

"That one," God calls, pointing to the Lady. "The Monk can stay. He's affiliated with an institution." Here God calls to monk. "You can sit here." God moves chair over, as Monk strides confidently past Lady. Flashlight beam goes back on high, and Guard drags Lady out. She is screaming, kicking, singing about natural forces flowing as she is carted away.

Zen Monk sits down, still carrying his stick with him.

"Is that enough justice for you, Louie?" God calls.

Before Louie can get a word in, Monk answers, "Justice, injustice, it's all the same, from the point of view of the gobbledy gook. That's the key. That's the key to what enlightenment is all about. The one thing that's fixed is nothing is constant. Nothing is fixed."

IV.

"Excuse me," Dan says, bumbling into the cafeteria. He removes Ben Franklin glasses, wipes them free of sweat. Jane clears off the briskit and marble cake to make room for him.

Dan pulls out a subway map and spreads it out across the table.

"Listen," Dan digs in, "can you tell me—"

Just then a 40-year-old man walks in.

"He's given up his life for his parents," Minnie informs him.

Dan digs further in. "I was on my way to Coney, second to last stop, I'm new here—never been to Brooklyn, must have been the wrong train, the wrong stop—" No response. Dan looks chagrined.

Jane dons glasses to help him. "Whatsa matter ya ain't got a date, kid?"

"Yes, I do, but—" Dan looks down.

"So who are you meeting?" Jane asks. "I know a girl—doesn't have much of a social life—hangs out around here—"

"Bapka?" Dan pops out.

"Yes." Crew looks perplexed.

"That's her! She's out here writing a novel. About her granddad, a death."

"No, she's out at the aquarium."

Dan: "Yes! Do tell me how to get there! That's where she said to meet her. She said D train, second to last stop. Somehow I ended up here."

Jane gestures. "No need to go all the way out there. We got it piped in here." She fiddles with the sound button on the set. Words sputter out across the table. Black, gray, and white lines uncross. Color dots form into shape. Big Jake adjusts cap with braid, still talking, pleading earnestly, grasping podium on the television.

"Who is that?" Dan asks.

"Some midwestern psychiatrist. Her family called him."

"We got bored, so we turned it off," Jane informs him, leaning back to reach into carpet bag to pull out knitting. "Put this over your hands, and spread out your fingers. That's right. Yes, good job, kid."

Dan looks around the cafeteria, caught in Jane's skein across his fingers. "Can I get corn-on-the-cob here? A can of tuna? Something American?" She makes a ball while he's talking.

"Bermann, did ya hear that?" over her shoulder Jane

calls to him. Her head shakes from side to side.

Bermann's still ladling cole slaw.

"Watch the show, kid," he calls. "We specialize in . . . *latkas*, meatballs . . . blintzes, livers . . ."

On the screen, Big Jake straightens up, beams at the audience, winks at the fishes, grabs the podium.

"Why is he on?" Dan asks.

"He's about to haul her off," Jane informs him.

Dan jumps up in alarm.

"Bapka's in trouble!" he calls. "I've got to rescue her!"

"Down, down in front," Jane says, and knits.

Dan looks bewildered. "But I've got to save her."

"No, no." Jane knits. "German men don't save Jewish women. They put rats in their stomachs and prepare them for ovens."

"No, that was my ancestors," defends Dan. "I'm American."

"Then why," Jane knits, shaking her head, "do you say you feel like you're with a foreigner when you're with Bapka? and other Jewish women?"

"I dunno," says Dan, hanging head. "Gee, you are right. She's been American—as long as I have."

"Well, if you've learned that much," Jane says, "you can go. Run along now, kid."

"Yes, yes," Crew supports.

"Yes, I'm off!" Dan jumps up. "Bapka! I'm off! I'm coming to you. Though it's way past two! Keep the story for me. We'll do it after I rescue you!"

Show tunes back in again.

V.

"Well, now, Missie," says Geezie, self-importantly, as the show picks back up again. "I'm going to synagogue."

"Why?"

"I dunno. Got the sudden urge to rock back and forth in ecstasy."

"Is that what the men do there?"

"Yah," he hitches up his checked baggies. "It's a tough lot being a woman. You wouldn't know what goes on there."

"No," I answer, remembering visits to the synagogue with Louie. "The women just watch the show, when they come in late, after cleaning up from the cooking."

"Yah, well, you just watch this one." He leaned up and winked, closely. "Besides, a little birdie or a big fish told me, ya got another date now." He and the oasis of old men clump out.

Just then Dan darts in, wrapped in turquoise star-studded pirate's cape, sword in air. "Excuse me," he asks the old men as they shuffle out, "Bapka, is she here?"

"Yes," points Geezie, pointing over his shoulder as he and the men puff out, chanting, *Odem, mee,* death, blood, death by fire, death by blood . . ."

"Thanks," Dan grins, and leaps out. "Bapka! I'm here!" he shouts, and lands, cape over chest, by my chair. "What's the story?"

I sniff, and pull away from him.

"Bapka, are you OK? I came as fast as I could . . ." He reaches to touch me.

"No, Dan," I say, and pull away from him.

"Have you been jogging?" Dan asks. Then "What's the story?" again.

"Yes," I answered, putting the toes of my filthy sneakers ahead of me on the back of the next row's chair.

"Good. Gotta keep healthy . . ." He determines to alter my mood for me. "Those are nice pants."

"What?" I look up at him.

"The white balloons," he points.

"Oh, they're from my aunt. I mean," I brush them off. "From Macy's, I guess. She brought them for me."

"Mind if I pull this golden string?" He tugged at the string on my waist.

"Yes," I answer, "I sure do."

Dan settles down, sword on seat next to him, polished Ben Franklin glasses, and asks, "What's the matter?" and

205

"What's the story?" again.

Zen Monk raises stick on stage, giving a commercial for Zen: "Do you talk too much at parties? Are you too intense? Try ZEN, as an aid in Assimilation . . ." he grins broadly, lowering stick to side of right ear. "It'll work, fast. You too can sit and stare at a wall for hours, contributing nothing to a conversation, free of silt and chatskahs." He lifts stick again.

"Oh, Dan," I scream, "I'm scared!" I threw my arms around his neck.

"Don't worry," Dan says, covering me with cape, "I'll save you." He raises sword to duel with Monk's stick, but by then I had blacked out on him, and found myself hurtling back into the mouth of Gold Neck, the fish I had seen at the door when I came in. I rose above and looked down, experiencing myself as another person. I watched my Bapka self look up and hold on to her hat as she sinks back, longing for safety, seeing only red, as Gold Neck broke out of his tank at the aquarium, swings the length of the boardwalk, turns right, and heads for the Statue of Liberty.

From above I view her, as inside she is swallowed down. She tried to kick and scream, but hears nothing save the waves' rush and the fishes' gurgle. She remembers the rapist's knife, raised then as the Zen Monk's stick was now. That whole winter in Boston waitressing had been so grim. She had been hitchhiking back from *Clockwork Orange*, and got into the car, without her friend . . .

Hurling down Gold Neck's throat, on her back, head first, it all came back to her in bits and pieces. As she passed his larynx, in a strange staccato her own long-stifled voice broke forth: No, not my mouth, please, don't hurt my mouth . . . *on her back she had pleaded with him . . . and the red walls of Gold Neck parted, and shuddered, and she appreciated the pulsating rhythm of them, and turned and slid onto her left side and sidled by.*

Oh, the winter itself had been so horrid, she remembered as she smashed her sisal hat down over her ears to hold it close to her head. Why do you insist on seeing everything as all black, the psychiatrist at Government Center had said to her . . . At 20, she had been living in the city, at the age of 20 she thought she would die. *Gurgling down Gold Neck it came back to her again and again* . . . when she gained consciousness in the car, he had her underwear removed, and had backed her against the far door of the car. He had ripped her dress off, piece by piece, at knife point too, and he had shoved her bared knees apart, leaving her knee-high boots laced up. He opened the lips of her vagina, staring as he spread her skins apart. "What," she had strained to get up, "wh—" not understanding what he was doing. "I like the color of it," he explained to her. "It's red—I like to look at it." He stuck his thumb into her. "It's so warm!" he frolicked gleefully. He stuck his face, with a toothmark on one side and a curious fang hanging down on one side of his mouth, between her legs. Exactly why, she wasn't clear. He picked his head up from between her legs, and spat. . . .

Yellow bananas issued forth, as Bapka came to in the fish again. Red and blue tank top, the gift of her aunt, came up, over her head and off. Yellow, she sensed, all around, but she lost consciousness again . . . memories came pouring out, as she kicked, and approached Gold Neck's middle . . . and the memories still came, next: Wrapping the rapist in an awesome spell, by talking on and on about how she had been so silly as to take seriously the social barriers in a society she didn't believe in anyway. "Well, no time to worry about it now," the rapist has said to her." "Why not?" she asked, shocked. "Well," he started to drive the car again, and she focused on the toothmark on his face from her position. "You were a good sport, kid, but now that I've raped you, I'm, uh," he hesitates again, and a turban appeared on his head. "I'm going to kill you." She gulped. No response. She gulped again. She turned to look out the window, and became aware of the details of the physical environment very slowly. "I'm going to take you to a pond, in the suburbs somewhere," he informed her, driving, holding her down, thumb in the middle of her. "I found a little pond in the woods, and I'm going to take you there, and I'm going to kill you."

She turned to look out the window as best she could and saw the snow coming from very far away, in the darkness, each white flake vaguely contributing to an iridescent white glow. He stopped at a red light, and got out a map. "Let's see, somewhere north." He turned on the car light. She shrunk away from him as he pulled his thumb out.

She came to in Gold Neck again. Another layer of clothing came off. "I don't believe in institutions, prisons, jails . . . you don't have to go to the trouble of killing me, I won't go to the police," she remembered she had said. *The bangles on her arm bounced off her. She had the sensation of lying on the bottom of a pool of green.* "I wouldn't do that to another human being," she had told him.

The memories, though choppy, spewed forth . . . suddenly she felt that Gold Neck was swimming in a school, or surrounded by other fishes. They were waving their tails and their fins to the pace of his heartbeat, though they were outside him; and she was setting the beat, or it all seemed to be in unison. And the beat beat more out of her, in great huge pieces.

Bapka felt the cold of a snowbank, all around her. She was lying, when she next came to, 30 feet from the car, motor still running. She pulled the shreds of her ripped dress closer to her, and cringed as he came towards her, brandishing weapon to kill her. "Listen, will you tell them," she had voiced inaudibly, "take down my parents' phone number, call them . . ." But he broke down all of a sudden, sobbing, and couldn't go on. He leaned against a tree. The steady stream of snow had stopped. "Why are you sobbing?" she asked. He came and presented the strange turban to her, loosened the fang, and the toothmark, as if to answer her question for her. Together they returned to the car. Barely dressed, he let her drive home.

And the fish outside gurgled, and the remembering part of Bapka came to again, and in another gulp, Gold Neck swallowed her one step further down. And everything turned to blue with alarming simplicity. An astral blue, shimmering as Bapka sat up somewhere in Gold Neck's lower portion. She protruded his belly, and a diamond ring appeared on her forefinger, but she threw it off, out into the school of fishes, and they clapped their fins, and shot one of them up to catch it. Gold Neck swam proudly in front, he was the apex; the other fishes took their places spiraling out on either side and everybody swam as one. Bapka sat up to mouth to the followers: "Trust me. He told me to trust him, but he still had the knife. I was petrified. For six hours, afraid for my life."

Bapka sat up in Gold Neck. She felt herself at one in a balmic fluid of purple. She looked out of the hole in front of her into the subterranean depths of an emerald and aqua ocean. Behind her, all the layers she had shed: bangle bracelet, shawl, man's shirt, tank top, sisal hat, even the sneakers, the diamond ring, and the white balloon pants . . . Bapka realized she was quite naked. She awoke next on a cloud. Everything was white. She had fallen out of the asshole of Gold Neck, and he had turned to suck her out of the waters and had taken her into his mouth to save her. He had spat her up into the air, as he realized she needed oxygen, and the Statue of Liberty had bent down to pick her up with one hand to place her on the tall torch tip. Bapka looked down. Gold Neck winked. "Thanks for the bath," she called dreamily, "I really needed it . . ." And as she waved goodbye, a white bunny fell into the crook of her smooth naked arm.

"Look at that," says Jane, nonplussed, knitting in front of television as Bapka plops down, naked and pure, on the screen. The Statue of Liberty, bending over and rubbing the small of her back, asks, "So where's the t'ai chi class? Do you know how long I've been in that position? What time is the work-out?" Jane knits. Minnie shoves her. "Jane, the Miss Liberty is speaking to you." "Hush," gestures Jane. "Action on the set again . . ."

VI.

"All those Jews who marched to their deaths in the concentration camps," Bapka, on her back in her grandfather's apartment, is shuddering out loud. "And I let myself be raped, just so I could live, perhaps—prostituted—and I wasn't even certain. On the mere hope that I could keep living . . ."

"It's OK," a voice breaks through to her. "Being alive, living, it's a good reason to risk anything . . ."

She draws herself up on the bed, comforted by the sound, she thought, and moves to a sitting position. She sits, feet on floor, head in hands, at the edge of the bed. Outside, one bird is chirping. She slowly realizes she is with Dan.

"Why, Dan," she looks up, bewildered, "when did you get here, and how?" She scratches her head. "I don't remember letting you in—did you find your way OK to Brooklyn? Right train and everything?"

"It's OK, it's OK," he said.

"But," she stammers, looks up.

"Let's get a clean start. Start all over again," Dan suggests. He stands up. "I'll go out, knock on the door, and then I'll come in. I'll ask you about the story then. Remember, that's why I came out."

"Um, OK," says the Bapka self, wanting to go along with him. She got up to let him out, putting on house slippers and grandfather's red, white, and blue checked bathrobe. She followed him to the door of the apartment and let him out. She came back to the kitchen, fiddled, putting water on for coffee, staring enraptured at the burner, musing about the rapist again. Forgetting about the water, she stumbled into the back room and fell asleep on her grandfather's bed as the memories jarred again.

Next she awoke as if into a dream, looking up to see a white fang on a golden string swinging back and forth, back

210

and forth. "It's absolute and relative," the Zen Monk suspended above her was saying, "absolute and relative . . ."

"Absolute and relative *what*—" Bapka asks, trying to sit up.

Zen Monk stops teaching and takes a meditative pose above her. She lies back, watching the white fang pendulum swing back and forth. Slowly, more voices and faces start appearing to her.

"Did ya get what ya need in the apartment, sweets?" Louie, in white gloves and tuxedo, sits out on the laundry line outside the apartment still trying to send everything she needs to her. "No, not yet?" She reaches up after him, with one hand, but he disappears before she can quite touch the strong image of the man.

Her father appears, and slowly she realizes a ring is being formed. They are encircling her. The Monk at her head, Louie out the window at her toes. Though visually she can't keep him in focus, still he is there somehow, she knows. And now her father at her left, stooping, as if an elderly gentleman. He holds his hands to his cheek, and sobs to her, in a moan unfurling as he did chanting kaddish at the grave when they put Louie in and threw the dirt after the funeral.

"I didn't mean you any harm," he was crying, "I was trying to help you get along, and your brother too, by telling you Jews were just like everyone else . . . if only I had known he had done this to you . . ."

She feels encircled, hands placed above her by everybody and feeling vapors as if from a steam room suddenly, and as the fang swings back and forth, to and fro, she wonders vaguely just who is holding up the golden string, whose strong arm, she wants to know, and the dawn comes and light is shed into the room and all the vapors and the mists and the faces and the voices and hands evaporate, and even the fang too, and all she can see is a rainbow streaming in through the window where once Louie had been. The kettle whistles, a knock is heard, and as she fails to answer immediately the doorbell rings. She struggles to the door, wondering, why this one, why Dan, now what lesson is she supposed to learn from him. She turns off the tea kettle, and welcomes him.

"Dan," Bapka mm's, contrite. "Let's go to the boardwalk, shan't we? I don't feel safe—Statue of Liberty was swinging a golden string, and everything." She looks cautiously around. "It's spooky in here. Let's get out."

"OK," says Dan. "Let's go exploring Coney Island. I'm up for adventure, and finding a story out of all this. Maybe I can write an article then. Got the key?"

He beams, and Bapka nods, obligingly. She starts to step out the door.

"Say there," Dan intercedes. "Don't you think you better put some clothes on?" She was still in the bathrobe.

"No, why bother. You're new to this borough, I know, but things are—less formal in Brooklyn than they are in Manhattan."

"What, how's that?" Dan asks, fumbling to hide his cape left over from his pirate-rescue costume.

"You'll soon know."

Dan asks for the key. Bapka hands it to him. Out they go, and he locks the door after them.

Bapka straightens the folds of her grandfather's bathrobe and tightens it around her as she hears the familiar bolt of the door of B4. She and Dan wade through the marble lobby, their footsteps resonating back to them. "Oh, it feels good to have my feet on the soil of Brooklyn again," she proclaims, as soon as they hit the pavement. The heavy door to Jericho Courts swings shut with a bang. They go up 15th Street, straight to the Highway and neighbors discussing, she's normal, she's seeing someone. Bapka turns to face Dan. They bump into each other, as Dan is following her very closely. He stops abruptly and puts sleuth magnifying glass back into his pocket.

"What's that?" she asks.

"Nothing, a glass, to magnify everything in case there's a good story about Brooklyn out here. I'm a journalist, you know. Got to keep my eye out for a story. Besides," he pauses, "you said soil of Brooklyn, and I was taking a good look." He bends down. "Seems like pavement, you know?"

When they reach the Highway, Bapka stops again. "Well, we're going to Coney, but which way do you want to go?"

"Well," Dan fumbles in his pocket for the map to Brooklyn subways he had armed himself with in Manhattan. "It says here—" he says, removing his Ben Franklin glasses gingerly.

"Oh, look . . . look out!" Bapka refrains a shout. Too late. The glasses fall to the sidewalk and shatter loudly.

"Oh no," moaned Dan, "what will I do now?" Trying to gather the pieces, he crawls on all fours around her.

"It's OK, I'm used to helping people. Towards the end, Louie couldn't see, but he'd always want to walk with me."

Again Bapka takes Dan's hand, after thus informing him. "But how do you want to go?" again she asks. Dan stands up. "The overground, the underground, or the round-de-round?"

"Let's see," says Dan, composing himself, "the overground, that's buses . . ." He holds up one finger on one hand and with the other hand he bends it to count the modes of transportation, "underground, two . . ." he bends back another one, "er, subway, I believe. But—three . . ." He squints his eyes in Bapka's direction helplessly.

She grabs the hand that had been holding down each finger and says, "Come with me."

Suddenly he inhaled an odor, a fragrance—of flowers. "Where are we, Bapka, at a florist's?"

"No," she called over her shoulder. "We're at the entrance of the round-de-round. You got blasted with a flower fragrance first, to cleanse your aura, instead of with radiation like they do at the airport before you get into that silver machinery. And listen," she said, turning to him, finger to pursed lips, "hear the sound?"

Dan tuned in to baritones singing, babies crying, teenagers revving motorcycles, sopranos, then to sea gulls squawking, bell buoys clanging, dogs barking, swing sets squeaking, the thud of balls against handball courts, though he didn't recognize them, and the clung-clang-clung slowly turned to sirens calling DAN!!!DAN!!!DAN!!! He heard melodies of the soul, finally.

"Yes, but," in a normal speaking tone, he was asking her, "where are you taking me?"

"Well, we're going to the ocean, eventually, and the way the transport works, or this mode of it, is, you have your aura cleansed by blossoms, then tune in, to sounds around you, then, in your inner ear, to the sound of where it is you want to be, then, you close your eyes, and go—it's a travel-through-time gift. You get there by entering another incarnation. It's a gift, my grandfather must have given it to me."

Trembling, Dan went along with Bapka. Visions of the story he could write for the *Times* kept swimming through his mind.

All of a sudden they were in the air, and then under the ocean. He was a pirate. And Bapka was a very lovely woman on a shipwreck, calling to him as if from the bottom of the sea, making the sound of a siren. He dove to the bottom of the sea to be with her. Then they re-emerged as one, splashing to the shores of Coney Island. They felt refreshed and lay in the sand, panting. A dog ran up and licked them.

"What's this?" Dan fumbled behind them.

"A sea chest," said Bapka nonchalantly, "full of treasure. We brought it up with us apparently." Dan turned, shivering, patting the dog. His teeth began chattering uncontrollably. "Bapka," he pleaded, "please show me the way—show me how to get to Manhattan. I'm scared. I don't care if I lose face with the *Times* editor. I'm too scared to go through with this. Help me."

VII.

"Now, now, now," Bapka clucked. "To think you were

214

doing this for fame, and fortune. I thought you came out of love for me. Not only for the story. And besides, it's not so easy. You are far, far into the outer reaches of Brooklyn with me." Though he felt trapped, she held on to him, straightening the costume as it was pulled on by the dog.

"Besides," she dropped both him and the issue. "There's more I want to see."

"I can't—see anything, much—"

"Well, you'll get the feel of it then—"

Following Bapka in his pirate's uniform, Dan prowled behind. The two of them walked up from the beach, up the nearest entrance to the boardwalk. The dog followed them.

"Where are we?" Dan asked in a grim tone. "Bapka, I can't see—" he stated nervously. The dog barked, running after them.

"Yes, you can. Open your eyes." When he did, he could see they were somewhere up high. Perhaps on the D train subway platform? He looked down and saw Bapka with a woman humming and sweeping. Her hair was tied in a triangular piece of cloth, a babushka which looked like it had been cut out of a tapestry curtain. "Sweep, sweep, sweep. I am the great soul-sweep of your life," the real-babushka woman started to sing out loud. She had a fresh white apron fastened over her waist, like a peasant, and he watched as the image appeared of this peasant babushka woman, standing back to admire her Siberian bearskin, which hung diagonally over the door to her kitchen. He watched, his consciousness of self fading in fascination as she went over to straighten the bittersweet green and orange plastic flowers which hung in great pots above from the rafters. She hopped onto a Persian carpet, as if onto a stage, still sweeping. Dog wagged tail, watching with them.

Just then Bapka and Dan heard a rumbling. "Something's happening," Dan cries, and white as a sheet, he holds on to her. He realized they *were* on a subway platform, and that they were very small, as the passengers waiting on the platform to board the train could not see them. They waited for the shattering sound of the train to pass, and crawled out to the railway again. Yes, they looked down, over the black-and-white-striped Rabinowitz drugstore ceiling, right through the roofs into the dwelling of this great soul-sweeper, who was still cleaning her Russian hut. She straightened up her shelves of *chatskahs* to open the establishment as a restaurant. Painstakingly she organized and reorganized the orange wooden horses, which still had straw on them. As she did, Bapka, with Aryan date, walked up.

"But isn't it?" asked Dan, raising his hand, pointing.

"Shh, yes," said Bapka, gesturing the need for silence. "You see, with this gift, we—" She stopped, straightened up, and turned to him. Dan was afraid, on the elevated, that they would swing off, if he did not listen to her.

"I see, simultaneously, in the same place, all sorts of occurrences happening," Bapka murmured to him. "And you can see too, since you came on the round-de-round with me." Dan fingered his beard, straightening out a ruddy curl one by one, and he held onto her. They looked down again.

There Bapka is in a prior self, visiting the Russian hut in the middle of winter with a Britisher. He is at least six feet tall, and carrying a bottle of Pinch scotch, attempting to carry his own liquor in. Bapka is worrying about her immigrant friends, afraid this will insult them. "Nevil," she says, pulling him by the tail of his trench-like overcoat as they start to go in. "Must you take your scotch in there?"

Nevil blinks. "Why not?"

"Batava will find it insulting. You know, the immigrant woman." Still no response from Nevil. He pulled back his trench-coat tails. "They drink vodka," from Bapka. "Stolichnaya. They're Russian." Nevil looked nonplused. "This place is rustic, Nevil," she continued to explain to him. "Batava's husband is a furrier. I come here often, just to talk to them. Four years ago they left Russia, and it took them all this time to get a passport to Brooklyn from Israel. Israel's supposed to be the home of the Jewish people, but many of the Jewish people," she slowly drops her eyes, "prefer to come here."

216

"So?" Nevil took a swig, and Bapka realized she might be dating not only a schmuck but a drunk. She had been hoping he could see for himself that his scotch would clash with the scenery. "It's Old World here, like Odessa," she tried to describe the backdrop again. "So don't bring your booze in." Suddenly she took a turn to nasty with him. "I don't want to colonize the atmosphere, although I know the British do that so easily."

"Now, listen here." Nevil turned toward the Avenue and took another swig.

"The people here like making everything Russian, they're homesick, so we do what we do to fit in, gracefully." She opened the door, and walked in ahead of him.

Nevil blinked his blurred eyes and stuck the Pinch in one of his pockets and went in after her. Batava in babushka greeted them. Many shots of toasted vodka later, Nevil says to her, "What fun! I feel like I'm on a holiday, actually." He grins at her.

For him it's like travel. For me, it's my heritage, thought Bapka ruefully.

And Bapka slowly noticed, tuning into the environment. She felt so remote, as if she were watching a Russian movie. The people, with whom out of love she had once merged, now, with the Britisher, no longer seemed to be part of the inner her: the Dostoevsky-like conspiratorial characters, with swooped-up noses and pockmarked faces; busty old ladies breaking out of black silk bodices, each clutching a single red rose to wave in the air; young eastern beauties staring eagerly, running red-painted finger tips sedately through the black rings of their Marie-Antoinette curled hair.

"Oh yes," says Bapka on the perch, turning to Dan, "this was the winter she got all this," Bapka put her hands to her ears on either side of her head in the memory of it, "Israeli Russian disco music." She shuddered. They looked down again, and ever-passing platters of food were bursting forth from the back kitchen.

"Oh look," about the beef stroganov up above they

heard Nevil remark. "She's serving it in butter dishes. What a lark."

Just then a wry little man came up. Though they were sitting down the short little fellah on his feet peered up at Nevil on his chair and began to shout, "You Yid?"

Bapka down below didn't have time to warn her date that he was being asked if he were Jewish. Nevil nodded his head, yes.

The little fellah began to lift his glass.

Nevil, jumping the fellah's gun, got up to toast him first.

"To Russia!" Nevil shouted, glass in air, drowning out the male baritone behind, who had begun to croon at the visitor's ignorance.

"To Israel!" Bapka blurted out to cover him.

"To Brooklyn!" the little fellah toasted back to her.

On their perch above, Dan shook the tracks with his belly laugh so full that Bapka thought another train had come. "That's so funny," he held his stomach and gasped. Bapka was beyond belief. "Maybe to you!" They looked down, as Dan changed his expression from laugh to frown. Babushka-Batava was running out from her kitchen with dessert: a platter of cream puffs, and all colors of grapes and pears and fruits from the kitchen. Although Bapka so longed to belong, she backed out.

Up above, Dan leaned back. "Wow," he was saying, "that's quite a story." He pulled Bapka over onto his lap after things settled down a bit and the scene they had just observed began to fade. "You know," he was stroking his beard, "I've been thinking. I'd like to take you along on my assignments, my adventures, as an atmosphere assistant." He paused now. "Wow, with that gift you have, how I could write."

"No, well, Dan," said Bapka getting up and looking over the railing to where her legs had just been kicking, "I mean, I appreciate your connections and everything, but I'd sort of like to write myself, not just be somebody's assistant. You know, I'd like to sell some work. I've been published too, though not as much as you."

Just then the sweep, sweep, sweep of Batava's masterful broom was heard, and all the restaurant characters—Nevil, the old Bapka, the wry little fellow, the Dostoevsky characters, the busty old ladies in bodices, the eastern beauties, and more—the Persian carpet, the orange wooden horses, the *chatskahs*, the platters of grapes, the Siberian bearskins, the stroganov in butter dishes—came flying out. Even including a male baritone, a singer. The door to the Russian hut was slammed closed, and Batava dimmed from Dan and Bapka's elevated vision, sweeping the door to a close.

"Bapka!" Dinah's parroting voice was the next sound they heard. Bapka looked up. There was Dinah, hovering in trench coat on her umbrella in the air, Macy's and Gimbel's bags on either hand. She fluttered near a telephone wire. "Look," she pointed animatedly to them. "Look. At the ocean. Something important is coming up."

Bapka and Dan looked to where Dinah pointed immediately. Sure enough, a rock on fire was coming up. First Bapka and Dan though it was a fire. They blinked. Then they thought it was a stone. They blinked again. Whatever it was, the shimmering red, yellow, and orange moving on a backdrop of the blue horizon and the thrashing green of the sea was approaching them. They backed off toward the D train tracks, clutching each other, afraid it should reach the sand.

The dog barked.

"Hush," said Bapka. "You'll terrify it. Uh. Them."

The dog barked again.

"Love," said the Fire Stone.

Bapka and Dan backed off again.

"Love," shimmered the Fire Stone again.

"Love issss," the Fire Stone added a hiss next. Bapka and Dan repeated, "Love hissss," as what she was saying remained a mystery to them.

"Love hisss, oh."

"Love is o," Bapka and Dan repeated after her.

"Love is o-press," the Fire Stone goes on. "Love is o-press-on . . ."

Her words billowed out from her, like thunder clapping over the sea. Bapka turned to Dan. "Love hiss oh press on . . . whatever does she mean?" Dan shrugs. "Gosh, Bapka, I don't know. We don't get messages from the sea in Manhattan. We listen to the radio mostly." On this line, the great Fiery Stone gave a gigantic shudder and returned to the sea. Giant pink polka dot socks beneath green denim trousers appeared on the line between sky and sea. "What's that on the horizon?" Bapka asks.

Dan shrugs his shoulders. "I don't know."

Big hands reached down to straighten up socks, and the brim of a blue Portuguese fisherman's hat came down over them, with a golden braid. The hat stayed on the head, miraculously. The socks were straightened, and what must have been a giant stood back up.

The dog barked.

VIII.

"Oooh, look how small we are," Bapka squeals when, jumping off the train rail, they land about as tall as dandelion flowers.

"It's OK," says Dan. "Take long strides." He brushes himself off.

"Long strides?" asks Bapka.

"Yes," Dan answers, acting as if he could explain anything. "It's got something to do with growing up," he goes on. He faced the sea, which turned from haunted green back to blue again. He arched his back, and then took long strides to approach the boardwalk. Sure enough, as he strode, he shot up and up. He called back to Bapka to follow him, explaining over his shoulder he was looking for a phone to call his *Times* editor, his service, and his agent. Bapka watched, wistfully, wondering how he would explain the situation to them. She followed, and she shot up too.

"I don't know," says Dan. "Wonder why I can't find a phone. Don't the Russians use them?" Strolling up on the boardwalk, he turns to her again, as they pass by a group of Israelis hawking fresh fruits and vegetables. "I know I've said this before, going out with Jewish women is like going out with someone from another country. That's why I agreed to come out. Thought I could whip off some sort of travelogue. But this is too much." Dan brushes off his still-clinging pirate's costume. "But why don't you just go to Israel then?"

"Look," says Bapka, pointing to a booth on the walk. "That Tattoo Lady with the Last Supper on her back—where have we seen her before? Was it somewhere on television?"

She steps closer, to have a better look, and Dinah, flying high on her umbrella, calls down, "Bapka, take this." She reaches into either a Macy's or a Gimbel's bag, and throws down a dress with frills, replete with petticoat under it. "And for your boyfriend, Dan . . ." she reaches into her bags again, and tosses down another pair of glasses to him.

"Wow, thanks," Dan shouts. "Maybe I can find the phone and reach my agent now!"

"Thanks, Dinah," Bapka calls up, where she can still see her aunt flying. "Dan could sure use those glasses, but a dress with petticoats—I'm not Alice in Wonderland."

"Well," says Dinah, still hovering low, "you never know." She waves and swoops off.

Dan, with glasses, and Bapka, fully re-dressed now, pass under the archway into Astroland. "Get your fruitcakes," a hawker calls after them, "now or never, fruitcakes, just back from . . ." Dan gets concerned about a phone again.

Bapka marvels in the coolness and silence of the wax museum when they step in. Then she gasps in horror, and turns to Dan. "The summer I was raped in Mississippi at a summer camp—by the rabbi—that's him!" She froze in front of a glass box.

She dropped on the floor between this scene from her

past and Jack the Ripper. Dan went out to try again to make a phone call. Dog, yipping at cape on pirate's costume, went out after him.

When Bapka came to, wax was melting out, telling a story in slow motion . . . signs of NO SMOKING and RICHARD SPECK faded in this Hall of Horrors, and CAMP ZIONSVILLE loomed into view. An arc in the sky, with curly lettering, Bapka got up, as if mesmerized, and walked through. She walked into the center, a ring of children dancing and singing in Hebrew. Bapka felt funny in her dress with frills and petticoats, but joined them now as she had then. Funny, she found her inner fires still burned with the desire to return to Israel, to make a pilgrimage. She remembered how she had gone to the rabbi of the camp. She walked back into the scene once again.

"I can buy you an airplane ticket, and call your father," the kindly white-haired man had told her. "Come to my cabin after your bunk is sleeping, and we'll talk about it."

Now, Bapka's own father had been a fine man. A doctor. How had she been prepared to suspect? So she wandered into Zev the rabbi's cabin. He sat on one twin bed, she on another. Between them stood a table, with a lamp and a Bible. He asked her a few questions, and then got to what he had brought her there to ask: had she ever made love with anyone?

Bapka was reluctant to answer him.

The rabbi continued to prod her. She went numb, frozen in paralysis. Zev didn't give her much time to explain anything. With one hand, he turned off the light on the night stand; with the other, he pushed her flat on her back by pressing roughly. Working quickly, he unzipped his fly, put on a rubber. When he was all done, in real life, Bapka had run out of the cabin, into a thunderstorm which had cleansed her forever of her desire to go to Israel. In this rerun version, the rabbi Zev hit the hardness of her plaster-of-Paris–like petticoats. This failed attempt to thrust into her bent his penis. *He* froze into paralysis this time, and Bapka pushed him to the ground where he lay in pain grimacing next to the Bible in the dark. Up above, Bapka heard laughter. "See," squawked Dinah, on umbrella, "don't say I never gave you anything." She flew off.

Bapka walked out of the glass box. To her surprise, the grimacing Zev, clutching his crotch, followed her. Bapka turned, looking vaguely for Dan, wondering if he had successfully completed his phone calls, and where the dog was. She heard the roar of the cyclone. And saw Elvis Presley and the Father of the Atomic Age shimmering. She turned to the rabbi. "Are you made of wax? Why are you following me?"

"Well, I had to rape you, I wanted to tell you, so you could go on your own spiritual search . . . and besides," he said, looking down, "I know your aunt is for chastity, but . . . this thing really hurts. Do you know anyone who can fix it?"

Outside, in the bright light, they run into Dan, with mutt, and Nevil.

"Say, where did you get this guy, and why is he holding his crotch?" Dan asks.

"Where did I get this guy? Where did you go? He re-raped me, in the replay, and bent his thing, and now he wants it fixed."

"Oh, that's too bad," flustered Dan. "Well, I went to look for a phone, or a subway, or something, and ran into Nevil here. I found him on the boardwalk. All he wants is his trench coat. And his bottle of Pinch back. And I want to go home."

"Yes," said Nevil angrily, "Dan found me wandering on the boardwalk. And I'm glad. When Batava swept us out, I lost my scotch and my trench coat and ended up in this silly changing of the guard costume." He fumed and looked angrier under a black helmet. "Dan here doesn't mind his cape, with the stars studded all over it, as long as he's got his glasses he'll deal with the silly pirate's costume. It doesn't really change his character. But this red, white, and blue diagonal trip, Bapka, it's too much for me. I give. What'll we do?"

"It's OK," said Bapka. "I know where to go next." She gestured. They formed a line, and skipped arm in arm, the dog following: she in her frilled dress, the rabbi Zev with the bent thing, Dan in his cape, looking for home, and Nevil in his changing of the guard costume looking for a way to get out of it. Arm in arm, they skipped away from the cyclone, onto the boardwalk, and due west, all the while Zev crying about the pain.

Behind them, in the air, silhouetted against the roller coaster, Dan spies Doris on her cigarette holder, enlarged to the size of a broomstick. He pulls out his magnifying glass, the better to inspect her with, and drops back from the line he had been skipping with. He ducked from a hailstorm of fruitcakes, fresh vegetables, and blintzes. The Zen Monk flies past next, calling, "Try Zen, it'll help you assimilate, dampen your intellect if not your spirit . . ."

"It's too crazy out here, Bapka, how do we get to Manhattan?"

Nevil stopped in his tracks too. "How do I get my trench coat, and my scotch?"

The rabbi stopped too. "How do I get my thing fixed?"

The dog barked. Bapka broke free and ran. She ran off the boardwalk, down a spiral staircase into the sand. She fell on her back, and looked up. God in his empty chair spoke to her.

"Bapka, get Brooklyn admitted to the UN as homeland for the Jews . . . Coney Island is the promised land."

Bapka breathed, "God, why me?"

"Don't fight it, it's destiny."

When her eyes opened again, she looked up at a giant man in a blue cap with a brim. "Where ya been, little girl? Having a vision? Don't worry, it happens to everyone." Giant squatted down to straighten pink socks. Green knees loomed.

Bapka struggled to get up, noticing she was without petticoat or dress with frills and back in the old man's bathrobe again. She grew fainter as white pellets started to fall from the barrel of a huge silver gun.

"It's just the sun, and the sand," she heard, and

suddenly she and the other characters were picked up in a giant hand. Dog barking, they were removed once and for all from the promised land. The boardwalk filled with tourists watching them go.

IX.

"I dunno," says Dan, stroking beard, relieved to find himself at least next to his khaki pants and striped shirt—his original clothing—in bed with Bapka next to him. "Maybe Jews are a tribe of their own," he contemplates. "Maybe Brooklyn should be admitted to the UN. That was quite a story out there. Although my chances for publishing something out of it look pretty grim. Can I use your phone, and call my agent for a minute?"

He dials. Hesitates. And hangs up again. "Gee, Bapka, how long have I been out here?"

"I don't know myself," she answers, stretching next to him. "But let me fix the blind, lest the baritone is watching through the window again."

As she hops out of bed, she hears a rattling in the kitchen. She jumps back in. "This place is haunted," she says.

"Yes, I believe you," Dan answers, his tone pretty grim.

Bapka pulls away from the comfort she might get from him. "I'm not sure about things between us," she announces.

Dan sits up sharply. "What?"

"Back in Manhattan, you've got other girlfriends, and don't even know who I am when I call you on the phone . . . you don't even care about me, you just wanted a story . . . I could forget about all that, with the calamity bringing us closer. But you're anti-Semitic really, and you think Jews are not like other people. And you probably don't even believe I talked to God, about Destiny . . ."

Dan smirked. "God, but you are so cosmic, I think not . . ."

"And," Bapka begins to sound threatening, "you just wanted me to be an atmosphere assistant, really . . ."

She hears his pants zip, and watches as he fumbles for

225

his Ben Franklin glasses. She lies on her back, and stares, not really caring who is looking in. "Love is oppression, love is oppression, that's what the message of the Fire Stone was about. You don't love, you oppress me, even in trying to rescue me. Now I see what the silly costumes are about."

"Honest, Bapka," Dan, fully dressed, goes down on his knees at the side of her grandfather's bed. "I was serious about trying to help you."

"Here's your glasses," she says, digging them up from under the sheets.

He lets himself out the door of B4, jogs down the stairs, and into the stone lobby of Jericho Courts, out past the lawn-chair civilization . . . he runs all the way into Manhattan, wings sprouting on his feet as he jogs over the Brooklyn Bridge, not stopping to call his agent, or the *Times* editor, or anybody. He just wants out.

"Look at that, look at him go, God!" says Jane, still knitting in front of the television set in Dubrow's where the Crew had been watching what seemed like cartoons or animated pictures. She puts down her knitting and pulls out her compact again.

"Not now, Jane," God calls to her from the screen again.

Nonplussed, Bermann continues ladling.

"And why not?" Jane looks up, disturbed. "I've got a right. I've got a brain. I've borne two children."

"Yah, I know," says God from the television. "But you're needed on the set. Now go."

"Yah? OK?" Jane answers him, adjusting spider on wig. "Yay! I've got a part!"

X.

CONGRATULATIONS! the old people shout, waving flags either for Simchas Torah, July Fourth, or admitting Brooklyn to the UN. Bapka hears the D train roar by, and

226

down fall the walls of Jericho Courts. She sees the whole Crew from Dubrow's parading around following Jane, blowing silver trumpets. Minnie hands out fruitcakes, potatoes, briskit as they finish their seventh round. "Here, kid," she calls, "try something nourishing. Didn't ya know this was a movie set? Old man set ya up to be rich and famous. That's what he did with his diamonds, his cash, his money. No?" Bapka wagged her head faintly, no. "Well, now ya know." Minnie falls back in line.

"Here, kid, have a new costume," Jane throws over gray wig as Bapka sat up, naked in bed, covering up to her chin in cotton. (Dinah was embarrassed; the sheets weren't linen. Louie comforted her.)

"Hurry up, get dressed," Old Geezie flips the brim of his visor and calls to her. "Didn't ya hear me cheering you?"

Gold Neck leaps up, wags his tail, and kisses her.

"Whew—" says Jane, handing binoculars to Southern Belle. "Look at the sprint on that kid."

"OK, everyone grab a lawn chair," Belle answers. "Sit down a bit. This is a shock for Bapka." Bapka's Mom and Dad, and brother and sister-in-law and kid walk up. "She'll need some time to reconcile herself to it."

The rest of the men, including the Jewish Minister, come back from the steam baths at Brighton dripping wet. By the cameras being rolled off, they know they are late for their bit on the set.

"Sorry we missed everything," they said.

Bapka struggles to get out of bed, forgiving them, even the Zen Monk, and the psychiatrist, and Zev. The rapist steps back, knowing in truth he had a secondary part. "Here, cover up," Southern Belle flutters and admonishes her. She covers Bapka with a sheet. Bapka's mom tries not to look upset.

"Well," calls Southern Belle, "it's about time for a ceremony, isn't it?"

Jewish Minister stands up with a prayer book, thinking this is a cue to him. Referee blows whistle, indicating it isn't.

"The young like to write their own ceremony, nowadays,"

somebody whispers to him.

"What are we celebrating anyway?" asks Lena's husband, the Listener, not sure.

"Bapka threw out the no-good *goyishe* man," Dinah quacks, passing out cole slaw and pickles to everyone. Bapka's mom stood up to help with that. "And up at the Empire State," Dinah continues, "Bermann, he's got a concession."

Applause breaks out.

"Well, then," Dinah says, feeling the end draw near, and wanting to help out. "How shall we get there?"

"Let's fly!" somebody calls.

"Yah," says Louie, "why not? That's Jewish. Even the young do it."

Atop the Empire State Building, they all land, en group. They watch the spirit of Macy's and Gimbel's fly by, and admire the fireworks down on Coney Island put up for the Fourth. They see dancing. The preppies, the Statue of Liberty, masses of people back to back . . . orthodox Jewish boys end to end with Russian immigrants . . . Batava sweeps up, and Israeli hawkers sell fruitcake and fresh veggies to Jack the Ripper. Dogs bark, babes cry, waves lap, and Tattoo Lady flies out from the House of Horrors. Li'l Jake goes back out, seeing a good market for his fundamentalist leaflets. Big Jake shrinks back down to the size of a man, and goes out shooting pistols in case anyone is suffering from delusion. A whole row of women with guns on their belts parades behind the dancers looking for Dan's forgotten magnifying glass, to help them locate Nazis. Dan's dad wanders around, looking for old neighborhoods; and befriends the 40-year-old man who gave up his life for his family, who had a breakdown when Bermann left.

And back at the top, Bermann is making a lot of money on a concession, selling hot dogs, since everyone in Manhattan came to celebrate Brooklyn being admitted to the UN. And if it doesn't rain, it pours: orange wooden *chatskahs*, Marie Antoinette beauties, busty old ladies from Batava's restaurant, tourists waving, platters of grapes, red roses, turbans, bangles, even the old Jam popped up. The rabbi had his thing unbent. And Nevil had a job, too, in the costume section, where tourists get pictures taken in uniforms of different periods. But at least he had his Pinch scotch back. The dog was enrolled with Jane in a special semester of studying knitting. The preppies with cameras were photographing that.

A wreath appears over Bapka from above, mysteriously, making her Brooklyn's Ambassador *to* the UN. The Ambassador *from* the UN, with his Wife, steps up and gives the results of surveys to her, so she can start work with a proper report. And the lady with white lipstick hands out *Yeats: A Vision*, mimeographed version.

"Oh, look," Bapka cries, feeling like she's on top of a grandstand. "There goes Dan!" Sure enough, there Dan goes, chased out by firecrackers and explosions in Brooklyn, one foot landing in Manhattan, the next in Jersey—right over 9th and 10th Avenue and the Hudson River in one step. And each foot has a wing continuing to grow on it. As Dan leaps over the West Side Highway, over Sunday morning joggers, someone tries to sell him a bagel. "Oh no," Dan cries, hands over ears, and keeps jogging—on through New Jersey, Kansas City, Nebraska, the Pacific Ocean, Japan, and China, as if through a Steinberg poster. On the borders of Mexico and Canada he is cheered by Texans and Chicagoans and everybody standing end to end, even though he missed the biggest story breaking forth on earth:

"EXTRA EXTRA, READ ALL ABOUT IT . . . BROOKLYN ADMITTED TO THE UN."

CONTRIBUTORS' NOTES

Alcina Lubitch Domecq was born in Guatemala in 1953. Her novel *The Mirror's Mirror, or The Noble Smile of the Dog* (1984), clearly influenced by Lewis Carroll and Jorge Luis Borges, describes the adventures of an eight-year-old Jewish girl who's left alone on a battlefield. The majority of her 30 stories, among them "Bottles," are included in *Intoxicated* (Mexico City: Joaquín Martiz, 1988). She now lives in Jerusalem.

Batya Weinbaum has published two books with South End Press and has another scheduled to appear from Clothespin Fever Press in Los Angeles. She has published prize-winning fiction and poetry in *Phoenix Rising*, *Realm of the Unreal*, *World of Poetry*, *Feminist Review*, *Key West Review*, *West End Review of Poetry and Politics*, and *Home Planet News*. She studied writing with Alix Kates Shulman, Marguerite Young, and Ann Waldman. As this book went to press she was working on a novel about Jerusalem.

The cafeteria in "Bapka in Brooklyn" no longer exists. It was turned into a Wrangler's jeans shop, and the old Jews there have either died or gone to Florida.

Conda V. Douglas: While I am not Navajo myself, I grew up with many experiences of The People, both on the reservation and at my home in Sun Valley, Idaho. My father, an artist, worked with the Navajo to preserve their sandpaintings. This childhood fostered in me a lifelong interest in other cultures and other lands. In pursuing these interests, I've traveled and lived in Europe and Asia. And as a film editor of documentaries, I've had the pleasure of researching such diverse subjects as the Dalai Lama and the waterways of Ireland. I also belly dance, and find that many of my best ideas come while shimmying.

I'm a fifth-generation Idaho native and though I've traveled all over the world, I always return to my Idaho home. I hope that this story shares some of my experiences and some of the joy.

Ellen Gruber Garvey is completing a doctorate in English at the University of Pennsylvania, where she teaches creative writing and literature. Her work has appeared in numerous short story collections, including The Crossing Press anthologies *Word of Mouth, Women's Glib*, and *Speaking for Ourselves*. She lives in a heated apartment in Brooklyn.

Gwynne Garfinkle: I am a Jewish feminist writer. I was born in Los Angeles, California, in 1965 and have lived there most of my life. My first book of poems, *New Year's Eve*, was published by Typical Girls Press in 1989. My work has appeared in many periodicals and anthologies, including *off our backs, Sojourner*, and *Along the Fault* (Resident Alien Press, 1990). I've worked for a women's bookstore and a feminist mail-order book company, been a temporary secretary and a data-entry clerk. Currently I'm working on a new poetry manuscript and a novel about vampires, suffragettes, witchburnings, and revolution.

Ilan Stavans, a Mexican novelist and critic, teaches at Baruch College, the City University of New York.

Kathleen J. Alcalá's stories of magic realism have been described as "illuminating and gently transcendent." They have appeared in *The Ohio Renaissance Review, The Written Arts, The Seattle Review, Seattle Arts, Calyx, Chiricú, Black Ice*, and *Isaac Asimov's Magazine of Fantasy and Science Fiction*. Two of her stories have been nominated for the General Electric Young Writers Award. Kathleen is assistant editor of *The Seattle Review* and was guest editor for the spring 1990 international, multicultural issue. She is currently working on a novel set in Saltillo, Mexico, circa 1870. She has a B.A. from Stanford and an M.A. from the University of Washington, and attended the Clarion West science fiction workshop in 1987.

Kathleen de Azevedo: I was born in Rio de Janeiro of a Brazilian mother and a Jewish father. In spite of my origins, I prefer to explore the uninhabited mountains or the desert rather than a crowded beach. My work has been or will be published in *Common Lives/Lesbian Lives*, *Other Voices*, *Sojourner*, *Creative Woman*, and *Visions International*. Before that, I worked as a playwright, which included writing and co-producing a folklore radio series for a National Public Radio affiliate station in San Francisco. I was also invited to participate as a librettist at the University of Minnesota's opera workshop, where I wrote the libretto for a short Brazilian opera about cleaning women.

Kristine Kathryn Rusch has published short fiction in science fiction, literary, and mainstream magazines. She has won the John W. Campbell Award for best new writer and a World Fantasy Award for her work as editor of *Pulphouse: The Hardback Magazine.* Her four novels will appear from New American Library beginning in late 1991. She lives in the mountains in the Pacific Northwest with Dean Wesley Smith (another crazy writer who shared that World Fantasy Award for his work as publisher of *Pulphouse)*, seven-and-a-half cats (the half is wild and refuses to admit that he's part of the household), and a large collection of books. (For information about *Pulphouse*, write P.O. Box 1227, Eugene, OR 97440.)

Lianne Elizabeth Mercer is a Texas poet who has spent a lot of time in mental institutions working as a psychiatric nurse to support her poetry habit and to maintain her powers of observation, compassion, and storytelling.

Lianne also writes fiction and nonfiction. "The Monument" is one of several short stories she has written about women who almost live in a small town on a curving river quite close to you. "The Legacy" appeared in *Common Bonds: Stories by and about Texas Women*, edited by Suzanne Comer and published in 1990 by Southern Methodist University Press.

The How-to of Great Speaking: Stage Techniques that Tame Those Butterflies, written with Hal Persons, was published by Circle City Press in 1990. And, oh yes, her poetry has been published in *Concho River Review*, *The Sow's Ear*, *The Harbinger*, *The Dan River Anthology*, and *Negative Capability*.

Lorraine Schein is a New York poet, currently working on various fictional projects. "My only comment on `Edgar Allan Poe in the Bronx,' and magic realism in general, is that 'truth is stranger than fiction.'"

Her poetry has appeared in *Heresies*, *The New York Quarterly*, *Bay Windows*, and *BLUE LIGHT RED LIGHT*, among others, and recently in the special SF issue of *Semiotext(e)* and the anthology *If I Had a Hammer: Women's Work in Poetry, Fiction, and Photography*, published by Papier-Mache Press.

Her story "The Chaos Diaries" was in *Memories and Visions*, the first volume of The Crossing Press's science fiction series. She has new poetry in Crossing's humor anthology *Women's Glib* and in *Home Planet News*.

Lucy Sussex was born in Christchurch, New Zealand, in 1957. After living in France and England, she moved to Australia in 1971. She has worked as a librarian and is currently a research assistant. In 1987 she solved the literary mystery of one of the first female crime writers, revealing the writer behind the pseudonym Waif Wander to be a Canadian-Australian woman, Mary Helena Fortune. As a result, she edited *The Fortunes of Mary Fortune* (Penguin, 1989), a collection of Waif Wander's autobiographical writing.

She has also published a children's book, *The Peace Garden*, and a collection of short stories, *My Lady Tongue & Other Tales*, the title story of which appeared in The Crossing Press's *The Women Who Walk Through Fire* (1990). She has just completed a novel.

Mary Rosenblum: A native of Pittsburgh, Pennsylvania, I became an avid SF reader at age 11, when I discovered a stack of old *Galaxy* magazines in the closet of a house we rented. I started writing sometime around then—but *everyone* knew that you couldn't really be a writer when you grew up. I dutifully got a degree in biology and did try out a variety of careers, including work in endocrine research, horse training, commercial cheese-making, and a stint showing livestock on the professional county fair circuit. Ultimately, I realized that what I wanted to be when I grew up was, indeed, a science fiction writer. By then, I'd stopped believing "everyone," so I attended the Clarion West writers workshop in 1988. I have been writing full time ever since and have sold stories to *Asimov's, Fantasy and Science Fiction,* and *Pulphouse.*

Rosalind Warren is a mother. She is also a writer, a feminist, and a bankruptcy attorney. Her stories have appeared in many magazines, from *Seventeen* to *Beatniks from Space,* and in numerous anthologies; she was awarded a 1990 Pennsylvania Council on the Arts Literature Fellowship for her short fiction. She also reviews books, for *New Directions for Women* and *The Women's Review of Books.* She is the editor of *Women's Glib: An Anthology of Women's Humor,* now available from The Crossing Press, and is gathering material for the "sequel"—*Women's Glibber.* Send her something funny at Box 259, Bala Cynwyd, PA 19004.

Stephanie T. Hoppe: Some years in environmental law showed me that the starting point lies in our ideas of our relationship with the Earth — a question for the imagination —and I turned to writing fiction. *The Windrider,* a fantasy novel grounded in the myths and landscapes of the Western mountains and deserts I know best, was published in 1985; an anthology on relationships with animals and the natural world, co-edited with Theresa Corrigan, followed in 1989-90 (*With a Fly's Eye, Whale's Wit, and Woman's Heart* and *And a Deer's Ear, Eagle's Song, and Bear's Grace*). A collection of thematically linked long stories/short novels set in different futures, *If Mirrors Asked Questions*, is looking for a publisher.

"Old Night" originated in 1983 in a frightening dream. It has taken years to effect the transformation from that private vision to sharable fiction: the negotiation between self, language, world, and society that I see as fiction.

I live in northern California and finance the above with free-lance editing and proofreading while I study t'ai chi, raise vegetables, make wine, and work at reconciling ambitions to both step lightly on the earth and set my mark upon the world.

Valerie Nieman Colander: In magic realism, other truths intrude upon that world accepted as ordinary life. As a writer, I find myself balanced between worlds marked out as "mainstream" literature and science fiction/fantasy. I have published one SF novel, *Neena Gathering* (Pageant Books, 1988), and recently completed *A Survivors' Affair*, a novel set in a West Virginia factory town in the early 1970s.

My poetry and short fiction have been published in literary and feminist journals, including *Calyx, Poetry, Southern Poetry Review*, and *Sojourner*, and in small SF magazines such as *Pandora, Space and Time*, and *The Magazine of Speculative Poetry*. A chapbook collection of my poetry was selected in national competition and published in 1988 by *Sing Heavenly Muse!* That same year, one of my stores was chosen in the PEN syndicated fiction series.

I've taught creative writing at workshops and journalism at my alma mater, West Virginia University; appeared at regional science fiction conventions; and read from my work on public television, at colleges and arts festivals.

A native of western New York state, I graduated from WVU in 1978 and am employed as a reporter/arts editor at a daily newspaper. My husband John and I own a small farm, on which we have built a home.

*The Crossing Press
publishes a full selection of
feminist titles.
To receive our current catalog,
please call —Toll Free—800/777-1048.*